imperfect heart

Amie Knight

An Imperfect Heart
Copyright © 2018 Amie Knight

ISBN-13:978-1717209931
ISBN-10:1717209939

Editor: Emily Lawrence of Lawrence Editing

Proofreading: Julie Deaton of Deaton Author Services

Interior Design and Formatting: Stacey Blake of Champagne Book Design

I wanted to write a romance for all the mothers out there. The stay-at-home moms. The working mothers. The empty-nester mommas. The tired, selfless women who put their children's needs above their own every day of their lives. We are amazing and one day our children will realize it.

But I especially wanted to dedicate this one to my momma, because even though you told me every day how much you loved me, I didn't truly understand the magnitude of it all until I held my very own child in my arms.

So thank you, Momma, for loving me so much. This one's for you.

Prologue

Kelly

"You're pregnant."

The doctor's deep voice resonated throughout exam room one in who the hell knew where we were Alabama. I barely heard his words. The acoustics were fantastic in here. I wanted to bring my band in and set up shop. Bang my drums a little. Rock out.

"Excuse me?" I pitched my body toward him in an effort to get closer, thinking surely I'd heard him wrong. A slight breeze coasted up the back of my paper gown and the blue vinyl I sat on clung to one of my ass cheeks.

He smiled and looked down at the iPad gripped in his big hands. "The test came back positive. You're pregnant."

What in the hell was he grinning about?

This time when my body rocked backward it wasn't of my own

doing. My head swam. My palms sweated. Oh, hell no. Surely this was a mistake. I'd only come to the doctor because I'd been throwing up for days and was hoping to get some drugs to help with the nausea.

I had a virus.

Not a baby.

The creepy smiling doctor was wrong.

I was fucking careful. I religiously took my birth control pills. I always used condoms. I drank. I rocked out. I traveled. I was a party girl, sure, but I was a responsible one. My momma made sure of that.

"I think we need another test." My voice sounded croaky. Nothing like the sultry voice that had captivated audiences in small clubs all across the Southeast.

He was still smiling. "We can do another test, but, Ms. Potter, the results aren't going to miraculously change. You're having a baby."

My body locked tight as I sucked in air through my nose. My life as I knew it was over and there he sat grinning at me like this was an episode of *The Price Is Right* and he'd just handed me the keys to a brand-spanking-new car.

He didn't know that children were never in my life's game plan. Yeah, I was a thirty-two-year-old woman, but I was a far cry from mother material. And my biological clock had never started ticking. Hell, I didn't even *own* a watch. To an outsider looking in, I might be the perfect picture of a mother-in-waiting, but I was anything but. I was a girl still trying to live her dream. Still trying to make it big. I just wanted to play drums and sing my life away, and I'd been doing that for the last ten years.

The doctor's face finally registered my panic and the smile was gone. Thank God.

He cleared his throat and diverted his eyes. "There are other options," he said, not meeting my eyes and grabbing one of the many pamphlets that sat on the counter next to him.

He handed it to me, but I didn't look at him. I just grabbed that folded piece of paper in my hands and slipped off the hard table beneath me. The paper felt all wrong in my hands, so I shoved it into my purse that sat on the only chair in the room.

"Thanks," I grumbled, slipping my jeans on beneath the gown. I had to get out of here. Pronto. I was going to suffocate if I didn't.

I tore the gown off over my head, not bothering to untie it.

"Ms. Potter. I—" The doctor's cheeks turned an interesting shade of pink before he turned away.

"Thanks," I gritted out. This conversation was over. I couldn't breathe. No matter how I looked to him, I simply wasn't ready for a child. Ever.

I'd fled that doctor's office that day like a bat out of hell. Then, I'd been panicked, so emotionally charged. I remembered it now with quiet resolve. That was the day I thought my everything had changed.

I'd been so wrong.

I'd gone to the hotel the band was staying at for the night, thankful I could be alone and not piled into the van with three smelly rockers while I had my breakdown. Pissed off that I'd been stupid and hooked up one too many damn times with my bandmate, Cash. And break down I did. I cried. I hiccupped. I sobbed into that flat pillow in that cheap hotel in Alabama. I read that pamphlet that made me sick. It made me sick because I wanted to do it. It made me sick because I couldn't. I just couldn't.

I just had to accept it.

I'd never get my dream.

But what I didn't expect was that I'd get a nightmare.

A mother's worse nightmare.

Because just when I'd come to accept that I wouldn't get to perform for millions under the colored, flashing, scorching lights of a sold-out stadium. Just when I'd come to accept that no one would call me famous or a rock star. No, I'd just be mom, and I was finally okay with that. Now. Just when I thought I'd figured it all out, I had the rug jerked out so fast and hard from under me, I had burns to show for it.

It was the twenty-week scan that really changed everything. Not that day in the doctor's office in Alabama that seemed so damn trivial now.

The ultrasound tech had looked so happy as she squirted the goop on my round stomach and my baby girl gave a kick that even made my lips tip up in a barely there smile. She was growing in me. She was growing on me, too. I already loved her.

So imagine my shock when ten minutes into that ultrasound the tech's face fell. She excused herself and came back with a doctor, and I knew. Something bad was wrong.

Things only got harder after that. Once again, I was handed that same pamphlet, only this time by a different doctor. It was equally awkward and still too damn wrong.

I still couldn't do it.

Even knowing what I did.

So, I pulled up my momma britches. They were ugly and had a huge elastic band at the waist, but at least they were comfy.

And I placed my child's heart in the hands of the lead pediatric heart surgeon at Duke University Hospital.

Dr. Anthony Jackson, heart doctor extraordinaire.

Anthony Jackson, the devil with dimples.

Anthony, the biggest asshole in the world.

Anthony fucking Jackson, my ex.

Sort of.

Chapter 1

Kelly

now. Fucking snow.

    I turned on my windshield wipers and blew out a long breath. I couldn't believe it. Yes, it was January, but I thought it didn't snow much around the Carolinas. Truth was I wasn't surprised. The snow was just icing on the shit cake that was my life right now.

"I know, baby girl. I know," I said, taking one hand off the steering wheel long enough to give my thirty week along belly a slow rub. She was a big one. If she grew much more, I wouldn't be fitting behind the steering wheel so easily. Lord knew I was already squeezing myself into sweats and leggings nowadays. The blissful days of cute jeans and crop tops were long gone. Hello, stretchy tops, elastic waistbands, and giant bras.

She gave me a good kick. It was like she knew I was a nervous wreck. She'd been rolling around in my stomach the entire four-hour drive from my friend Ainsley's house in South Carolina. The signs for Raleigh, North Carolina, that sat along the side of the interstate only seemed to send my anxiety higher. Pulling off the exit for Duke University Hospital, I swallowed hard and clenched my teeth. A slight pinch in my chest and hitch in my breath sent me turning off the main road that led to the hospital and straight into the parking lot of a McDonald's.

I parked and tried to breathe through my nervousness. The heat in the car blasted, and I cranked it down, feeling like I was burning up. It was the shame. It was like fire in my veins, all-encompassing and so very hot. The shame of swallowing my pride and begging for help from someone I didn't even really like. No, that wasn't true. I'd really liked him once. For one single night. I might have even more than liked him. But I couldn't think about that now. I couldn't think about how that night had ended.

I had to think of the baby girl growing inside of me. I'd learned quickly that the moment you found out you were going to be a mom, pride and shame and embarrassment could fuck right off. Little else mattered in comparison to the sweet life that seemed to mean more to me every day.

Every hour.

Every minute.

"You can do this," I whispered into the stifling air of the car. "Go to hell, pride. Fuck you, shame."

I'd been giving myself this pep talk the entire way here. It wasn't working. I was still terrified of what I had to do, but it didn't matter. I'd do anything for her.

I placed both of my hands to my round stomach. I glanced down. My small but strong drummer hands didn't cover her anymore. I was running out of time. In there, she was safe. Once she arrived, once she was out here, things were too uncertain. Tears stung my eyes, and I hated them. I'd never been a crier, but I was now. Damn pregnancy hormones.

Looking up at the car ceiling, I blinked back my tears before staring back down at my stomach. "We got this. You and me. Together, we're gonna be a force, baby girl. Team hope."

I was talking a lot to my girl lately. Since leaving the band and the road, I'd been spending a lot of time alone. Just her and me and a slew of doctors except for my quick visit to Ainsley. I'd kept playing with the band for as long as I could. Until I started to show, until the diagnosis. Then, I'd stayed with Ainsley for a couple of weeks, garnering up the courage to come here.

I patted my tummy. "He's gonna be a dickhead, but we can handle it. We can handle anything."

I nodded and prayed that even if he was a dickhead, he'd help me. He was my last hope. My only hope really.

A ring sounded out in the silent car, causing me to jump. A breathy "fuck" flew past my lips as I rolled my eyes at myself and reached for my cell phone.

Ainsley, the screen said, so I hit the green button. It was like she knew.

"Hey," I said softly into the phone.

"How's it going? Did you make it? How's the weather? Have you seen him yet?"

"Fucking Christ, Ains. Take a damn breath." I laughed out.

"Language, Kells. You're having a baby. You have got to tone it down. You want her first word to be fuck?"

I honestly didn't care as long as she got a first word. I needed that first word like I needed my breath. I mean, did I really want her first word to be fuck? Absolutely not. But I didn't have the same luxury as most expectant moms. I didn't get to look forward to all the firsts. I only got to pray and hope I actually got them.

Her first smile.

Her first tooth.

Her first step.

God, I wanted them.

I didn't share that with Ainsley, though. I held my feelings close to my vest, too scared to voice them. Too afraid I'd jinx it all.

"You think she understands now? You think she can hear me? Should I start playing her a little Metallica now?" I asked, smiling. I knew she could hear me. I knew she was 15.7 inches long and weighed three pounds. I knew she was about the size of a large cabbage. I knew it all. I had the damn Baby Center app like every other expecting mom out there. I just liked to fuck with Ainsley.

Ainsley laughed. "You're an asshole, you know that?"

"Hey, watch your mouth around my baby!"

She giggled harder at my pretend outrage.

Her laughter eventually grew quiet and faded out to nothing, and my smile fell. Silence hit the phone line like an anvil, the mood instantly somber.

"Have you seen him?" she whispered.

I let out a hard laugh. "No. I'm a chicken shit, so I'm sitting at a McDonald's a block away according to my GPS." I held the phone tightly in my hand.

"You're doing the right thing." Her voice was quiet.

I nodded. "I know, but the right thing isn't always easy."

"You got this. You're the bravest person I know. You've traveled and performed all over the United States. You're a rock star, Kelly Potter. "

I had a snarky response right on the tip of my tongue, but it just sat there as my lips trembled slightly. I had wanted to be a rock star and spent the last ten years of my life giving that my all to no avail. I might not even get to be a mother either. It was almost too much to bear, but I couldn't sit here and feel sorry for myself. I needed to get my shit together. Or my stuff together. Ainsley was right. I needed to start watching my mouth. She'd be here soon and then I'd be fucked. Eh, fudged.

"Thanks, Ains," I breathed.

"That bastard better not be mean to you. I will drive up there and kick his smarmy ass." She paused. "I wish you had let me come with you."

I laughed. She was always so good at making me laugh when I needed it. "I know, but I need to do this on my own. You can come when the baby is born. I'll really need your help then. Okay?"

"I wouldn't miss it. She's going to be beautiful and fun and the kindest person I know. Just like her momma."

I rolled my eyes, but I still grinned. "God, let a girl borrow a set of sheets in college and she'll wax poetic about you the next fifteen years," I smarted.

She was quiet when she replied. "I borrowed a lot more than your sheets that year, Kells."

I thought of how sad Ainsley had been our first year of college. How isolated. How I'd pushed her to be my friend even though she'd just wanted to be alone. She'd just lost a loved one and was mourning so horribly.

"I'm here if you need me. For anything. Sheets, shoulders, hugs. Anything you need." She finished quietly.

"I know. I'll call you when I get settled tonight."

"Speaking of calls, have you called your mother yet?"

I groaned over the line. "I'm not ready, Ains."

She blew out a long breath and I could just picture the eye roll she was giving me on the other side of the phone. "I don't care. It's time. You'll need her. You don't think you will now but you will, I promise. Having that baby girl is going to change things. You'll need your momma more than ever before."

She'd been giving me this same speech for weeks now. How being a mother changed how you saw your own mother. I didn't see how it could. I loved my mom. We were totally cool. We lived our lives and talked every few months. She traveled. I traveled. We were close in our own way, but I was definitely independent. I didn't need to talk to my mother every day the way Ainsley did with hers. We just had a different kind of relationship.

Also, I wasn't ready to tell her I'd gotten knocked up. I'd been an unplanned pregnancy after all. My mom had only been nineteen. She'd never wanted that for me. She wanted my career first, marriage second, babies third, and even though I was thirty-two, I still wasn't married. I hadn't even really had the career yet. I didn't want to let my mother down. She'd never let me down once.

"I didn't realize it either, Kelly. I didn't know how much I'd understand my momma and all she did for me. All she gave up. How much she loved me until I had children of my own. Just think about it, okay?" Ainsley implored.

"Okay, I gotta go. It's getting late, and I'm losing my nerve."

"Drive safe, and call me."

I hung up the phone and pulled out of my parking space with a firm resolve. The worst he could say was go to hell, right? He'd basically done that to me before and it had crushed my heart and soul. So, the worst had already happened, and I'd lived through it. I'd even managed to move on. I could do it again.

The huge hospital came into view and my heart kicked up a notch. Finding a parking space proved difficult and took longer than I expected, but I found his office easily enough. It wasn't even five o'clock yet, but it was already starting to get dark outside when I took the elevator up to the sixth floor.

I stepped off and into an office that looked beyond nice. My palms sweated. I was wearing too big gray sweats and my hair was in a knot at the top of my head. I didn't have a stitch of makeup on. I probably should have dressed for the occasion, but honestly I didn't expect much to come of this. All I had was hope. And you couldn't put hope in a dress or make her up. You couldn't fake hope. She was real and deep and there I was, huge and messy and sad, and praying for something big to happen. Me and hope.

A woman who looked to be in her fifties slid open a glass partition at the front of the room and leaned out of it a bit. She was put together, well dressed, blond hair sprinkled with gray, bun firmly in place, lipstick deep red and perfectly applied. She looked me up and down. "Can I help you?"

God, I needed help, but she couldn't help me. Only one man could.

"I'm here to see Dr. Anthony Jackson." I lifted my chin and prayed she couldn't hear the nerves in my voice.

Her brow furrowed as she checked a computer in front of her. "Do you have an appointment?"

I shook my head and shuffled my feet a little. "No."

She looked up at me, eyebrows raised.

"I'm a friend," I tossed out there. "I'm passing through town and thought I'd stop by."

God, I was a liar and a cusser. I patted my belly.

Good luck with me as your momma, little one.

She looked me up and down again and pursed her lips. She didn't believe me and rightly so because I was lying through my teeth. I hadn't spoken to Anthony Jackson in over ten years. We were not friends. I wasn't just passing through town. If things worked out the way I wanted them to, I would move here. I would start a new life with my daughter here. And Dr. Jackson would be the one to save her. Save us.

"I'm sorry, but he's gone for the day. I'm sure since you're friends you can contact him on his cell phone?" Her eyebrow hitched up and her lips puckered knowingly.

My whole body deflated. I'd missed him. And I sure as hell didn't have a cell phone number. I'd have to do this again tomorrow. I nodded at the woman and turned on my heel and left the office, making my way to my piece of shit car.

I wouldn't give up. I'd find a place to stay tonight, and I'd be here early in the morning so I could catch him as he was going into the office. I'd swallow my pride yet another day.

Me, baby girl, and hope would be back tomorrow and the next day and the day after that until I'd gotten what I'd come for.

Chapter 2

Anthony

The heart is exquisite. Other doctors might tell you different. An ophthalmologist may say it' all in the eyes. And the eyes, they are beautiful. A dermatologist will preach how the skin is the largest organ of the body. A neurologist will tell you how damn fascinating the brain is. And while all of those doctors have very valid points, nothing is as magnificent as the heart.

The heart starts beating merely four weeks after conception, long before the formation of skin and way before the eyes develop. And most certainly before the brain matures. The heart beats on average one hundred thousand times a day and pumps nearly one million barrels of blood during an average lifetime. It does more physical work than any other muscle during that lifetime.

The heart is what the kids call freaking cool.

You'll never hear anyone become increasingly verbose over an organ quite like they do the heart. A place where you store your memories. The spot in your chest so big it can hold every ounce of your love. The only organ that can "break" and still keep beating. If you're lost in the world? What's the old saying? Follow your heart. And when your love for someone is unwavering, unparalleled, and unprecedented, what do you give them? Ah. That's right. Your *heart*.

Yes, the heart is amazing, indeed. And everyone knows it.

It is somehow both strong and yet unfailingly delicate.

It's the leading killer of both women and men.

And nearly one in every one hundred babies is born with a congenital heart defect.

The heart giveth life.

It taketh away.

And I knew that better than anyone.

Chapter 3

Kelly

It was early as hell, but it didn't matter, really. I'd hardly slept a wink anyway. I'd spent the night tossing and turning on that lumpy bed in the cheap ass motel room only a few blocks from the hospital. I was a ball of worry. I had a feeling that worrying was pretty much all that moms did. I had a lifetime of this coming to me, I hoped. It sucked.

I wasn't hungry, but I ate breakfast anyway. After all, I wasn't eating for just me anymore. I squeezed myself into my too small coat and got into my car. The drive to the hospital was impossibly long for such a short drive. Small snow drifts peppered the side of the road. I fiddled with the radio more times than I could count on the less than five-minute drive there. I told myself it didn't matter what Anthony Jackson thought of me, but I couldn't help but be nervous.

Daylight hadn't even come, but there I sat in the parking lot with my car running to keep me warm. Still, I shivered, but it wasn't from the cold. The bouncing of my leg rocked the vehicle a little, offering me some small comfort. The sun finally made its appearance as a black Lexus pulled into the parking lot.

It figured he'd appear with the sun. *Hilarious, God. You're so funny.*

And my stupid heart, it leapt in my chest. That should have made me anxious, but all it did was remind me of another heart. One that was inside me, too, but below my own. One that was way more important than mine. So, I pushed out of my car and made my way toward the Lexus with the kind of determination in my step I only felt when I was behind a set of drums. I'd have to remind myself of that feeling a lot over the next couple of months. I'd need to conjure it up time and time again to get through the coming times.

The black car door opened long before I could waddle my way over to it and a blond giant of a man unfolded himself from the vehicle with the kind of grace I'd never had. Not even when I was thirty pounds lighter and a hell of a lot cooler. I paused on the sidewalk. I could only see the side of his face, but nonetheless I knew it was him. He was bigger. His shoulders broader. His hair a little darker. His chin more square, but there he stood, the sun over him just like the golden Greek God I remembered. He turned and started toward the building, and for some reason I became frantic. Worry filled me that I'd never have this moment again. I rushed forward.

Before I could stop myself I yelled out, "Dr. Jackson!" When he didn't immediately turn I panicked, shouting, "Anthony! Anthony Jackson!"

He turned around just as I came up on him, nearly barreling him over. I stopped precious inches from his body and looked up and up some more because Anthony, he was an unbelievably tall man. At least six feet five inches. And I was itty bitty, in height anyway.

I stepped back, embarrassed at how close we were, and took in his green eyes, remembering they somehow seemed magical that one night we'd had together.

"I'm sorry," I breathed out, feeling the need to explain, but also realizing I was out of breath from trying to catch up to him.

Those green eyes stared down at me, piercing me, splitting me wide-open because they didn't smile. They didn't say that he remembered our night or even me. They just seemed hard and confounded and mostly impatient.

"I don't mean to take your time. You probably don't remember me. I'm K—"

"I know who you are," his deep voice interrupted, sharp and to the point.

I looked down, embarrassed at having nearly tackled him in the parking lot and ashamed that while I'd been nervous but excited to see him, he seemed aloof and ready for our meeting to be over. I felt my hackles rise as my eyes did. I took in his shiny, fancy shoes and black slacks. I got to the light blue dress shirt and was shocked to see he had on a green bow tie with light blue polka dots.

My eyebrows rose, and my smart ass mouth couldn't stop itself "Nice tie."

I mentally rolled my eyes. I'd never been able to shut my mouth, not even when I was supposed to be full of grace and kissing ass.

He arched an eyebrow down at me. "The kids like it."

I nodded and felt like a complete ass.

Of course they did. And I was a bitch.

This time he cleared his throat. "Is there something you needed, Ms. Potter?"

Ms. Potter?

Ms. Potter?!

If he remembered me, which he obviously did since he threw out my last name easily enough, then he should remember I was never Ms. Potter to him. Kelly? Yes. Baby? For sure. As in "Come for me, baby. Right now." It grated on me. This Ms. Potter business. For some reason it pissed me off. The whole thing. The fact that he made me like him entirely too much that one night ten years ago. The way he ended things the next morning. Yeah, that pissed me off, too. Really bad. But what really chapped my ass most of all was how his pompous, unfeeling, Ms. Potter calling ass was behaving right now. And my ass hadn't been chapped in a long damn time. It was foreign, this passionate feeling of being so angry at someone. It almost felt good.

I tilted my chin up at him and stepped closer, feeling like I was on fire. For the first time in months, I wasn't sad. I wasn't worried. I was fucking angry.

"Ms. Potter, huh?" I spat at him as his eyes widened.

I thumped that ridiculous bow tie he was wearing "for the kids" and said as close to his face as I could with his height and mine, "I think you can call me Kelly, Anthony. You know, considering you've seen my lady bits and all. Come to think of it, you've more than seen them, you've tasted th—"

"Okay," he said, backing away a step and running his hands through his hair grumpily. My Anthony had never run his hands through his hair like that. He'd been fun and carefree and sweet.

"I get it...Kelly." He ground out my name and I smiled, glad I'd made him as uncomfortable as he'd made me.

Baby girl did a somersault I couldn't ignore, and I immediately placed my hand over the bump covered by my coat. Anthony's eyes tracked my movements and the exact second I laid my hand to my pregnant stomach, the shock registered on his face followed by a bit of softening that made me the opposite of angry.

His head fell forward, and he let out a long breath that had me holding mine. His eyes met mine again, and he ran a large hand through that angelic dirty-blond hair again. He said nothing, but his eyes were brimming with questions.

I had the answer. "You," I whispered.

His brows furrowed. "Me?" He angled a long finger at himself.

"You," I said louder this time. "When I typed in Hypoplastic Right Heart Syndrome, your name came up in all of the search engines on the amazing inter-web." My words felt stuck in my throat, too thick and hard to say, but I pushed on. "It almost seemed like a joke, or maybe if you were a person who believed in fate, like some kind of destiny that was written in the wind." I huffed out a sarcastic laugh. No, I didn't believe in fate or destiny; those things wouldn't make my baby girl better. I wasn't leaving her life up to some divine intervention. I was here, instead, begging for her life.

"It's what you do and it's what my baby needs for a fighting chance. A series of three surgeries over the next few years that could save her life, and from what I understand, you've trained under the best doctors around here to do these surgeries."

Yes, as soon as I'd found what was wrong with my baby, I'd done what any other crazy ass grief-stricken mother does. I'd scoured the web for hours, bound and determined to learn as much as I could about the heart defect my baby would be born with. I was more than surprised to learn that yes, Anthony had become a heart doctor. A pediatric heart surgeon that specialized in exactly what my baby needed. Fucking Fate. She was a sick and twisted, sometimes cruel bitch. But, I was hoping against all hopes that this time, she was on my side.

Siphoning every bit of courage I could from the cold air around us, I breathed deeply in before starting, "I don't have any money. I don't even have a place to live, but none of that matters but this baby girl. None of it." I slashed my hand across the air in front of me.

Half of his mouth hitched up in an almost smile. "A girl?"

"Yep. Me and baby girl. We're a team. And we're gonna do this thing. With or without you, but I hope it's with you because I hear you're good and I need someone who can deliver a miracle." My lips trembled as I said the words and I covered them with the tips of my fingers.

He held up a hand, staving me off. "Of course I'll help you."

I rocked back on my heels. "You will?" I couldn't quite believe it was that easy. I hadn't told him everything. I had a whole speech prepared. And he said yes just like that?

"I don't have insurance. Just Medicaid and I can't trust that Medicaid is going to give me the best, but you, you're the best. I trust you."

He leaned over and grabbed my hand. "I said I'd do it. I'll do anything I can to help you and your baby girl."

Relief settled in my chest like a soothing balm and I let out a breath I didn't realize I'd been holding. I used shaking hands to push the hair out of my face that had come loose from my ponytail. Tears threatened to spill out of my eyes and over my cheeks, but I couldn't let them. I had to be strong. For me and her. Weeping wasn't an option. Being fearless and brave was my only choice.

So I choked out the next words, feeling more than I could say. "Thank you. Thank you so much."

He held up a hand. "Don't, it's fine, but I have a full docket today and I don't like to be late for my little people. Can I get you to come in tomorrow? Where are you staying? Maybe I can come by there after work?"

"Oh." I didn't want to tell him I'd stayed at that shitty motel less than a mile away. I looked around, praying for some interruption. I turned and noticed people pulling into the parking lot.

A black BMW pulled up next to us, and the lady from Anthony's office from the day before got out of the car, studying me and my baby bump a little too close for comfort. Anthony gave her a pointed stare and she turned away, abruptly making her way into the building.

"Kelly," he said, pulling my eyes away from the lady and back to his. "Where are you staying?"

I fidgeted with my coat.

"I'm staying at the hotel with the blue roof a few blocks away." I looked away. For some reason I knew he wouldn't like that, and I didn't want to see the judgement in his eyes.

His hands went back to his hair, and I had the feeling he wasn't about to say anything good.

"You can't stay there again."

My eyes snapped back to his. He couldn't tell me where to stay. He needed to keep his opinions to himself and by opinions, I meant everything he ever thought about me and what I should do.

I rolled my eyes and gave my lips a smack for effect. "I can stay wherever I like. Believe it or not, I've stayed in far worse places, and I'm just fine. And besides, it's what I can afford. Not everyone is rolling in the dough, Dr. Jackson." That was a lie. I'd stayed in places just as bad, but I didn't think it got much worse.

I wasn't being nice. I was hitting below the belt. I shouldn't have brought up money. It was rude and mean, and even though I was being petty because he'd succeeded at his dream and I'd failed at mine, I couldn't stop myself.

He stood straighter and taller and reached his hand out, wrapping his elegant fingers around my wrist. "Listen, Ms. Potter," he said my name with snark, clearly proving a point that he could call me whatever the hell he wanted to call me as long as he called me. And wasn't that the damn truth. I needed him. He didn't need me.

"You won't be staying in that hotel tonight. It's not safe. You're an old friend, and I would never permit a friend to stay at that shithole."

I was confused. I was an old friend? Was that what he considered me? It sure didn't seem like I was, considering how our one hell of a one-night stand ended. It had felt like it that night, but the next morning had sure been one heck of a wakeup call.

He let go of my wrist and fished around in his ridiculously expensive slacks. "Lucky for you, I'm working an overnight at the hospital tonight, so you can stay at my place." He held out a set of keys, and I took a step back.

Nope. Just nope. I might have been poor and needy, but I sure didn't want him giving me any more handouts than he already was. I was already asking too much of him. I couldn't let him give me a place to stay, too.

He jangled the keys in front of me, and my eyes widened in horror. What in the hell was going on? I didn't even think this beautiful, successful man had remembered me and now he was trying to give me the keys to his house.

"Wipe that crazy look off your face, Ms. Potter, and take the keys. It's only for one night until we find more suitable accommodations for you."

Taking another step back, I shook my head, but he took a giant step forward. And let me tell you, for every five steps of mine, he probably would only have to take one. It didn't take long for him to catch up to me and grab my hand again, this time turning my palm up and placing those damn keys right in the center, using his other hand to curl my fingers around them.

"You'll stay at my place tonight and you won't give me any more shit about it. This conversation is over."

He rattled off an address and told me he'd be in touch while I stood here shocked. And I was hardly ever shocked. I was the shocker. Not the shockee, damn it. It took a lot to surprise a girl who'd been on the road for ten years with a rock band. He turned on his heel and marched toward the medical building like he was king of the fucking world, his pricey shoes clacking against the pavement, his swagger unbelievably cocksure. King of the fucking world in a ridiculous bow tie. And he still looked good. Shit.

Chapter 4

Kelly

That Night Ten Years Ago

"Jesus. You're fucking gorgeous, you know that?" He ran a large hand from the spot right in the middle of my shoulder blades past the small of my back before landing on my ass where he squeezed hard enough to make me giggle.

"Less talking, more petting, Doctor," I said through laughter.

"Not a doctor. Yet." His voice was cocky, and it made me hot. "Still a ways to go before that happens."

I could hear the smile in his voice even though I couldn't see his face. I was lying on my stomach on top of his white plush down comforter naked as the day I was born. And not shy about it at all. He'd just laid his mouth, his tongue, his hands over every inch of this body several times and he'd seemed to enjoy every second of it.

I looked out the small window next to his bed while he was propped up on one hand beside me and using the other to rub every available surface of skin on my body he could find. It was phenomenal. I wanted to purr like a damn cat, but instead I stretched out further along his bed.

"I can't believe you came home with me tonight," he husked out.

I couldn't believe it either. I wasn't the type of girl who did one-night stands. I didn't really have boyfriends, either. I was married to the music. Anthony Jackson wasn't even really my type per se. I liked moody guys with tattoos and piercings. Boys with darker eyes and even darker souls. I was a walking cliché, but I liked the tortured musician types. After all, we were kindred spirits. Me and my hard, banging drums, them with their soft guitar riffs and raspy lyrical voices.

I rolled to my back and gazed up at Anthony. He waggled an eyebrow at me, and I bit my lip to hide my smile. He may not have been my type, but I was positive there wasn't a girl out there who'd turn him down. Vivid and inquisitive green eyes stared down at me and God, I wanted him all over again.

And I'd had him plenty that night. We'd met at the club only hours ago. I was visiting my friend Ainsley in Columbia, South Carolina, and we'd run into Anthony and his college friends at a nightclub. Ainsley introduced him as an old friend. He'd come on strong. I'd come on even stronger. Hardly any alcohol in my system and yet I'd let him drag me back to his small apartment, between my legs aching with want. We'd barely made it through the door when he picked me up and placed me on the entry table and pushed his massive body between my thighs. Slick skin, hot hands, wet mouths. And the rest was history. Or maybe not.

No, Anthony Jackson wasn't my type. He was *every* girl's type.

Chiseled to perfection face.

Wide smile complete with full pink lips and deep dimples.

Square jaw that somehow managed to be both soft and hard.

Blond hair that was so thick and shiny I wanted to ask him what shampoo he used.

Not a tattoo or piercing marred the bronzed skin of his muscular body.

For fuck's sake, even the man's cock was pure perfection. Thick and long and cut just as beautifully as the rest of him.

He was surprised I'd come home with him. I couldn't believe it, either. I realized in that moment, him over me. Me under him. The sweat still glistening on our bodies. His ruggedly handsome good looks beaming down at me like the sun on a bright day. For the first time in my life, I'd had a man. An actual real man. Not boys playing men. No, Anthony was all fucking masculine beauty and he'd picked me at the bar. I was one lucky girl.

I ran a finger down the middle of his chest, and when I reached his abs I felt them jump under my hand.

"Well, are you gonna feed me, Doc, or are you going to sex me to death?" I breathed out. I could feel the pink on my cheeks, but this man made me feel bold. Beautiful and wildly sexy.

Leaning over, he pressed a kiss right between my breasts and whispered against my skin, "Can't I do both?"

"Mmmhmm." I stretched again. "But first you have to feed me."

And before I knew it, I was up and off the bed and being carried wedding style to the little kitchenette that sat in the corner of the apartment. Anthony sat me gently down on the counter, bare bottom and all, and I startled at the cold against my ass.

Pushing his body between my thighs, he pressed his lips to mine. "What do you want?"

"Now, that's a loaded question," I said, my grinning lips pressed to his. Because it was. A girl could learn to want a lot from a guy like Anthony.

He backed away and opened the compact refrigerator a few

feet away, and I took in the small apartment. It wasn't dirty or old looking, just bare, like a bachelor lived there. Just a couch and a large TV with a comfy king-sized bed pushed up against the opposite wall. The small kitchen was along the back wall. A tiny studio apartment was all a college guy like him needed.

"Eggs?" He held up a gray carton and I nodded, but I wasn't looking at the eggs. I was looking at his beautiful and still very much naked body. I guess we were doing some birthday suit cooking. It should have felt ridiculous, him standing there, naked in the fluorescent lights of the kitchen, but it didn't. It just felt comfortable. Easy.

He had breakfast going at 3:00 a.m. and I had a lot of questions.

I pulled an apple out of a basket on the counter and asked, "How long have you known Ainsley?"

He was stirring the eggs, but his eyes looked distant like he was lost in a memory before he answered. "I guess most of my life. We grew up together."

I smirked. "Did you date?"

He looked back at me, surprised. "No, she's always had a thing for Adrian. As long as I can remember, anyhow. I was never on her radar."

"But you wanted to?" I crunched into my apple.

A bark of laughter flew past his lips. "Maybe. At one time. She was always nice to everyone. I liked that about her. But when I realized she only had eyes for Adrian, I mostly just flirted with her to piss him off."

"Why?"

"Because I was an asshole when I was a kid."

"And now?"

He grinned charmingly at me while stirring the eggs. "I like to think I've toned down the asshole."

I nodded. "So why a doctor?"

"You sure do have a lot of questions."

"What can I say? I'm inquisitive." I was, too. It drove my mother nuts when I was a kid. I was always the girl with a million questions. I still was.

Spooning eggs onto two plates, his face looked serious. "I've always wanted to make a difference."

God, this guy. He was perfection.

"What kind of doctor?"

"I'm not sure yet. I'm thinking the heart."

"A heart doctor." I nodded, thinking on it. "Yeah, I could see that."

"Grab some forks and meet me in bed." He winked and took off toward the bed with our plates.

With two forks in hand, I climbed into bed beside him, his naked hip pressed to mine. We sat propped against the pillows, white duvet covering our laps, the plates on the bed between our legs. I passed him his fork and we dug in.

We were sitting in relative silence when he looked over at me and asked, "Why could you see it?"

My eyebrows furrowed as I looked over at him. "See what?"

"See me as a heart doctor?"

I smiled and looked away shyly before answering. "It would take somebody brave, bold, yet tender and caring to hold someone else's heart in their hands. Someone special." My face flushed hot before continuing. "I think you could be that person." I felt my lips tip up at the thought of gorgeous, blond and beautiful, God-like Dr. Jackson going around saving people's hearts. Like some kind of superhero in a white coat giving people second chances at life.

I shrugged, playing it cool. I'd known him only a few hours and already I was smitten. "Yeah, you'd make a great doctor, granting second chances all over the place. I can already see it."

His smile fell and the laughter slipped out of his gaze. His face was too serious when he asked, "Second chances?"

Feeling my head tilt to the side, I studied his grave face. "Yeah, Doc, I believe in second chances. Everyone deserves them. Even hearts."

His facial expression was tight, his eyes too intense, so I looked away to the half-eaten plate of eggs in front of me.

"And what about you? Would you trust me with your heart?"

I smiled despite myself even as I blushed. I cleared my throat before answering. It was chock-full of feelings. "Yeah, I might," I whispered.

He didn't say anything, so I looked up, anxious and nervous. And out came his dimples in full force, almost knocking me clear off the bed with their perfect sweetness.

"You're pretty smart for a drummer girl, you know that?"

I nudged my shoulder against his and glanced up at the starry green-eyed gaze I'd decided I'd never get enough of. "And you're pretty cool for a smarty pants doctor."

Chapter 5

Anthony

Kelly Potter. I still couldn't quite believe it. It shouldn't surprise me how she'd shown up today. It was so her. She'd moved across that parking lot toward me like a gentle storm. Her now long hair slipping out of her hair tie and blowing around her face. Her gait slow at first but her steps firm in her resolve to knock me over with her presence. I hadn't seen her coming—just like ten years ago. Fuck, I couldn't believe she was here, and it made me think of that night we'd had together so long ago. The best night of my existence. The worst morning of my life.

She'd looked good today. Better than good really. Even without trying. Her fresh face had glowed in the light of the morning. Her hair was longer and thrown haphazardly into a ponytail at the nape of her neck, but I could still see how dark and shiny it was as the loose strands whipped about her face. Her blue eyes shone in the sunlight and rendered me speechless. Yes, drummer girl Kelly Potter at twenty-two had rocked my world, but the woman who stood in front of me this morning captivated me. She was fucking stunning. Yes, I'd thought of her over the years, but nothing, and I mean nothing, compared to the real thing.

I pushed the elevator button for the sixth floor of my office building and thought of her messy hair, her makeup-free face, her disheveled clothes. I should have known something was wrong right away, but all I could think of seeing her standing there was that night, and I tried my damnedest not to think about her or that night or how it ended. Because it made me bleed emotionally. It made me feel weak and flawed and vulnerable, and I fucking hated it.

She thought I didn't remember her. The truth was, I couldn't forget her.

I stepped into the elevator, thankful I was alone so I could stew. Stew and think because I was an idiot. She'd come for help, and I'd been cold. Cold because I was good at it. I had ten years of practice. No friends. No attachments besides family. Work. Work was life.

My shock had made me a bumbling idiot barely capable of words. But then she'd laid that delicate hand of hers to her stomach, and I'd seen the soft curve of Mother Nature's greatest gift and I'd immediately known what she needed. After all, I'd seen the panic etched in the features too many times on the faces of too many women seated across from me in this damn building.

I'd been shocked. And stupid. So incredibly dumb. My stomach had dropped at the innocent gesture of her rubbing her stomach. A slight ache had taken up residence in my chest. Just a pinch. And that had surprised me, too. That feeling. I damn sure didn't like it. It hadn't been me. No, I wasn't the father. I'd let that ship sail. I'd been too entrenched in my grief to think of anyone other than myself when I'd had my chance.

Where was he? The father? Why wouldn't he be here with her?

I'd never abandon her, I told myself. Only I had, hadn't I? Why was she here alone? The longer I stood there listening to her, the angrier I became. She was alone, penniless it seemed, and scared to death for her baby. I'd probably been too harsh, but someone had to take care of her, damn it.

I realized as I walked into the office that I was a fucking mess. Kelly had managed to completely throw me off my game. I got up early every day, worked out, made my coffee and toast, and got out of the house in record time. Every second away from my little people felt detrimental to their health and sometimes it was.

I tried to breeze past the reception office quickly. I didn't want to deal with questions when I still had so many myself, but I should have known I wouldn't be so lucky.

Lucille was like a pit bull with a bone. She never gave up.

"Anthony," she called out, exiting the small reception area up front and practically chasing me to my office in the back of the space.

I picked up speed, hoping to close the door and lock it before she made it there. I was just about to push it shut when the front of one pointy black stiletto kept the godforsaken door open.

She slid in between the door and the jamb, and I sat at the desk, unloading my bag and trying to pretend like hell she wasn't there.

She humphed before taking a seat across from my desk, but I didn't look up. I wouldn't give her the satisfaction.

"Anthony," she tried again.

"Dr. Jackson," I corrected her.

I could feel her eye roll, and I felt myself smirk.

"Will you talk to me if I call you Dr. Jackson?"

"No."

"Why not?"

"Because you're being a damn snoop."

She brought her hand to her chest on a heavy inhale and this time I rolled my eyes.

"You wound me."

"Bullshit."

"Watch your mouth, young man." She leaned forward. "Who was the girl?"

"I'm not doing this, Lucille. I'm working." I stood up and gently grabbed her arm, pulling her out of the chair with one hand and opening the door with the other. "And you're leaving."

She paused in the doorway, looking up at me. "Just tell me you didn't make a mistake. She showed up yesterday, soaking wet from the snow, looking plain pitiful. Just tell me you didn't do that to that poor girl." Her eyes were full of worry, and it finally occurred to me what she thought.

I barked out a laugh. "Jesus, no! Of course I didn't do anything to her. She's a friend. She needs help."

And I was going to help her. Because it was what I did every day. Helping Ms. Potter wouldn't be any different from helping the other countless moms who'd walked into my offices.

She let out a relieved sigh, and I gave her a death glare that should have sent her skittering to her desk at the front of the office.

"Don't you have a nail to file? Or a gossip magazine to catch up on?" I asked, goading her.

She threw a red-tipped finger in my face. "Don't you dare. I work hard for my measly wages. If I want to file my nails or read in between patients, that's no concern of yours. I get the job done."

"Oh, I think it is."

"It isn't," she argued.

"It is. This is my office."

"And you wouldn't know what the hell was going on without me, Anthony. I'm the glue that holds this place together. Besides, let's be honest, you may own this practice, but this office, it's mine."

I laughed at her dramatics, but she had me by the balls there. She did get her job done, even if she did spend too much time on the phone with friends and polishing her nails during work hours.

The worst part? The patients adored her.

"Go to work. I have patients to see." I pushed past her to get to exam room three, but she grabbed my arm.

"We aren't done talking about this."

"There's really nothing to talk about. She's a friend. Her baby has a problem, and she thinks I'm the man to help with it."

She nodded. "Where is she staying? What can I do?"

"Tonight, she's staying at my place. Tomorrow, I'll have to find her another place."

She gave me a hard stare.

"Don't look at me like that, Lucille. I'm working an overnight at the hospital."

"But you're not scheduled to work tonight."

"I am now." I breezed past her to make my way to exam room three and my first patient, in hopes she'd drop it.

I could spot another question on her lips as I skirted into the exam room and closed the door behind me, a smile already on my face for my coolest patient.

"Ian, my man!" I said loudly, holding my hand up for a high-five. The Filipino four-year-old smacked his hand against my own and grinned at me with all of the innocence of a child from the examination table.

"Sup, Doc Jackson?" Ian went in for a second round of hand-shakes that the kids referred to as dap that I'd learned long ago so I'd look the coolest. And I was. The kids loved me.

His mom sat in the corner, a small smile on her face as she rolled her eyes.

"Alright, buddy, let's check you out." Ian was two months past his third heart surgery with me and he was doing amazing.

"Let's see those big muscles."

His arms flexed at his attempt to make muscles. "Okay, guy, put those guns away before you have all the nurses in here checking you out."

28

His mom giggled as I examined the rest of his body before finally getting to the nitty gritty. "Okay, show me your superhero badge."

He pulled open the front of the gown to reveal the thick, long scar that ran the length of his chest.

"Looking good, my man." I checked the healing wound and let his mother know that everything looked great before heading to my next patient and then my next, all the while trying to keep the image of a glowing, pregnant, blast from the past out of my mind. It didn't work at all.

Chapter 6

Kelly

"I'm in his apartment," I whispered to myself, standing in the small foyer right inside the door where I'd been standing for the last fifteen minutes. I was going to have a panic attack. My bag with all of my belongings still hung from my shoulder heavily, but for some reason I just couldn't make myself move. I looked around the apartment, equal parts bewildered and awed. He'd come a long way from the small studio apartment I'd spent one night in with him long ago. I stared around at the lavish space. The nice leather furniture and expensive rugs, but still I didn't move.

"Why am I in his apartment?" I still couldn't believe it. Somehow, our conversation had gone from 'please help me with my child's failing heart' to 'go stay the night at my apartment'. Anthony and I didn't keep in touch. We really weren't old friends. We'd had one amazing night together that had ended so badly I'd tried to block it from my mind.

I was actually standing in the foyer trying to block this very minute from my mind, too. Who does that? Hands someone they had a one-night stand with the keys to their damn home? Was he some kind of saint? My heart fluttered at that. Good, I needed a saint right now.

Light blues and browns surrounded me, and I thought the place definitely had a homey feel. Even though I didn't really know the Anthony Jackson of now, I could somehow see him lounging on the big, plush leather sofa that took up most of the living room. The TV would be on and his big body—whoa, Kelly. Let's not think about Anthony's big body because that was just asking for trouble and I already had trouble in heaps.

My phone rang from inside my bag and I was never more glad for the distraction. I sat my bag on the perfectly polished dark wood floor and rummaged through it, breathing like a goddamn elephant. I gave up and finally slid down the floor onto my behind and leaned against the front door, taking deep breaths. Being pregnant was no joke. I'd never been so tired, so out of breath, so clumsy in my entire life.

I finally found the phone and smiled at the screen before answering.

"Hello."

"Jesus, why the hell do you sound like that? Ohhh, are you finally getting some? You shouldn't have answered. You totally could have called me back." She snickered.

"Ha-ha. You're hilarious, Miranda. No. I'm just over here huffing and puffing because this is what I do now. You don't know my life."

She laughed. "Oh, I know your life. I know it times five. So, suck it up, buttercup."

That's why I loved Miranda. Everyone else was babying my

ass, telling me everything was going to be okay and that I just had to pray, but not Miranda. Praying wasn't going to do shit. Actions. That was going to make a difference in my baby's life. Miranda was right. I needed to suck it the hell up. She was also crazy as hell. Who the hell had five kids? Miranda, that's who.

"I'm sucking all right," I breathed out and rocked my head back against the door and closed my eyes. What the hell was I doing here? Maybe I should have just gone with the doctor Medicaid told me to. Maybe this was all a big mistake. Maybe I was already completely fucking up this mother thing.

"You okay?" Her voice was soft over the line.

My head shot up, and I took in the overly nice room I was sitting on the floor of.

"Nope, don't do that. That's not what we do. You give me shit. I come back with a sarcastically brilliant remark, and we laugh and laugh and laugh." I didn't say it, but I didn't need to. I needed the normal, and she knew it.

"Okay, fine. Sit around feeling sorry for yourself and don't tell me a damn thing about it. I couldn't care less, you know. I've got twenty million kids and a ridiculous husband to tell me their problems, anyway. I'm all booked up. You're actually doing me a favor."

We laughed and laughed and laughed until we didn't and the line got quiet.

"So, did you do it? Did you go see him?"

She said him in a whisper that made Anthony seem like the villain in a movie. And again I thought of him in that ridiculous bow tie. It made me giggle.

I knew who she was talking about, but I couldn't help but tease her. "Him?"

"You know exactly who I'm talking about, Kells. He who must not be named."

"Yep, I talked to him. As a matter of fact, I'm standing in his apartment right now."

She sucked in enough air I could hear it over the line. "What? Why are you there? Did he kidnap you? Is he holding you hostage in his basement? How did you answer the phone if your hands are tied? I'm on my way."

"You're insane. You know that?" I laughed, but I was thankful for her crazy antics at the moment. I couldn't even take a step out of the foyer I was so overwhelmed with the mess my life was. No money. No home. And now I was mooching off the person who could save my baby's life.

"Yeah, that's what they tell me. But, you know, they don't know my life."

I laughed again at how she turned my own joke around on me.

"But, for real, why are you there?"

Hell, I didn't know why I was there either. He'd handed me those keys, and I didn't feel like I had much of an option. I needed him right now.

"He didn't want me to stay at the hotel I was at. He handed me his keys and rattled off an address, and here I am."

"Huh…that actually sounds admirable."

I smiled into the phone. Miranda, Anthony, and Ainsley had all grown up together, and honestly Miranda couldn't stand the guy when they were kids. Even he himself had admitted to me he'd been an asshole.

"Yep, says he's gonna help me."

"I'm glad, Kells. So glad." I could hear the relief in her voice, and I knew she'd been worried about me.

"So what's the devil's lair look like, anyway?"

I groaned. "I wouldn't know. I've literally been hanging out in the foyer for over twenty minutes."

"Why? He gave you the keys, Kells. Have a look around. He's not home. Have a peek in his pantry and fridge. Ease on over to his bedroom and look in his bathroom cabinets. Have a look in his underwear drawer. It's your big chance to totally invade his privacy."

She muttered, "It's like I don't even know you."

I laughed, but part of me really wanted to do that. I wanted to know what he was like now. What kind of shower gel he used and if he wore boxers or briefs. God, I hoped it was boxer briefs. The other part of me was terrified I'd like what I'd learn by snooping a little too much and I wasn't here to be all swoony over Anthony Jackson. It would never work anyway. He was some high profile heart doctor and I was a knocked up, washed up musician who needed to find a job. He probably thought I was a hot mess and he'd be right.

"It's not nice to spy on people, Miranda."

"Again, who are you? Come on, at least take a peek in his closet. I want to know how many dead bodies he's hiding in there."

I picked myself up off the floor with an eye roll, but I knew what she was doing. She was getting me up off my ass and into the apartment. I needed to get over my shit, and if I had to snoop around for Miranda to do it, I would.

I grabbed my bag and headed for the kitchen that was all gleaming white cabinets and gray granite countertops. It didn't look like it had ever been used, so I opened the refrigerator and was surprised to find a good bit of food inside.

"Sorry to disappoint you, Miranda, but the kitchen is sparkling. No murders have taken place in this room."

"Is there food?"

"Yep, already checked the fridge."

"Sweet, I knew I could count on you."

I chuckled at our game a little before going back out into the living room and past the dining room that was attached. There was a little hallway right off those rooms that had a guest bathroom that seemed virtually untouched.

The farther I made my way down that little hall, the more I smelled it. And it smelled good. Really good. My pulse kicked up a notch as I entered the bedroom that reeked of testosterone and musk and pure, unadulterated man. It did all kinds of dirty things to my already hormonally addled brain. Still I pressed on into the light brown room, past the large king-sized bed and heavy dark wood dresser to the closed door in the corner. I pressed my hand over my nose and mouth, trying not to smell the goodness that was Anthony Jackson.

I pushed that door open and if I thought for one second it smelled good before I was wrong. A woodsy scent poured out of that closet and into that bedroom in two seconds flat and I found myself taking in the small space for all of a millisecond before turning and running right back toward the living room.

"Abort, abort!" I shouted to Miranda on the phone that was clutched in my hand like a lifeline.

"Oh my God, how many dead bodies?" she shouted back.

"None. Not a damn one." I sounded disappointed, and I was because no man should smell that freaking good, especially not the one I needed in a medical capacity.

I threw my bag on the floor and myself onto the living room couch and fanned my face, because I was on fire. God, I was hot.

"Well, what happened? Don't keep a sister waiting. It was handcuffs and whips, wasn't it? Did he have a red room of pain? I knew that fucker was into some kinky shit."

"Jesus, you have got to stop reading so many romances."

"Holden doesn't mind."

I smirked. "I bet not."

"Well?"

I rolled over on the couch and buried my face in the back pillow, pressing the phone into my ear and I mumbled, "Thedeversroonmellsikeheaven."

"What the hell did you just say?"

I pulled my face out of the couch pillow and groaned into the room. I was in physical pain. No pregnant woman should ever, ever have to smell a smell like that in their lives unless there was a willing man within five feet.

"The devil's room smells like heaven. How is that possible?"

Miranda's maniacal laugh over the phone snapped me out of whatever chemically-induced fog Anthony's cologne had put me under.

"Oh, goodness, those pregnancy hormones got you all messed up," she said through giggles, and I could picture her wiping tears of laughter from the corners of her brown eyes.

"Go to hell."

She laughed some more before offering. "What's the address? I'm going to send you some presents to get you through the hard times."

Oh, no no no, I didn't need those kind of presents coming to Anthony's house. Could you imagine my embarrassment? Besides I wasn't even sure how long I was staying here. As far as I knew, only a night. Although, he did say something about finding me suitable accommodations. Ya know, in that hoity toity way that pissed me off.

I settled back onto the couch and brought my feet up, feeling completely exhausted. I sighed into the phone.

"I don't know where I'll be staying. I think this is just temporary, but honestly I'm feeling so thankful for a safe place to stay for the night. I'm exhausted."

"I'm glad Anthony put you up for the night. Even if he is a grade A douche." The line was quiet. "Do you need anything? Do you need me or Ainsley? We can come there. You're only a few hours away."

God, my friends. They were amazing. I hadn't thought about how lucky I was in a long time. Not since the heart diagnosis. It had me feeling like the unluckiest person in the world. But I was wrong. I had people who loved me and cared about me. Even a man who barely knew me, who put me up in his house for the night. Yeah, I was damn lucky.

A doorbell rang that sent my body shooting straight up. I

cringed a little at the pinch in my back.

"What was that?" I guess Miranda had heard it, too.

"I have no idea. I think it's a doorbell. Let me go, so I can check out who's here."

I got up off the couch and headed toward the front door.

"Don't open it. It could be a murderer, a human trafficking ring—"

"Lay off the romantic suspense, too, lady," I cut her off. "Call me later, love you."

I hung up and looked through the peephole in the door, curious if I should even answer. The teenage boy standing on the other side of the door looked safe enough, so I opened the door.

"Can I help you?" I hoped he didn't say yes. There was nothing I could do to help him. I couldn't even help myself at this point.

"Kelly Potter?" he asked, holding out a paper bag that smelled suspiciously like the most delicious food ever.

"Yes?" I eyed the bag, thinking I was going to have to steal it because I definitely didn't order it. I would have remembered. I was crazy, but I wasn't that crazy. Yet.

He handed the food over, and I took it because I wasn't stupid, but I was also honest, so I said, "But I haven't ordered any food."

He shrugged. "I'm just the delivery guy and if your name is Kelly Potter then that food is yours." He turned and headed back toward the elevator and said over his shoulder, "It's already paid for."

I closed the door and took the food to the kitchen, opening the containers to find grilled chicken and rice and Greek salad with a side of hummus and bread. Oh my God. I'd died and gone to heaven. Right on cue my stomach growled and I searched Anthony's cabinets for a plate before I ate this food right out of the cartons like a savage.

I wasn't a fool. He'd sent me food, but he wasn't here for me to refuse, so I was going to enjoy it. I was going to close the door to that bedroom that smelled like the manliest man ever and grab some blankets, cuddle up on the couch, eat, rest, watch TV, and relax for the first time in months. I needed it. Just a little time to recuperate. Just a little time to get my footing again. Just a few worry-free hours.

Chapter 7

Anthony

I adjusted my polka-dotted tie as I stood outside of my apartment door and fidgeted with the cufflinks of my jacket for the millionth time. Should I knock? Just go on in? I had an extra set of keys. Fuck, I was nervous. I didn't like it one damn bit. I was never fucking nervous. I was a goddamn rock star in and outside of the operating room. To think I was letting this tiny woman throw me off my game was fucking comical. If you were the laughing type, that is.

I'd spent the night tossing and turning on one of the stretchers in an extra room at the hospital, and it wasn't just because I was uncomfortable as hell. Kelly was back. Only she was different and so was I, and for fuck's sake, I was supposed to save her baby's life. She was just another patient's mother, or at least that's what I told myself. But I knew better; she was the one who got away. The one

I'd let get away. It had been a mistake.

I was being ridiculous. I was just here to drop off her intake information and tell her the arrangements I'd made for her. This was my home. I had absolutely no reason to be nervous.

I pushed the door open and stepped inside. Placing my keys in the basket on the foyer table, I walked toward the bedroom expecting to find her asleep in my bed, but before I even made it to the back hallway, I noticed a big lump under two sets of covers on my couch.

It couldn't be. Why in the hell would she choose to sleep on the couch instead of my comfortable bed? Stepping closer to the couch, I investigated the piles of covers more closely and sure enough one of her hands was hanging out of the bottom and off the couch.

The words were out of my mouth before I could stop them. "What in the ever-loving hell are you doing sleeping out here?"

A blur of dark hair and milky white skin shot up on the couch and the covers fell back, revealing a rumpled and ridiculously cute but angry Kelly. Her eyes glared at me from behind thick locks of dark hair.

"Jesus fucking Christ, you scared the shit out of me."

I raised an eyebrow. "I hope not, you're still sitting on my couch," I deadpanned.

"Ha-ha. Hilarious. Are you going on the road with that act?" she asked grumpily, lying back and pulling the covers over her head.

I looked around the room for the first time noticing the absolute mess that was my living space. Two plates with leftover food and a couple of empty glasses littered the table and it looked like Kelly's bag of clothing had exploded all over the place.

I pulled the covers from over her head and stared down at her. "Why didn't you sleep in the bed? You had the whole damn apartment and yet you chose to sleep on a leather sofa? And what the hell happened in here?"

Even at thirty-three years old women fucking baffled me.

I sounded like an asshole, but I couldn't help it. It seemed like I had one speed with this woman, and it was firmly set to bastard.

She let out a long breath and sat up. "I couldn't." Biting her lip, she averted her gaze. "It didn't feel right. I didn't feel comfortable."

I couldn't put my finger on it, but something seemed off. Was she lying? Why? My bed was comfortable. I'd paid thousands and thousands of dollars to make sure of that. I needed my rest. It was more than important to my job. When a baby's life hung in the balance, you couldn't be tired.

I looked at the leather couch with disgust. "This couch couldn't have been comfortable."

She yawned. "Oh, it was. Trust me. I haven't had such a peaceful night of sleep in months." She smiled and I softened. "Thanks for letting me stay."

She pulled the covers back and placed her feet to the floor, revealing pink-tipped feet and legs that seemed ridiculously long for such a short woman. I wanted to tell her to put those damn sticks of dynamites away. They were inappropriate and sexy as hell. I cleared my throat and made sure to keep my eyes off those legs and my temper in check.

"Did you get dinner?" I tried to soften my voice. See, I was making an effort.

"Oh, yes, I did. Thank you for that, too. You've been so incredibly awesome about everything. I really appreciate it, but I'm going to pack my stuff up and get out of your hair. My guess is, you're ready to have your apartment back."

Who was this gushing, sweet woman? Did she think she had to butter me up because I was helping her? I already told her I would. I wouldn't go back on my word if she didn't kiss my ass. I pulled at the tie around my neck. It felt tight. She was being too nice. The Kelly Potter I remembered from years ago asked a million questions and not a one of them was appropriate or timely. She was snarky and unashamed. She was magnificent.

"Well, actually, I'm not staying," I clipped out. "I just stopped by on the way to the office. I have to work today, but I wanted to drop off all your intake and release forms. I'll need all the information from the doctors who diagnosed your baby's heart problem. If you fill everything out, I'll have Lucille pick them up tomorrow and then we can get you in for an appointment and workup."

She smiled and pushed the hair off her face. "Lucille? Is she the lady from your office?"

I nodded. "Yep, one and the same."

"Okay, I'll get them filled out, but I can just bring them by tomorrow. I have a few errands to run, anyhow. You don't need to inconvenience Lucille."

I arched an eyebrow. "But I love to inconvenience her." It was true. I lived for it most days.

She giggled. "Somehow that doesn't surprise me."

I headed toward the kitchen. "Come on. I'll whip us up something for breakfast."

She followed me, shaking her head. "No, please, you don't have to do that."

The kitchen was crowded with both of us in there and it reminded me of the last time I'd made us breakfast. It may have been ten years ago, but it could have been two nights ago the way I recalled it. It was so clear in my mind. Her naked form perched on a different set of counters but still mine nonetheless. She'd been young and carefree and wild. So sexy.

I pulled out a carton of eggs and she stood there awkwardly, her hands fisted in the bottom of the sweatshirt she was wearing. I could see something was on her mind, and I wasn't one to mince words or try to dance around questions.

Giving her an imploring look, I asked, "What is it?"

She dragged her plump, pink bottom lip into her mouth and even though I didn't want to I noticed. I noticed it a hell of a lot, but

I told myself I'd noticed plenty of beautiful women doing provocative things before. It had never affected my job. And it wouldn't now. I wouldn't look at her lips or legs. I'd be safe then.

"I don't want you to think I came here expecting you to take care of me. I just need you to do the surgeries. The doctors said she would need three sometime during the first five years of her life." She paused, and I took a break from whisking the eggs to look at her face. Her bottom lip trembled, but tears didn't shine in her eyes, and I thought of how brave she was being for her daughter. I was impressed and I wasn't easily impressed. I had to give it to her. She was giving it a fighting try, but she still needed me.

"What I'm saying is, I'm here so you can save her life. I'm not here for you to save mine. I don't need saving. I need an amazing doctor. For her. That's it."

Inwardly I rolled my eyes and ignored the drivel she was spouting. She was a mess. It was clear she needed my help.

I poured the eggs in the pan and stirred. I wasn't even going to acknowledge how ridiculous she was being. "So, what are your plans for today?"

The woman was stubborn. She didn't know it, but I was more stubborn, and I'd had way more practice at it.

"I don't know. I need to find a long-term place to stay and a job."

Let's just jump right into this, shall we? "Speaking of working." I looked at her while I finished cooking the eggs. "We need to talk about that."

She pursed her lips and a fire lit in her eyes that made me strangely giddy. Anything was better than the pretend nice she'd been spoon feeding my ass all morning.

"No, we don't."

Oh, yes, I really liked this girl. "We do."

I wasn't an easing into the things type of guy. I was a man with facts, and the facts were she needed my help and I was going to give it. And maybe, just maybe, I enjoyed getting her riled up. Maybe I wanted to piss her off a little. Light a little bit of fire under her ass.

"No working. No heavy exercise." I spooned the eggs onto plates and turned toward her, ready for the fight.

Her face fell in shock just as her eyes lit up, and they were sparkling for a fight.

And stupid, stupid me, I couldn't help it. It was like second nature. My hand just flew out and grabbed her own, clutching tightly. Her hand hung limply in mine and it pissed me off. For some reason, I wanted her to squeeze mine back, accept my help.

I met her eyes head-on. I held her hand tighter. She needed to hear me out. "You're going to have to stop being stubborn about this. I need you to take care of yourself right now for your baby's sake. Do you understand what I'm saying? We can't afford to put any undue stress on your baby girl's heart right now, and if that means you have to take a little help from me, then you need to just accept it. There's no other way." There, I'd put it out there as plainly as I could.

She pulled her hand from mine and ran both of her palms over her face before leaning against the counter. "Fuck."

And just like that her fire was doused. I didn't like it one damn bit.

I swallowed hard. I didn't want to upset her. I just wanted her to understand what was at stake—her baby's life.

"I get it's not ideal accepting help from a virtual stranger, but I want to help you." I grabbed her hand again. "Let me."

I gave the meaty part of her palm one more hard squeeze and let go, because what I was about to say was going to thoroughly piss her off, but she cut me off.

"I think I need to call my mom," she whispered.

I nodded, feeling like one of those ridiculous little figurines people kept in the front windows of their cars with the wobbly heads. Just bobbing my head whether someone was just cruising or having a life-threatening crisis. Christ, but I didn't know what else to do but nod. Why was she here alone? It infuriated me. Where was the man who got her pregnant? Had she not already called her mom about all of this? I had a million questions, but a professional courtesy to her privacy kept me from grilling the hell out of her.

I wanted to save the rest of our conversation for another day. She seemed distraught and visibly upset, but it couldn't wait. There just wasn't time. The sooner we got her settled, the sooner she'd have less stress, the healthier her baby would be.

I pretended not to notice the beginnings of an epic meltdown, and I could see one coming a mile away. I'd delivered enough bad news to patients over the years to see the signs, and I could tell a tsunami of tears and hysterics were headed my way.

The way she kept wringing her hands. The frown line in between her eyebrows. The slight quiver of her bottom lip. They were all dead giveaways.

But I couldn't baby her. I'd already grabbed her hand in a moment of weakness. I couldn't let it go further than that. I didn't hold patients' hands or hug them. I was a straight shooter. I'd tell them like it was and then save their child's life.

Walking around the bar and toward the dining table, I said, "Sit. Let's talk."

She followed slowly behind me, the frown line on her forehead deepening, her lips turned down in what could only be described as a scowl.

She sat down in a chair heavily, and I placed her food in front of her.

I sat down across from her and sipped my coffee, studying her face. "No work. No exercise. The end."

She didn't say anything at all. Only stared at her food and bit her lip every now and then. I wasn't even sure if she heard me.

"Surely, the other doctors told you to take it easy?" I couldn't believe how upset she was. It was as if she was hearing this news for the first time.

She nodded as she stared into space before answering. "Yeah, they told me to take it easy. No heavy activity, but I at least thought I'd be able to work."

"Well, that's out. Now eat." I inclined my head toward her plate of food she'd barely touched and started in on my own.

Her eyes widened. "Excuse me?"

I wanted to smile. This was the Kelly I remembered. The one who took no shit. I'd liked her so much. It could have been more, but fate had other plans.

"Eat your food."

"I heard you the first time, Doc. I'm not deaf. I'm also not dumb. So, I don't need anyone to remind me to eat," she snapped at me.

Doc. And that hit me right in the chest. Just a tiny pinch. But that was all it took. Doc. The memory settled over me so heavily. How she'd called me that so affectionately with a bit of pride and teasing laced throughout her voice. I'd missed it, damn it. I'd missed her. After only one night. It made me irrationally angry. It was my fault, but still, the circumstances of how that night ended almost seemed completely out of my control.

I looked at my plate, feeling too many things, mostly overwhelmed. "Eat your food, Ms. Potter, and then I'll escort you to your new home for the next few months," I said to my plate of eggs.

I felt her eyes snap to me even though I was avoiding looking at her. "What?"

"I told you I'd find suitable accommodations for you and I did."

"I didn't ask for you to find me a place to stay."

"I'm aware."

"Then why the hell did you?"

I grabbed my coffee and plate and headed for the kitchen. I was putting my plate in the dishwasher when I felt her behind me.

"Well?" she asked the back of my head.

I stood on a sigh and looked at the ceiling of my apartment, praying for patience to deal with the most beautifully infuriating woman I'd ever had the pleasure to meet twice.

My prayers didn't work at all. "Because I fucking felt like it." I pushed past her and started grabbing the dirty dishes off the coffee table in the living room and loading those in the dishwasher, too.

It was a comfort knowing some things didn't change. The woman could still make a huge mess in two seconds flat.

"You fucking felt like it?" she yelled. "You felt like it?" she repeated, sounding crazed as she followed me around the apartment, and I couldn't help but smile. I liked her like this. Like the Kelly I remembered. Full of life and spunk and heat.

I turned to her, gesturing to her explosion of clothes and toiletries all over my living room floor. "Yes, I felt like it. Now pack your shit. I have to get to work."

Her mouth fell open. "You did not. You did not just tell me to pack my shit."

"Are you going to repeat everything I say today?" I picked up a white, lacy bra hanging off the side of the couch.

She snatched it from my hands and stuffed it into her bag along with other clothes off the floor. "You're impossible. I should have known. Miranda warned me."

I smirked. Oh, Miranda and I had grown up together, and I enjoyed torturing her. "Of course she did. Chop-chop. You need to get dressed, and we need to get going."

She paused and glared at me below the waist. "Oh, I'll chop-chop, all right."

I decided right then and there this was exactly how this was going to play out. She could hate me. She could literally loathe the sight of me, but she wasn't going to cry or have nervous break-downs. She wasn't going to shout or scream. She was going to fight and if that meant she was fighting me, then so be it. I'd be her out-let. If I had to call her every day and rile her the hell up until her daughter was whole, I would.

Yes, I'd keep her fire lit and her storm raging. We'd get through the rain together.

Chapter 8

Kelly

This man was out of his ever-loving mind. I stood in the middle of an apartment that was identical to Anthony's besides the decor, of course. Which shouldn't have been a surprise since it was only two floors above his.

"I can't afford this place. You are out of your mind."

"The rent is taken care of."

I stormed up to him, ready to pull every single hair out of my head. The sheer audacity of this man. I couldn't even believe it. He'd been bossing me around from the moment I'd asked for his help, and it didn't seem like he had any plans on stopping any time soon.

"You are not paying my rent, Anthony Jackson."

I hadn't depended on anyone but myself since I'd graduated college. I was a strong, independent woman. I didn't take handouts from men.

He smiled down at me. It wasn't a nice smile, but instead an asshole smile, but it was still sexy. God, he was pretty, damn him. Standing toe-to-toe with him, I had a pretty sweet view. He was better looking than he'd been ten years ago, and it just wasn't fair because he'd been so handsome and breathtaking then. Why did men age so damn graciously? The slight lines around his eyes only made him look more distinguished. How did he have stubble today already, and why did it look like it needed a good lick? And damn it, but he smelled like his bedroom, and I found myself holding my breath even while wondering how he managed to make that absurd bow tie hot. I could have screamed.

"Chill, bite size. I'm not paying for anything, so put a pause on your conniption fit. I have a doctor friend in Syria who's away with Doctors Without Borders. He'll be gone for the next six months. He said it was cool if you stayed here."

Did he just call me bite size? Conniption fit? The man could drive a saint to murder. "I can't stay here."

I couldn't explain it, but I didn't feel right about Anthony calling in favors for me. Besides, it was way too nice of a place. I could find a crappy studio apartment to stay in for the next couple of months. I had a little money saved up, and if I played it right I could make it work for a little while.

"You can and you will."

"No, I can't. I can't even afford a portion of the rent on a place like this."

"It doesn't matter. It's paid for already. All you have to do is keep it clean. I know that's asking a lot, but I think you can manage if you try really hard."

Oh, the condescension in that sentence almost really did send me into a conniption. Asshole. I rolled my eyes. I backed up and grabbed my bag off the floor and headed toward the door. I didn't have to stand here and listen to him despite what he thought. I only needed him in a professional capacity. Nothing more.

"Uh uh uh," he said from behind me, lifting the bag from my shoulder filled with all of the belongings I owned, and carried it to the hallway off the living room.

"What the hell are you doing?" I knew what he was doing. He was taking my stuff to the bedroom. And I knew what I was doing because he was pissing me off so I was making a scene.

I stood at the foot of the bed with my arms crossed and looked at the bag he laid on the bed.

"What does it look like I'm doing?" His eyes met mine with a dare even as he unzipped the bag slowly, seductively like he'd unzipped the back of my dress that night so long ago, and a shiver started in my toes and slipped right to my nipples. He must have seen it because one side of his lips hitched up in an almost smile.

Damn hormones. I couldn't be held responsible for my body's actions. I mean, the man was wearing an ugly bow tie, for goodness' sake. Clearly I was out of my mind.

He reached into the bag and of course found that lace bra again and held it out. "I'm helping you unpack." He smiled at me.

I snatched the silky piece of material from his hands and quickly shoved it under my shirt. "You are doing no such thing." It was embarrassing the first time, even more so this go around. That bra was huge and not pretty. It had been a while since a man had seen my bra, and of course it had to be a giant, ugly pregnancy bra. I moved closer to the bed and blocked his path to my bag.

His jaw ticked. "Unpack the bag, shortcake. Now," he gritted out.

Shortcake? He was just full of all kinds of short girl nicknames, wasn't he? I flicked that bow tie again because it was fun. And it annoyed him. "No."

His hand shot around me and dragged my bag off the bed and onto the floor. He pulled the handle toward the dresser and opened one of the big drawers at the bottom.

Grabbing my bag off the floor and holding it in his arms, he looked at me. "I was going to do this the easy way, but since you seem to like things hard." He paused with a smirk and a raise of the eyebrows, and I rolled my eyes at his emphasis on the word hard because even though he was a thirty-something-year-old educated man, he had the sense of humor of a thirteen-year-old boy.

I pursed my lips, and he grinned evilly before turning my bag over and dumping all the contents in the bottom of the dresser drawer. "We're gonna do things your way, Ms. Potter." He gave the bag a final shake. "The hard way."

I walked quickly toward the dresser drawers, jaw slack as I looked at all my toiletries and clothes thrown in the dresser haphazardly and spilling out over the side.

He slammed the drawer closed even though half of my shit was hanging out and then looked at me. He eyed me up and down, frowning at my stomach, and then bent over, opening the drawer again before standing back up and reaching under the bottom of my shirt and snatching the bra I'd hidden down there minutes before and tossing it in the already too full dresser drawer before slamming it closed again.

He'd been too quick for me to do anything but stand here like a fool. My eyebrows smacked my hairline. "You're insane!" I screamed two inches from his face.

He dusted his hands together and started walking to the front door. He was certifiable. He was not leaving. I was leaving.

He laid his hand on the doorknob and turned around to look at me. "I'm insane." He halfheartedly laughed. "I'm insane? You're the most stubborn, infuriating woman I've ever met in my life!"

"I'm stubborn? That's hilarious, Doc. You're the absolute king of stubborn." I pushed his hand off the doorknob. I was being immature; I just couldn't summon the will to care. The man drove me nuts.

Hands low on his hips, he turned to me. "I'm the king of a lot of things, baby, but stubborn isn't one of them."

"You're not leaving. I'm leaving!" I shouted, trying my damnedest to ignore his ridiculous sexual innuendo and him calling me baby. I didn't like it at all. Not even a little bit.

"You're not leaving. You're going to sit your ass on that couch and relax. Because it's what's best for your baby."

He stopped, looking at me because he knew he had me.

"Doctor's orders," he clipped out, adjusting his stupid tie and pulling at the cufflinks under his navy-blue blazer. He opened the door, giving me a final look before closing it quietly behind him like we weren't just having the throw down of all throw downs. And I knew a throw down when I witnessed one because I was a throwing down kind of girl.

I stood here, staring at the door, mad as hell, mostly because I hated how much I loved that blue blazer on him.

"Stupid tie, stupid blazer, stupid Dr. Anthony Jackson," I muttered to myself as I stomped back to the bedroom and pulled my stuff out of the dresser and placed it back on the bed, folding everything neatly.

I'd teach his ass. I'd call my momma and get the hell out of here. He couldn't tell me what to do. There were other doctors out there who could help me.

Baby girl somersaulted around in my stomach, and I smiled down at my belly despite the crazy day I'd had.

"Team Hope," I whispered to her, rubbing my hand over my belly.

Then I thought of all the diapers, clothes, and things I'd need to care for her. I thought of all the money I'd need to buy those things. And I realized I was standing in a very nice apartment. For free. So I took all the neatly folded clothes from the bed and slipped them into the dresser drawers Anthony had thrown my belongings in earlier.

I may not have wanted Anthony's help, but I needed it. It sucked, but I was just going to have to get the hell over it because this entire situation sucked, and I just needed to make the best of it. And that's what Anthony was. My best bet. My arch nemesis.

After I finished putting my clothes away I texted Miranda and Ainsley my new address for the next couple of months and put my shoes on, deciding I'd need to get groceries. It took way longer than it should have, and I was huffing and puffing by the time I actually got it done. As I went to open the apartment door, I heard a knock, so I looked through the peephole to find the same teenager from yesterday there with a bag of food. I opened the door and he gave me a look like I was going to argue with him again.

Instead, I grabbed the food from his hand and grumbled out a, "Yeah, yeah, I know the drill."

I closed the door, pushed my tennis shoes off with my heels because I was done trying to bend over anymore today, and opened my food and ate out of the containers on the sofa, savage and all.

The man wasn't going to let me do anything for myself, but I wasn't about to turn down food. I was starving and pregnant and until you actually were growing a baby you didn't quite understand what starving meant. Which meant I was hella hungry. All the time.

The bastard. He'd known exactly what I needed and he'd been ready to offer it up to me on a silver platter even though I didn't want it.

Yes, Dr. Anthony Jackson had won today, but tomorrow I wouldn't let him get me riled up. Yes, I'd be cool and I'd keep a calm head.

Tomorrow, I would win.

Chapter 9

Anthony

That Night Ten Years Ago

"Siblings?"

"One. Brother. And you?" I asked.

"Only child. Favorite movie?"

"That's easy. *Forrest Gump.*"

"Really?" Her forehead scrunched.

"Am I not allowed to like the movies I like?"

"I'm just surprised."

"Why? A lot of people like that movie."

"I don't know. You don't strike me as the kind of guy who likes the kind of movies a lot of people like, Doc."

I smiled at that. She thought I was special. I thought she was, too.

"Okay, what's your favorite movie?"

"*Steel Magnolias*, of course." She made a duh face.

"How cliché," I threw back at her and she tossed a piece of popcorn at me. The woman was destroying my apartment. She was like a one man wrecking team. There was evidence of her all over my apartment, from spilled food to pieces of popcorn. Her clothes were strewn about along with the plates from our dinner earlier.

"It's not cliché. It's a damn southern classic. You can't be a woman in the South and not have seen it, and you most certainly can't help but to love it." She clutched a pillow to her naked chest. "Gah, it makes me cry."

Damn, she was pretty. I wanted to keep her. She was almost small enough, I thought maybe I could stick her in my pocket and take her everywhere with me always. She'd make for good entertainment, that was for sure. She was funny and sweet and had this innate kind of happiness people hardly ever possessed anymore. She'd be the type of girl you wouldn't have to try to please all the time. No, Kelly was pleased all on her own.

She rolled over onto her back and her breasts were on full display. I loved that she wasn't ashamed of her body, and she shouldn't be because there was absolutely nothing there that wasn't fucking magnificent. And, God, my cock was already hard for her again and I'd just had her. We'd spent much of the night like this. Tangled up in each other, naked, and hot and whispering into the dark room of my apartment.

I'd never had a night like this before. Where I felt so completely connected to someone. Where it seemed there was only us in this dark space, talking in quiet voices, making love in hushed tones, not because we were afraid someone would hear, but because we didn't want them to. This night was just ours. Me and Kelly Potter, we were like fucking magic. I wanted to keep the glamour going forever.

I ran a hand through her hair. If I was learning one thing, it was that the woman loved to be petted, stroked, touched. And I'd be lying if I said I didn't really fucking enjoy obliging her.

"So, now that you're done with school, what are you going to do?" I asked, toying with the ends of her hair that grazed her neck.

She let out a low laugh. "Piss everyone off, I reckon."

I smiled at her. "Why?"

"Because I don't want to teach music. I don't want to be stuck in a classroom all day. I want to travel. I want to see the world. I want to make music."

That didn't surprise me a bit. The thought of someone trying to pin down this beautiful butterfly's wings made me sad. "I take it your family doesn't want you to do that?"

She shook her head. "No. I mean, I went to school for music education, but it was always a backup plan for me. I have a few friends I'm in a band with. We do okay. I thought I'd travel a bit with them. My mom isn't crazy about the idea, but she does want me to see the world before I settle down. My dad isn't really in the picture. He took off when I was a kid, so she was a single mom my entire childhood. She wants me to have a plan. A career, then a husband, then babies." She let out a long breath. "Her dreams aren't my dreams, though."

"And your dreams are to be in this band and travel the world?"

She pursed her lips and then smiled. "No, my dreams are to make it big, Anthony. I'm talking about roaring crowds, blinding lights, deafening music, and my drumsticks. I want to play for millions. For as long as I can remember, I've wanted to play music. When I was only eight I'd begged my mom for a drum set. She knew it was going to be hella noisy, but she'd finally caved and that was all she wrote."

Fuck, she was amazing. "Those are some pretty big dreams. What will you do if you don't make it?"

She pulled that plump bottom lip into her mouth and sucked before letting it go with a pop and looked me in the eye. "I don't know, Doc, but if your dreams don't scare you, then you aren't dreaming big enough."

I must have been losing my mind because if I'd been a woman in a Jane Austen book I would have been swooning my ass off. This woman and her words. They overwhelmed me. Her goodness, her maturity, her sincerity, they were the sweetest thing I'd ever witnessed in my life and even though I'd laid my lips to her countless times tonight I felt a need to kiss her like I'd never experienced. The want rushed over my skin like a thousand tiny stars shooting across the sky.

I leaned over her quickly, but it felt too slow. I needed her now. "Kiss me," my lips whispered across her own, breathlessly, wantonly.

Sparkling aquamarine eyes stared up at me. "Where?" she whispered back.

"Everywhere." And I didn't mean the warm spot behind my ear that she'd already realized was my weakness. Not the dimples in my cheeks that she couldn't help but to smack sweetly as we lay in bed and talked. No, I wanted this woman to ravish my spirit, my heart.

Kiss my soul, my eyes begged.

I wanted our bodies, our lips so entangled you couldn't tell one from the other. Until we were just floating—one. Terrified, exhilarated, but dreaming big, together.

Her mouth touched my own with unwavering intensity, her lips meeting mine, searing through me, tearing me down and all the while building me up. Just like I needed. Of course. It was like she knew me better than I did and all in a few hours. I was a goner.

Chapter 10

Kelly

Oh my God, I could have kissed Anthony. And not because he was so good-looking. This bathtub was freaking amazing, that's why. I'd passed out last night, sleeping like the dead and doing the pee pee dance all the way to the bathroom, only to spot the most amazing bathtub I'd ever seen in my life.

It was huge and when I say huge it was big enough for me to sprawl out and it still completely covered every inch of my body, even my bowling ball belly. Every woman knew how special and rare a bathtub was that completely submerged your body in water. And this one did. It even had jets. I was in heaven.

I spent longer than I should have in the tub, refilling it twice with hot water and still lounging about when I heard what I thought was a woman's voice from the other room.

I froze, not daring to move for fear of making a splashing sound.

"Hellooooo," I heard called out from the other room, and my eyes immediately zeroed in on the bathroom doorknob, which I hadn't bothered to lock because I somehow thought that locking the front door was good enough. Silly me.

I jumped out of the bathtub as quickly as possible, which wasn't very fast at all, leaving a trail of what felt like three gallons of water behind me. I grabbed a towel from the vanity and wrapped it around me just in the nick of time. The door flew open and there stood a perfectly coifed middle-aged woman in a startling and superb red dress suit that made me somehow feel underdressed when in truth I was as naked as a jay bird.

"Lucille?" I squeaked out.

She smiled. "Yes, dear, but you can call me Lucy."

She just stood there in the doorway, taking me in like we were standing in the middle of the living room and I was fully clothed, which definitely wasn't the case.

She walked toward me and my body locked tight. She reached out and ran a hand through the side of my wet hair, lovingly. Creepily as hell, too. "Well, you're quite lovely, aren't you, sweets?"

What in the hell was happening?

"I'm naked," I finally said, not knowing what else to say.

"Well, I can see that, honey. But you don't have anything I haven't seen a million times in a million different ways."

And I almost laughed because I in no way wanted to know how many different million times or ways Lucille had seen naked girlie bits.

She turned and looked at herself in the mirror, patting her blond-gray hair into place and wiping the red lipstick from the corners of her mouth like she hadn't interrupted the most amazing bath of my life, like I wasn't stark-ass naked wrapped in a white towel that did not cover my baby bump.

"Go on and get dressed so you can help me put away the groceries, would you?" she clipped before turning on black heels with red soles and leaving the bathroom the way she'd entered. Very quickly. And I wondered how the hell a woman who worked as a receptionist at a doctor's office could afford those heels and that perfectly fitted red suit.

And more importantly, how the hell she'd gotten into the apartment even though it was locked.

So I just stood here and stared for no less than a full two minutes before the clattering of cabinets being slammed snapped me out of my daze.

I hustled my ass into some panties, black yoga pants, and a tank top. I skipped the bra because let's be honest, she'd almost seen me buck ass naked anyway, so what did it matter at this point.

I walked to the kitchen, not quite understanding what was happening. Grocery bags littered every available surface of the kitchen and the fridge and cabinets were wide-open. "What are you doing, Lucille?"

"Lucy," she immediately corrected me as she placed a loaf of bread in a stainless-steel bread box on the counter.

I nodded. "Okay, Lucy. What the hell is going on?"

"I brought groceries."

Oh, hell no. I was winning today. And letting Anthony buy me groceries was not winning. It was losing. And I wasn't losing anymore. I'd written that off yesterday after I'd pigged out over the meal he'd sent me. I was done with his handouts.

"No, no, no. I don't want Anthony's groceries. Pack them up and take them down two floors to his place. Come on, I'll help you."

I picked up a couple of bags and started toward the front door.

"Oh, no, Anthony didn't send me over with these. I just thought you might need them and since I was coming over to pick up your intake papers, I thought I'd kill two birds with one stone."

Oh, no. It was the sting of my nose that told me what was going to happen before it started. The burn in my eyes was the next indication, and I immediately sat the bags down back in the kitchen and tried to suck back the tears that threatened. Why was everyone being so nice to me? Why were they helping me? It just didn't make sense! And it was overwhelming. It was making me feel too much. Sad that I couldn't help myself but most of all I felt relieved, and I didn't even realize it until that moment standing here in the kitchen with gorgeous, perfectly groomed Lucille in her red suit and red-soled shoes, looking like she'd stepped off the pages of a fashion catalogue and me looking like a drowned, pregnant, braless rat. I was so relieved.

I involuntarily choked out a sob I hadn't felt coming. Damn hormones.

"Oh, honey." Lucille came toward me and wrapped her arms around me, enveloping me in the scent of expensive perfume and hairspray. She was hugging me. She was freaking hugging me! I wasn't a hugger. I hated hugs, but her hugs weren't so bad, so I leaned into her a bit.

"Don't be upset. I just thought I'd bring you some groceries since I knew there were none here. I didn't want your little one getting hungry." She patted my round stomach.

I'd learned quickly that I didn't like strangers touching my stomach once it started to grow big and round. I felt weird and oddly violated, but I didn't feel that way with Lucille. She seemed to genuinely care, and she'd brought me groceries out of the kindness of her heart. And I thought maybe she was just a little crazy, which for some reason I really liked.

And even though tears shone in the depths of my eyes, I backed away from her and smiled. I sucked back the wetness that threatened to fall. "Thank you, Lucille. Lucy," I corrected myself.

She started putting groceries away again, and I helped her. It was silent for about five bags until she asked, "So you'll accept my groceries but not Anthony's?" She had a small smile playing at her lips.

I shook my head back and forth, exasperated. "That man. He's a big tyrant in a tiny bow tie."

She laughed and nodded. "Yes, and he's so bossy."

"I've been here less than two days and he has literally done nothing other than tell me what to do."

"Oh, sweetness, he loves to be in charge. He lives for it."

"How do you do it?" I asked and she raised her eyebrows questioningly. "Ya know? Work for him?"

She chuckled low. "I don't know. Some days I want to murder him. He's pushy and dictatorial." She laughed again. "I've quit five thousand times and he's probably tried to fire me five thousand more, but I've worked for him since he opened his practice." She shrugged.

"Yeah, he's a pushy bastard."

"He is."

"And he's high-handed."

"Mmmhmm," she agreed.

"He's sneaky, too." He was. The man just brought me up here and was like here you go. Welcome home! "And he wears those ridiculous bow ties!" I continued.

She placed the cheese in the fridge and turned back to me with a small grin on her face. "But he does look handsome in them, doesn't he?"

I narrowed my eyes at her before turning away and placing the chips in the pantry. "I guess," I huffed out.

"He has really nice eyes, too," she said softly.

I thought of Anthony's nice eyes. They really were pretty. I'd adored them ten years ago and now they were just as pretty and a bit wiser.

I found myself nodding even though I didn't want to agree with her. Because, damn, those eyes. *What? I was pregnant, not dead!*

"He works out every day, too, so he's nice and fit."

I got big eyes. Oh, God, I didn't want to hear about how fit

Anthony was, because I couldn't think about that. I couldn't think about the muscles and abs he was probably rocking underneath those sexy blazers that seemed to fit him like a glove. He'd been pretty damn fit ten years ago, too.

Before I knew what was happening, "Oh, I remember," slipped past my lips.

I paused, putting away the groceries in shock I'd said that, but also praying like hell Lucille hadn't heard me. I'd said it quietly, after all.

That woman didn't miss a beat, though. I should have known.

She arched a perfectly drawn on eyebrow at me. "Oh, do tell, darling."

I blushed under her scrutiny. She worked with the man. I couldn't tell her we'd had dirty, mind-blowing sex one night ten years ago.

"From the flush of your cheeks, I'd say whatever it is you're trying not to tell me is pretty juicy," she sang out, and I laughed.

"Well, let's just say ten years ago, before he was all of this"—I gestured around to the apartment even though it wasn't his because he had an identical one right below me—"we had a little bit of fun." I laughed because I felt ridiculous talking to this older woman about mine and her employer's sexual escapades.

"And now he'll be the one to save your baby's life. Seems serendipitous to me."

I sobered at the thought. Was it fate? Would Anthony be able to save my baby's life?

"Will he?" I swallowed hard, feeling like every bit of my fear and doubt was somehow lodged in my throat.

She cleared the last of the bags away and put them in the pantry and stood directly in front of me before taking my hands. "He's a bossy bastard, but he's good at what he does. He will. My boy won't let you down."

Her words eased the knot in my throat. If this brash, overly posh woman could believe in Anthony then I could, too.

"Well, then," she said, letting go of my hands. "Why don't I make us dinner? And I brought ice cream! We can watch a movie and eat and chat and get to know each other."

She was adorable, and I instantly wanted to be good friends with her. But I had a very serious question first.

"I never turn away food, so yes, but first, how the hell did you get in here, Lucy?"

Her evil laugh had me shaking my head.

"I took the key off Anthony's ring. At least we know he won't be barging in here tonight."

I laughed along with her and thought to myself that of course that butthole had an extra key to the place he'd shacked me up in. So he could sneak in and boss me whenever he wanted. Well, Lucy had shown him.

At least that's what I thought. Until around 8:00 p.m. when there was a quiet knock at the door.

Lucy and I were curled up on opposite ends of the plush brown sofa in the living room under thick fleece blankets with bowls of ice cream in our laps. She'd long since ditched her heels and suit jacket. She'd told me she was single. She and her husband divorced nine years ago. She followed it by saying that some marriages just couldn't handle when things got really tough. We talked for hours. We were thoroughly invested in the movie *Sweet Home Alabama* like we hadn't seen it a billion times when we heard it.

We both stared at the door and then stared at each other and did it one more time.

"It's the devil with dimples," I whispered.

"What on earth?"

"That's what my friends Ainsley and Miranda call him. That and thou who shall not be named."

Lucy snickered. "Doesn't surprise me." She stood up and placed her bowl on the table before heading to the door. "It might not be him."

"Oh, it's him. I can feel him trying to telepathically tell me what to do through the door."

She giggled, putting her face to the small hole in the door.

"It's him," she confirmed.

I placed my bowl next to hers. "Told ya."

"Open the door, Ms. Potter."

We gave each other big eyes and giggled behind our hands quietly.

"Now," we heard barked out from the other side of the door.

"Shall I open the door and put him out of his misery?"

I shrugged and pulled the blanket farther up over my shoulders.

She gave me one final look before opening the door and doing a grand sweeping gesture with her hand that made me giggle again. "Please, do come in, Anthony."

One step in and already he was frowning. He was going to ruin my ice cream and movie. I could see it coming a mile away.

"What are you doing here?" he questioned Lucille, and I got my hackles up.

"What are you doing *here*?" I interrupted. I wanted Lucille here. Him. Not so much.

His eyes cut to mine. "Just wanted to make sure you got settled." He glanced over the blankets and bowls before eyeing the TV.

"We're fine, as you can see," I pointed out and his face was a mix of relief and disappointment. I couldn't figure out for the life of me what he had to be disappointed about.

"I do see. Do you need anything at all?" he asked, shoving his hands into the pockets of his navy blue slacks and rocking up on his heels, and that's when I noticed he'd ditched the tie and the blazer. The top two buttons of his white dress shirt were unbuttoned, revealing tan, taut skin at the top of his chest, and my mouth watered a little.

His hair wasn't as neat as it had been this morning, and he'd obviously gone to his apartment before coming here to take off his jacket and tie. And then he'd come to check on me. I felt myself soften at the thought that he was worried about me needing anything.

"I'm good, Doc. Lucy brought me some groceries and we've spent the entire afternoon chatting."

He turned his closed mouth smile to Lucille. "She did, did she?" He gave her a reprimanding look. "I was wondering where you disappeared to. Jackie was a mess on the front desk today."

She shrugged. "I had more important things to do."

He looked back at me and said, "I see that, and I'd like my keys back." He held his hand out and my eyes shot to Lucille.

Don't you dare, my brain screamed at her, but I stayed quiet, hoping she could read my panicked expression.

If she read it, she didn't care because she marched over to her expensive black bag on the counter in the kitchen and pulled out a set of two keys. She walked back over and held them out, but as soon as Anthony's hand made to grab them, she snatched them back with a smile.

"Uh uh uh. Not until you lay one on me, darling," she said, tapping her right cheek with her index finger.

And me, I sat here stunned. What in the hell was going on?

He rolled his eyes and let out a long, "Oh, Mother."

Mother?! Did he just call her mother? What in the hell was happening? Lucy was my friend. Oh my God. I'd been duped. She was a sneaky devil, just like her devastatingly handsome son. I'd been had. All. Damn. Day. I'd told the woman I'd had sex with her son! What in the ever-loving hell? Embarrassment set my face on fire.

"Come on, then. You know you aren't getting these keys without giving your momma a kiss."

"You're insufferable," he said, but his eyes told a different story. They were sparkling with affection and filled with a bit of teasing before he leaned over and wrapped his arms around her waist, dipping her low and laying a smack on her cheek, I'm sure the neighbors in the next apartment could hear.

Lucy giggled, and I smiled even though I was supposed to be mad as hell. They were sweet and adorable.

Anthony stepped back with the keys dangling from his index finger. "Time for you to head home, Lucille."

She let out a long breath and looked over at me before acquiescing. "I suppose so. I do have work in the morning."

She collected her jacket, shoes, and purse while Anthony stared at me intently from his spot still next to the door.

A blur of red blocked my view of him, and Lucy's face leaned into mine, fully blocking my view. "I hope you're not upset with me, sweets." She rubbed her hand along the side of my face. "I was going to tell you, but we were having such a fun day and I didn't want to ruin it. I want us to be friends. Okay?"

She was so genuine, so sweet, I couldn't help but lean my face into her hand and whisper back, "Okay."

One final brush of her thumb over the apple of my cheek and she was gone, throwing a knowing smile over her shoulder at me but talking to Anthony.

"You behave yourself, young man."

"I always do."

She gave him a look that said she knew different.

Anthony closed the door behind him and stared at me for a beat before toeing his shoes off and making his way to the couch.

I watched him like a hawk. Because what in God's name was he doing?

I eyed him as he pulled the blanket back and sat in Lucy's spot on the couch.

"Hit play, yeah?"

"Huh?"

"Hit. Play."

I'd had enough. He'd chased off Lucy and now was bossing me again. "Does everyone always do what you say, Dr. Jackson?" I was being a snarky bitch, but I didn't care.

He gave me a pointed look. "Anyone who has any sense does."

Dick.

He picked Lucy's half-eaten bowl of ice cream up and scooped some into his mouth. Were we watching a movie and eating ice cream together? Did I miss an email or memo or phone call or something because I was confused as hell.

Since I was sitting here stunned and annoyed, Anthony reached around me and grabbed the remote from the arm of the couch on the other side of me.

He watched the movie and I watched him. What in the hell was he doing here? He finished Lucy's ice cream and then reached for my uneaten bowl.

"You gonna eat that?" He raised his eyebrows at me.

I shook my head, and he started in on my bowl of delicious-ness. I shouldn't have watched him eat it. It was a huge mistake. He made ice cream look sexy as hell.

Still, I continued to stare at him until he finally finished eating and placed the second bowl next to the first on the table.

He turned his big body toward me on the couch and he took up way more of the space than I did. He was long where I was short, burly where I was petite, and I took in his long, slacked legs with my eyes.

His socked foot nudged my thigh and my eyes snapped to his.

"She didn't tell you, huh?"

"Hmm?" I couldn't concentrate on anything but his body so close to mine.

"Lucille." He smiled. "She didn't tell you?"

I smiled despite myself. Because I was pissed that she hadn't told me. I'd shared with her that I'd had sex with her son, and she'd just smiled and acted like it was just an average day. The woman was crazy.

"Your mom's a nut."

His head snapped back and a deep, booming laugh filled the room and I was a goner. That laugh ghosted over my skin like the sun on a cold day, lighting me up, setting my blood aflame. It was over. I was done for. And in that moment, I knew I'd never win again against Anthony Jackson.

Chapter 11

Anthony

It was Friday. I loved Fridays. I only worked until about noon since the office shut down early, and I'd always head down to the French-inspired café near my apartment for lunch, and I'd pour over paperwork with a hot cafe au lait and a slice of my favorite quiche often followed by macaroons or an eclair, or maybe both. I loved sweets. They were my one vice. I didn't smoke. I only occasionally imbibed in the social drink. I didn't fuck random women. No, I ate cookies and cakes, and I fucking loved them. Work and sweets, they were my only vices. I worked way more hours than most doctors in my field, but I was committed to the cause—more invested than most of my colleagues.

So, there was a certain pep in my step as I exited my car and walked across the street to the café, and it had nothing to do with the fact I had to walk past Kelly's car to get there. I wasn't happy she was there two floors above me. I was just excited to be off for the rest of the day even if it really wasn't off. It seemed that something always came up. Or that I was always swamped in piles of paperwork I needed to do. I still fucking loved what I did.

I was halfway across the street when I saw her. Or I should say felt her. My skin prickled with an awareness and my eyes shot around and somehow I just knew she'd be there, and sure enough she was. It was a brisk fifty-degree day, but the sun was shining and she sat right in front of my beloved Friday café bundled up in a big coat that was almost too small for her and a hat pulled low over her ears to block the chill. Her hair was down and hung over her shoulders, and she was writing on a piece of paper in front of her furiously, the wires from what looked like earbuds dangling from her ears. Those small ears of hers. I wanted to lean over and run my lips over the tiny lobes. They were as precious as I remembered from years ago.

I was interrupting, but I couldn't seem to help myself. I couldn't seem to stay away. I had little willpower when it came to this small girl. Just like I hadn't been able to stop myself from going over to see her the past couple of nights. Often, she just sat there and ignored me, but last night she'd tossed me the remote and said, "Watch whatever you want."

It had felt like a victory. Maybe a small one, but one nonetheless.

In fact, I'd only seen her hours ago at the office when she'd come in for an appointment. We'd poured over her files and come up with one hell of a game plan. But seeing her there, I couldn't stop myself.

So, I slid into the seat across from her slowly as to not scare her and leaned back in the seat even though the metal was cold on my back and ass even through my shirt and coat. Pushing my big legs out underneath the table, I crossed them at the ankles and knocked my ankle to hers. It felt good, so I foolishly kept it there and that's when her blue eyes drifted up slowly from the piece of paper and looked me in my own.

She stared at me for what felt like an hour but was probably a full minute, her expression beyond annoyed. One side of my mouth hitched up. I couldn't help it. She was beautiful and adorable, even more so when she was riled up.

Plucking the earbuds out of her ears, she said, "This is getting awkward, Anthony."

The other side of my mouth hitched up, too, now. "How so?"

"This whole stalking thing. It's getting out of hand." Her face said she was bored, but I could read the playfulness in her eyes. She loved it when I bothered her.

I crossed my arms over my chest. "Is that what we're calling it?"

"That's what *I'm* calling it."

"Well, I call it friendship." I said it nonchalantly, but I realized right then that I meant it. I liked her so much, back then and now. I couldn't resist her.

She pursed her lips. She had a habit of that whenever she was displeased, and I thought it was possibly the most hilariously cute thing ever. "Is that what we are?"

Raising my eyebrows, I asked sincerely, "Isn't it?"

She looked away from me and scanned the street like she was looking for answers in the cars that drove by. She didn't consider us friends and part of me was overjoyed. I could do my job without entanglements. That was the best outcome here, but I knew better even then. Even with her only being back in my life for mere days.

"Besides, you're at *my* café," I shot out there, trying to lighten the mood, which had turned somber.

Her eyes flew back in my direction before she got up and walked toward the street and turned around, looking up at the front of the building.

She was almost in the street and she was making me nervous, she and her precious basketball belly standing in the road, her coat gaping open at her stomach.

"What are you doing? Get out of the road."

She stepped forward, smiling. "Just looking for your name on the front of the building, Doc."

Standing up, I reached for her instinctively, grabbing her hand in mine. "It's not on the front of the building, little bit."

She tried to pull her hand from mine, but I held it tighter, realizing how cold it was.

"Your hands are like ice," I said, grabbing her other small hand also and cupping both of them in my big hands. I brought them to my mouth and blew warm air on them softly.

I didn't think about it. I just did it. It was intimate. Something that only a significant other or a family member would do to someone, but it all just felt too right with her. Normal.

She watched, her hands in mine, seemingly fascinated with the sight.

I dropped her hands, embarrassed, when I noticed her watching me so intently with her palms held in mine and almost pressed to my lips.

"Come inside. I'll buy you lunch." I grabbed her papers she'd been working on from the table and clutched them in my hands awkwardly.

Her cheeks were pink, and I wondered whether it was from cold or me.

"I think I'm gonna head home. I'm a bit tired."

She was good. She knew that whatever was happening was a bad idea. She was being smart. I wasn't, but I found myself giving less of a fuck and wanting to feel more. It was an awful dilemma, but matters of the heart usually were. And unfortunately for us, too many hearts were involved.

"I won't take no for an answer. They have the best desserts ever. You gotta eat, right?" I grabbed her hand again, but this time I knew what I was doing as I opened the door with the small bell that dinged so familiarly. I walked in feeling like I was home.

Pulling her behind me, I dragged her to my booth and scooted in, laying her papers across from me where I expected her to sit.

"Get in, Kelly."

She stared at me for a bit before she sat with a huff, looking around the booth before her eyes zeroed in on the plaque below the window that read, Dr. Anthony Jackson.

She rolled and then narrowed her eyes at me.

I smiled, all teeth.

I pointed to the small gold plaque below the window. "See, my café."

"Duly noted." She huffed out a laugh. "I can't even with you."

I grabbed the menus from the small holder on the table and held it out to her.

She shook her head. "Nah, just order me whatever you usually have. I'm guessing you know what all the good stuff here is."

Placing the menus back in the holder, I asked, "So, what are you working on?" I motioned to the papers in front of her.

"Just music." She shrugged.

"Like writing music?"

"Yep."

I was frustrated. I wanted her to open up, elaborate. I wanted more than one-word answers and nights seated too far away from her on a couch that seemed way too big.

"You're a woman of very few words. I remember a time when I couldn't get you to shut up."

Her eyes flashed with anger. "Yeah, well, Doc, that was a long time ago. I was a kid then."

I realized it then. She was still angry with me. About that night. It shouldn't have surprised me, but it did. My memories of her were laced with lust, heat, laughter, and something on the cusp of young love. She remembered the ending. Not the beginning or all the good stuff in between. It was my fault.

I swallowed hard. "About that night—"

Her wide eyes snapped to mine. "What night?"

I leaned forward, closer to her across the booth. "The night," I whispered.

Shaking her head, she whispered back, "Don't."

I was frustrated. I wanted to tell her. I wanted to talk it out. I wanted it out in the open. Free. So we could move the hell on.

"Why?"

"Because it doesn't matter anymore. It was a long time ago." She smiled sadly. "We were young and stupid, and we both made mistakes that night."

I knew what my mistake was, but what was hers? "What was—"

"Anthonyyyy," Isabelle, the owner, sang out, placing two glasses of water in front of us.

I turned to see her striding toward us and looked back at Kelly. Her face was full of relief. We'd talk about this later.

"Hey, honey," I said, standing up and meeting Isabelle right outside the booth. We hugged before I settled back in the booth.

"The usual?" Isabelle asked.

"Yep, 'cept make it a double." I motioned toward Kelly. "Isabelle, this is my friend Kelly."

"Nice to meet you." Kelly smiled up at Isabelle.

"You, too."

Isabelle waggled her eyebrows at me. "She's pretty, Ant," she sang out.

I looked at Kelly with her hat pushed down over her eyebrows, her cheeks red from the cold weather, her blue eyes shining with intensity. Her creamy white skin begging for my touch. "She is."

Isabelle giggled. "Okay, well, I'll leave you two to it and get your food started. Let me know if you need anything."

She sashayed away, and Kelly just stared at me.

"What?" I questioned.

"Ant? What's with the hugs? The booth?" She gestured toward

the plaque with her head.

"ASD, also known as Atrial Septal Defect."

Her face was confused. "What?"

"It's a common heart defect in babies. That's what Isabelle and Marco's baby boy was born with."

Realization dawned on her face. "And you saved his life."

"Me and an amazing team of doctors I worked under."

"When?"

"Six years ago."

She laughed. "I'm surprised they didn't give you the entire damn restaurant." Then her face got serious. "I would have."

I bet she would have, too. I could tell her baby girl meant everything to her.

I smiled. "Well, I do have my own booth, and all the food I can eat, which is pretty damn good. Besides, I don't have a fucking clue how to run a restaurant."

"But you said, you were *buying* me lunch. And now you're telling me you eat for free."

"Ahh...but I am. With my expert doctoring skills."

"And I thought your mom was a nut."

I laughed.

"So what kinda music are you working on?"

"I don't know." She paused, studying the sheet of paper in front of her. "It's not anything special. I just sometimes write when I'm feeling anxious."

She had every right to feel anxious. "Is that what you did these past ten years? Write music?"

A sarcastic laugh fell from her lips. "Nope. I took off with my band, traveled the world. Followed my dreams. And guess what, Doc?"

"What?"

"Ten years on the road, countless nights slept in a packed van, and I have shit to show for it."

"Except the experience."

Her gaze flew to mine. "What?"

"Except you followed your dreams and you traveled and you got to play music. You may not have a lot to show for it, but you did it, and you'll remember it forever."

"I guess," she said softly. It made me sad that she never made it big. She had such passion. She loved playing the fucking drums.

"I didn't see your drums in the apartment. You storing them somewhere?"

"Nah. I sold them."

"Why?" I was shocked. She needed those drums like I needed my stethoscope. They were a part of her.

"I needed the money. And I don't need them. I need a crib. Diapers. The drums just aren't a priority right now."

She was sad, I could tell, and it broke my heart. I wanted to push into the other side of the booth and pull her into my arms. I wanted to tell her everything was going to be okay. That she could have her music and her baby. But I couldn't even promise that.

The heart was fickle, fragile even, and one moment everything could be smooth sailing and the next arduous. All I could do was promise I would try, and I'd already done that.

Isabelle delivered our food, and I was glad for the distraction. Kelly was so melancholy. I imagined her sitting around the apartment all day bored and thinking and worrying over the baby in between all of her doctors' appointments. No music. No friends. It was a good thing she had me around, I told myself.

Isabelle finished placing all the plates on the table, and Kelly's mouth fell open. "Dear Lord, you did not order all this food."

Isabelle laughed as she left our table, and I looked at all of the food. Four large pieces of quiche. Six macaroons. Two eclairs. Two tarts. I'd ordered double, so it looked right to me.

"I did," I confirmed.

"Why?" she almost yelled out.

"Because I'm hungry?"

"Doc, there's no way in hell you can eat all of this, even with my help."

I completely disagreed. I could eat all of this even without her help. "Sure I can. I'm a big guy, bite size, or haven't you noticed?"

Her cheeks turned a pretty shade of pink, and the pink in those cheeks told me she had noticed and that she liked it and for some reason that made me ridiculously happy.

"Eat."

She rolled her eyes, her lips pursing.

"Doctor's orders." I smiled mischievously.

At that, she ate.

And I watched her. I'd never sat across from anyone at my favorite café before. I hadn't realized I was missing anything special before that day. Until I watched her moan around a mouthful of cheese and crust. Until she laughed when she dropped a bit of cream on the front of her jacket. Until she smiled and chatted with Isabelle like they were old friends all afternoon. I'd thought my life was full. But in that moment, I was acutely aware of how wrong I'd been. I'd been missing her all these years and didn't even realize it.

Chapter 12

Kelly

"**I** smell cookies."

The man was going to eat me out of house and home, which was pretty hard since I didn't really have a home. "Maybe," I said from the kitchen.

I'd made cookies for me today. Not Anthony. It was just pure coincidence that they were done right around the time he came by every night. It was also just a coincidence that he'd mentioned chocolate chip were his favorites as he ate an entire pack of Oreos on the couch next to me the night before. The man loved to eat and the truth was I started to enjoy seeing him snack on the sofa next to me every night.

At some point over the last couple of weeks, I'd come to think of him as a friend. My only friend here really, besides his mother, who stopped by periodically to check up on me. Our friendship scared me as much as it elated me. I didn't want to depend on him for more than I already was.

I didn't know if he'd somehow end our friendship how he'd ended that night so long ago.

I didn't know how it would affect our patient doctor relationship either. I tried not to think about all of that as I spent the last two hours on my feet baking cookies. If he wasn't worried about it, and he clearly wasn't since he stopped by every night to hang out with me, then I wouldn't worry about it either.

Anthony came around into the dining room and sat on one of the stools at the counter that separated the kitchen from the other room.

His eyes scoured the countertop, taking in the hundred or so cookies I'd spent the afternoon and evening baking.

He brought his tender eyes to mine. "You baked for me."

I looked away. I concentrated on cleaning the counter I was so obviously trying to put a hole in with my dish rag. "I didn't. I baked for me."

"You baked a shit ton of my favorite cookies for yourself?"

"Yeah," I said, rubbing my pregnant belly. "In case you missed it, I'm pregnant and I was craving some cookies."

"*Some* cookies? There has to be over one hundred cookies here, short stack."

I turned, hiding my smile from him as I unloaded another batch from the oven. "I made some for Lucy, too."

He chuckled low and deep, and it rolled over me hot and heavy. I turned to the sink away from him, gripping the edge of it. I closed my eyes for a moment, praying for my damn hormones to calm down. My skin felt itchy, tight, and hot, and I wanted to vault over that counter and tackle him to the floor.

And just when I thought I got myself somewhat under control, I felt a hot body behind mine, too close, and I smelled him and God, he smelled divine. I wanted to lick that spot behind his ear that he loved so long ago. But, it was a bad idea. I closed my eyes, pretending he wasn't just behind me a breath away. Too close and still way too far.

"So, you'll give Lucille your cookies, and not me?" His breath teased me close to my ear and the tiny hairs on the back of my neck stood at attention.

One small sentence said softy into my ear and my core was aching, throbbing, pounding.

I didn't answer. I couldn't. I was afraid my voice would betray me. I was afraid it would tell him I wanted him to get down on his knees right now in this kitchen, jerk my pants down, pull my granny panties to the side, and do dirty wicked things with his mouth between my legs. I leaned forward more on the sink on a small groan.

"Are you okay?" he said from behind me, and I had just enough sense to pipe out a quiet yes.

"Come on," he said, grabbing my shoulder and turning me toward him and tucking me under his arm, which wasn't hard because as Anthony said on many occasions, I was bite size and he was huge.

"I think you wore yourself out." He pushed me down onto the couch and sat close to me, his thigh to mine, and I thought I was going to go out of my mind.

"Maybe," I lied through my teeth. I knew what was wrong with me. I had a sexy ass doctor parked next to me every night. I was a sex starved pregnant woman. I wanted him. I'd had him. I knew it was good. I knew we were good together. I wanted another round.

I looked down at my pregnant stomach and thought of the stretch marks there. The beautiful man across from me could never be attracted to me right now and probably not after the baby. I had a feeling I was going to be sporting love handles and stretch marks forevermore.

I pushed myself into the corner to get a little farther away from him and the fire that was blazing in my body.

He smiled from the other end of the sofa. "I can't believe it. I'm finally getting in there."

I narrowed my eyes. He looked too smug.

"You like me."

"I don't."

"You do. You baked for me."

"Fine," I groaned out between my teeth. "I might like you a little."

He laughed. "Just a little?"

"Don't push your fucking luck, Doc."

"So I can have some cookies?"

"Jesus, yes. Please, for God's sake, go get a damn cookie before you die." I was secretly so dang pleased he wanted my cookies.

I smiled to myself as he got up off the couch and went to the kitchen. He came back with a plate that contained no less than ten cookies, and I shook my head and giggled.

"What? I'm a big guy," he defended and I felt my eyes about to do it.

Please, I begged them. Do not look at his junk. Just don't. Don't think about it and don't look, but still my eyes drifted down and to the plate of cookies that thankfully covered his lap.

My cheeks flamed at the thought of cookies and cock because both sounded pretty damn good right about now.

I felt warm eyes on mine and looked up to find Anthony staring at me, a strange expression on his face that told me he definitely thought I was checking out his goods.

With one eyebrow raised, he asked, "Hungry?"

Christ almighty, but I wanted to tell him. I was starving but not for cookies.

"For a cookie, of course?" he finished and I nodded my hot head, embarrassed beyond embarrassment.

He passed me one and I took a bite, thankful for the distraction.

Leaning over, I rubbed my foot with my free hand. "Jesus, my feet are killing me."

Anthony sat his plate on the table and grabbed my foot from my hand. "They look swollen. You were on them too much today. Are you drinking enough water?"

I shouldn't have been embarrassed. He was a doctor and he was just checking out my feet since I'd complained, but still I tried to yank my foot away.

"Hey, calm down there, shorty." He pulled my leg until I was lying horizontally on the couch and both my feet were in his lap. He cupped one of my small size six feet in his big, warm hands and you could hardly see it. I lay here, my spine stick straight, paralyzed by my shock, cookie still poised at my mouth, but my other hand frantically gripping the arm of the couch. What in the hell was he doing?

That's what I was thinking when he took the pads of his thumbs and rubbed them roughly from the ball of my foot into the arch and all the way to the heel. And I melted into the couch, like butter.

"Oh my God," I moaned.

He laughed low. "That's Dr. God to you."

I didn't even have a snarky comment ready. All I could do was lie here with my eyes closed while one of the most beautiful men I'd ever seen in my life rubbed my fat, swollen feet like they weren't the most disgusting thing in the world.

I decided to take the moment of bliss even further. With eyes still closed, I took a bite of cookie. "Mmmm."

"Living the life over there, huh?" He laughed.

I opened one eye and narrowed it. "Stop talking. You're ruining it."

He laughed harder. "How have you been feeling?" He seemed genuinely concerned.

"I've been good, actually. Me and the baby, Team Hope, we got this thing in the bag."

"And me," he said quietly.

I didn't understand. "I'm sorry?"

"I'm on your team, too, right?"

I stared him at him stunned. I hadn't had anyone on my team in a long damn time. His eyes practically pleaded with me to say yes. And I wanted to, but I didn't want to let him all the way in. He'd disappointed me before. Would he do it again?

I laughed and pretended there was no way he could be serious. "You want to be on Team Hope? My team?"

That infuriating man had the audacity to not even pause. "Most definitely."

"Hmm," I hummed, not knowing what to say. Damn it, I wanted him on my team, too. But I was scared of him. Scared of what could be. Scared it wouldn't come to be at all.

His face was anguished when he said, "It's okay." He rubbed the arch of my foot softly. "Whether you like or not, I'm already on your team. I've been on your team for ten years, and I'll be on your team for ten more."

I didn't know what to say. The moment was too intimate. The rational part of my brain said not to say anything at all, so I didn't speak again until my cookie was gone and my breathing was slow and I felt like I was floating on a cloud somewhere in the sky. I wanted to tell him there was no one else I'd rather have on my team than him. That even though things hadn't ended well between us in the past, as of right now, he was my very best friend and I'd be lost without him.

"Where is he?" he asked quietly.

My eyes opened slowly to see him sitting there, staring at me like I was a puzzle he'd been wanting to solve his whole life. His red dress shirt was open at the collar, and I noticed the color really suited him.

"Who?" I asked just as softly.

"The man who should be rubbing your feet when they're sore.

The person who should be taking you to all your appointments. The one who should be sitting next to you at night while you watch your trash TV? Where is he?"

His jaw ticked while he waited on my answer. He was angry, mad that I was alone. I was relieved.

"My guess is he's still traveling with a band in a van across the US, only with a brand-new drummer. It's all for the best. He has a bad temper and a bit of a drug problem. Like most musicians." I swallowed. It hadn't been serious between us, but it had still hurt how it had all ended.

"He didn't want her. It wasn't a relationship, really. We just messed around. It was convenient and easy, but I'm starting to learn that convenient and easy aren't always good. Ya know?"

He nodded, his face solemn, urging me to go on.

"When I found out, I cried and cried. I was so sad. I didn't want a baby. And when I told him, he told me to get rid of it. It, he'd said. Like it was an object. Like a piece of trash in the back of the van. Just a thing to be tossed away. And I knew I couldn't do it. Because to me, the it he'd so casually mentioned was already a baby, a person. I couldn't do it, Doc. Not even after they told me she was sick."

Leaning over, his hand reached for my face. He rubbed his thumb across the apple of my cheek just like his mom had done weeks ago, his face soft, his eyes fierce.

"I'm glad you couldn't do it." His hand dropped and found mine. He wrapped his huge pinky around my small one and whispered, "Team Hope."

That was all he said. He tucked a piece of hair behind my ear and went back to my feet. And I went back to my cloud, only this time I felt a little bit lighter.

Chapter 13

Anthony

That Night Ten Years Ago

"You're a bed hog."

She giggled and my heart skipped a beat and I felt dumb, ridiculous, and utterly head over heels. I shouldn't like her this much already. She was a musician, for fuck's sake. She was going on tour, and I was going to medical school. We were headed down two different paths in life, but my body, my mind, and my heart didn't seem to give a flying fuck. She was gorgeous in that eccentric way that had never really appealed to me. Until now. Her adorable heart-shaped face framed in short dark hair and big blue eyes drew me in. Music notes danced in the form of a tattoo from the middle of her back across her side and up onto her ribcage. I wanted to show them how pretty I thought they were with my tongue.

"Hey, I totally resemble that remark." She punched me in the arm and I fell over onto my back, my head hitting the pillow with a grunt. I was putting on a show for her. She weighed all of a buck ten soaking wet. There was no way she'd ever be able to knock me over.

She laughed harder and leaned over me. "Need some mouth to mouth, Doc."

I grinned up at her. "Hell yeah."

Climbing over my body, she giggled before straddling me and leaning forward. She rubbed her nose along mine and then her lips. God, her lips. They were the color of fresh cherries against her pale skin, deep, pink, and luscious. I dragged her bottom one between my teeth and gave it a firm suck.

She pulled back and sat up on top of me, her cheeks a gorgeous shade of pink, her smile wide and uncontrived. Freedom and a wildness I'd never witnessed before sparkled in her eyes down at me, and I thought to myself in that moment that I'd never met a girl this real, this raw, this damn special.

I averted my gaze, feeling too much, too soon and it embarrassed me. It made me feel foolishly young and naive, something I'd always prided myself on never being. I ran my hand over the tattoos that spanned the length of her side.

"This is nice," I said without thinking, because I liked this tattoo. It suited her.

She pinched my nipple, snapping my eyes back to hers.

"Thanks." Her eyes flickered across the clear skin of my torso. "You don't have any, huh?"

"Nope."

Placing one of her hands over mine and the tattoo, she pushed both of our palms up until mine cupped her small but ample breast. She brought her hand up, tweaking her nipple and arching her back, offering her breast to me, and I obliged, leaning up to take one nipple in my mouth and giving the other a pinch. She gasped and rocked on me, making me rock-hard. And I thought for sure I was spent for the night. I'd been inside of her in every way imaginable and it seemed my cock couldn't get enough of her. My mind either.

"How come?" she breathed out a question, still rocking her wet cleft against my now slick cock.

Pausing my assault on her breast, I looked up at her, confused. "How come what?"

She stilled and placed her hands on my chest. "How come no tattoos?"

I grunted out a laugh. "You *really* do ask a lot of questions." My head fell back to the pillows on a sigh. This girl gave no fucks about timing when she asked her crazy questions. It was somehow both refreshing and frustrating as hell.

"I guess I'm just not a tattoo kind of guy."

"Hmm." She nodded her head in thought before meeting my gaze again. "Or maybe you just haven't found something that means enough to you, yet."

I quirked an eyebrow. "How so?"

"You know, I love music. It's my life. It's not just what I want to do. It's who I want to be. It lives inside of me. It's only fair that it live on the outside of me, too." She gestured to the music notes splayed across her side. "Maybe you haven't found your something."

I studied her face, surprised again. This girl. She'd done nothing but surprise me all night. How could she be so perfect? So beautiful, intelligent, thoughtful, and damn sexy, too. It just didn't seem possible.

"Maybe," I said quietly, contemplating what she said. Maybe I didn't have something yet. The thought was depressing. Maybe I'd never find it.

I changed the subject. Kelly was only here visiting friends and then heading out on tour with her band, Nocturnal Rose. I didn't want a second of our time together full of depressing thoughts.

"Why the drums?"

At the mere mention of her beloved instrument, her face lit up and I didn't need her to tell me why she chose them. It was written all over her features.

"Well," she said, biting her lip through her beaming smile, "the drums are kind of a big deal, ya know?"

"Yeah?" I laughed at her dash of coyness sprinkled with excitement. God, she was adorable.

"Uh-huh. The drums set the pace for the entire band, Doc." She leaned forward, pressing a kiss to my lips before using my chest to prop her upper body on with her elbows. "I control how fast or how slow the music is, and if I'm off my game, the entire band is, too." She ran her nose down mine. "The drums are the heart of the band, Anthony."

She lay down, pressing her ear to my heart, and heat flashed through me that had not one fucking thing to do with us being naked and in bed together and everything to do with the sheer intimacy of the moment. It made me uncomfortable and hot and flushed, and it felt amazing and I didn't want that impactful moment to ever end.

I breathed in her hair and our sex all around me while she listened to the sound of my heart silently. She lay there for long moments until I lifted my hand and ran it though her short hair over and over.

A quietly whispered "boom, boom" stopped the movement of my hand right over her head, so I held my hand there, listening to the voice.

"Boom, boom," she whispered over and over again to the cadence of my heart.

I closed my eyes, completely sucked into the moment, listening to her whispered booms that were synched up to the rhythm of my heart until it seemed I could feel her voice vibrating in my body like my heart and her words were one and the same.

"Boom, boom," she kept on and I was lost. So deep that I almost missed it. And if that had happened I would have been devastated because as she started singing the lyrics to "You Are My Sunshine" to the beat of my very heart I was swept away. Her voice. Her spin of the classic song somehow seemed more sultry. More sad. Maybe it was the deep undertones of her voice or the bit of raspiness, but I was enthralled, hanging onto every lyric of a song I'd heard a million different times in a million different ways. Because somehow this time, it felt brand-new.

Her voice. My heart. The sweetest lyrics I'd ever heard. Heaven. I never wanted to leave.

She finished the song and I breathed out, realizing I'd been holding my breath because I didn't want to miss a note of her voice.

She still lay there, her ear to my heart, her warm body pressed to mine. "See, Doc. I'm the very life of the band, just like the heart is the very life of the body.

"Boom, boom," she whispered again and finished with a quietly said, "The drums give life to music. And the heart, it's the music of life."

Chapter 14

Kelly

I woke to the sound of birds chirping. Rolling over, I glanced at the clock. It was 9:00 a.m. I looked around my bed, wondering how I'd gotten here. The last thing I remembered was Anthony rubbing my feet and me confessing the shit storm that led me here.

Oh, crap, I must have fallen asleep while he was rubbing my feet. I ran the tops of my feet over the covers, remembering how good it felt. I hadn't had anyone take care of me in forever. It felt nice to be cared for, even in a small, simple way. And he was on my team. It wasn't just me and baby girl anymore. I felt like a weight had been lifted.

He must have put me to bed. Crap. I lifted the covers to check and make sure I still had on my tank top and yoga pants. *Whew. Still good.*

But he'd put me in bed and I'd slept through it all. Wow. I must have been really relaxed or either zonked out tired from baking all of those damn cookies.

I was feeling great after that foot rub last night, so I decided to head out for the day, hoping the fresh air would do me some good. I even took the time to dress nice, throwing on my one pair of maternity jeans that were still comfortable and a nice maternity top. Light makeup and a brush through my hair and I was off.

I walked the streets near my apartment in a daze, breathing in the crisp air and appreciating the subtle beauty that was North Carolina in the winter. Almost spring. It was cold today, but there were small, white flowers budding on the streets that lined the sidewalks. I could picture myself staying here. Living in North Carolina. The summers were hot as hell, but if the winters were this mild it would be worth it. Plus, Anthony was here and he'd become quite the friend over the past few weeks. And with the baby's future surgeries I'd need to be here, near him.

I was walking past a building that looked ancient, and I couldn't help but notice a display of guitars in the front window. I stopped and looked up. Mo's Music, the sign read, and I couldn't help myself. I pulled the door open and the musty, earthy smell of instruments hit me. I breathed them in deep, feeling at home for the first time in months. The music store was filled with every instrument you could imagine, from clarinets to guitars, and I walked around for an hour, running my hands over pianos and drum heads alike. I thought I might like to work in a place like this one day when I was able to. It wasn't the dream, but it could work.

Along the back of the store there was a small clothing section full of all kinds of music apparel. I scanned the racks, knowing I really couldn't afford anything. A small rack to the side caught my attention and I smiled as I picked up the tiny scrap of cloth on it, grinning from ear to ear. It was black and covered in white music notes and treble clefs. It was a little of me and a little of him and his kids would love it.

"That's a nice one." I heard a deep, gravelly voice from behind me and I turned to find an older black man standing behind me, gazing at the bow tie in my hand. He had to have been in his eighties, but you could tell he was a musician through and through. He wore a black suit, white-collared shirt, the top buttons popped. He had on a black fedora hat with a white stripe around the middle of it. He was too cool.

"I think so," I said, looking back at the tie.

"For your man?"

I faced him, the bow tie clenched in my hand. "I'm sorry?"

"The tie. Is it for your man?"

I laughed awkwardly. "Oh, no, I don't have a man." And then I could have slapped myself in the face. Here I am almost eight months pregnant and I'm all like no, I don't have a man. Why didn't I just say yes and move on?

He looked down at my stomach and back at me. "That's a shame. Your daddy, then?"

I shook my head. "Nope, don't have one of those either." And I was on a roll today.

"Well, now that's even more of a shame. So, who's the tie for then, Ms...?"

A name. He wanted my name. "Oh, Kelly. Just Kelly, no Ms."

"All right, Kelly. Who are you getting the tie for?"

"A good friend."

He nodded and smiled as he put his arm through mine, leading me on a slow walk through the store. Damn musicians, they always charmed me. Even at eighty years old the man had me smitten in two seconds flat.

"What's he play?"

I grinned. "He doesn't."

He chuckled. "I'm Mo."

"Nice to meet you, Mo. This is a pretty nice place you have here."

He looked around, obviously impressed with his business. "It is. I've been here almost forty years."

"Wow."

"So you're the musician then?" he asked with a wink.

"Sure am."

"What's your pleasure?"

We paused next to a huge drum kit, and I motioned toward it. "That. I mean, I play a little of everything, but the drums, they're my jam."

Shaking his head, he laughed. "A little thing like you. I would have never thought. I'd figured you for flute, maybe piano."

"I hear that a lot."

He let go of my arm. "Well, you're welcome to give the kit a try if you want. The drumsticks are just over there." He pointed behind the kit.

I looked the kit over lovingly, ran my hands over the snare head, thumped the top of the high hat, and tapped the cymbal with a knuckle. No, I didn't need to be playing the drums. I needed to be focusing on the baby.

"I think I'm good. I'll just take the tie." I moved toward the register and Mo followed me.

I checked out and Mo walked me to the front door and opened it for me. "You come back and see me now, Ms. Kelly."

"I promise. I will."

"Maybe you'll play the drums for me next time."

I smiled. "Maybe. Your store is beautiful." I took one last look around.

"Thank you," he said as I passed by and out the door, but before he closed it, he said, "Tell Dr. Jackson I said hello." And then he was gone.

I was left here standing on the sidewalk confounded. It was like Anthony knew everyone in this damn neighborhood and they all so obviously adored him. It was the tie. That's how Mo had known most likely. Damn Anthony and his innate ability to make everyone love him. He annoyed me. It made me think the world of him.

On the walk home, I stopped at a gift shop and picked out a pretty box to put Anthony's tie in. Once in the house, I set about wrapping the gift and making lunch. I thought of maybe making a lasagna and salad for dinner, and then I'd give him his present. We'd watch TV and eat snacks.

I guess I was preparing a thank you dinner. Anthony had done a lot for me since I'd been here. He didn't have to help me like he did. I'd come to the decision that he was seriously a nice guy. Maybe what had happened those years ago was just a fluke. I didn't know what I'd do without him now. He was my only friend here and he seemed to know it, since he kept me company almost every day. I would've been lost without him.

I was just sitting down with a sandwich and a glass of iced tea when I heard a knock at the door.

Grunting, I went to the door, thinking that soon someone was going to have to roll me there. Baby girl was getting big and, in turn, so was I.

I looked through the peephole. I didn't want to be kidnapped and feed into Miranda's pretend drama. Two teenagers were standing outside. I opened the door.

"Can I hel—"

I didn't even get to finish my sentence before they barreled in.

"We're here to deliver the drums." I thought I heard one mutter. Sure enough they started to set up a drum kit right in the living room, but I didn't order any drums.

Out and in they went, carrying pieces of the kit, and all I could do was stand here and stare. I didn't understand.

"But I didn't order any drums," I finally managed to squeak out.

"Are you Kelly Potter?"

I rolled my eyes. Not this again. "Yeah," I said simply, deciding not to kill the messenger, or in this case the delivery guys. Nope, I'd kill the responsible party. Anthony.

When all was said and done a freaking beautiful, phenomenal, amazing, drum kit stood in the middle of the living room like a beacon of light in a dark, dark world. And I wanted to play the hell out of it, but I wouldn't. Because it was going back.

I gazed longingly at the handmade DW Performance Series 7 Piece Kit. Yes, I knew my drums like some people knew their cars and this kit, well, it was the Corvette of drums.

Damn him.

I fired off a text to Anthony. I'd never so much as thought about texting him before, but he'd programmed his number in for me weeks ago under the name Doc. It had made me smile at the time. Now I wanted to strangle him.

Me: I'm going to kill you dead.

Doc: ?

Me: Don't pretend you don't know why you're going to die!!

Doc: Short stack, you wanna kill me at least 7 times a week.

Me: But this time I'm really gonna do it.

Doc: ?

I didn't appreciate his cuteness. Now wasn't the time.

Me: Stop trying to be cute!

I was always fighting smiles when it came to this man.

Doc: How am I being cute?

Me: I don't know how you do it but I want you to stop!!

Doc: You think I'm cute.

No, I didn't think he was cute. I thought he was beautiful. Inside and out. Which made it damn hard to resist him.

Me: I want you to come get these drums!

Doc: Oh, the kit arrived! Awesome!

Me: Not awesome. Very not awesome. I don't want them!!!

Doc: That's a lot of exclamation points there, bite size.

Me: !!!!!!!!!

Doc: How can you not want them? It's an awesome kit. Mo cut me a fantastic deal.

It was really a shame because now that adorable old man with the amazing store was going to have to die, too.

Me: We will talk when you get home.

I sent it before I thought about it. Home. I'd said it like we lived together. Like we shared the same space, but we didn't. Did we? When had I started thinking of Anthony as my home? My pulse picked up along with my breathing. He scared me. This gentle man with hands so tender hundreds of people trusted them to hold their babies' hearts and he frightened the hell out of me.

Doc: Nothing to talk about. You're keeping the drums. Doctor's orders.

Anger soothed my fear like a balm. He couldn't just throw out doctor's orders anytime he demanded I do something. I mean, he did it, but it wouldn't work.

Me: You can't just throw out doctor's orders whenever you want and expect me to comply!

Doc: And yet, I just did.

Me: !!!!!!!!!!

Doc: ? ;)

Bastard. Gorgeous, caring, thoughtful damn bastard. I didn't care how sweet he was. How bossy he could be. I wasn't keeping the freaking drums.

I threw the phone on the table. I was done arguing with him especially since he was being cute again.

Throwing myself on the sofa with a huff, I noticed the bow tie sitting there. I turned my eyes to the drums and then back to the bow tie again. He'd made my gift look like poo. I couldn't give him this measly tie now.

I got up off the sofa and hid the beautifully wrapped gift in the kitchen in the junk drawer where it belonged.

He was going to save my baby's life. He'd found me a place to stay. He bought me a fucking drum set.

I'd bought him a damn bow tie.

And then I thought of all he'd really done for me. Spending every waking moment he wasn't at work or in surgery with me. Sparring with me every day. Laughing at my ridiculous jokes. Taking me to dinner. Watching romantic movies with me on the couch. I got it now. He'd been distracting me from the raw deal that life had given me—a sick baby.

And it had worked. I'd forgotten how terrified I was before him. The more I thought about it, the more I realized how I depended on him. And not just for his medical expertise. For everything.

In my mind my life was severed into two distinct pieces. BA and AA. Before Anthony and After Anthony. Before Anthony, Kelly Potter was terrified, cold, homeless, sad. And After Anthony, she was happy, so, so happy. She was warm and fed, and she just knew her baby girl was going to make it. And it was all because of him. Doc.

But what happened in the third piece? Ya know, the AAA. The After, After Anthony. When he was gone and I was alone again. Because it would happen eventually. When we didn't need him anymore and he was done with us. And the very thought of not having my Doc hurt me to my core, and I realized how deep I was and how very, very stupid I'd been to depend on him for so much.

Because the AAA was coming and when it did, I'd be crushed. And I didn't have the luxury of being crushed. Not with a sick baby. Not when I needed to face the reality of not being able to depend on Anthony. No, this had to stop. I couldn't let it continue. This playing house. This thing we were doing. This game. Because whatever game we were playing, it was dangerous, as games of the heart usually are.

Chapter 15

Anthony

I couldn't wait to get home so I could see Kelly play the drums. I was dying to see her in her element. She was going to be amazing, but my girl was passionate and anyone with that much passion had to be damn good at what they loved. My girl. Fuck, when had I started to think of her as mine? I'd never thought of her as mine, not even that night so long ago. It terrified me. It elated me.

I paused before pushing my key into the lock of her apartment, half expecting to hear her pounding away, but all I heard was a whole bunch of nothing, so I went on in. The sight that greeted me wasn't a welcome one. Usually, I came home to find the aroma of dinner wafting through the space and Kelly in the kitchen plating me up something. Barefoot and pregnant in the kitchen was actually a thing in my life and while I was liberal and all for women's rights, I loved that she cooked for me. Took care of me in the seemingly small but really big ways that she could.

So, when I saw her sitting on the sofa in the dark staring at the drums, I knew something was very wrong. I walked over to her, my heart somewhere in my stomach, which was an impossibility, but my body told me differently.

I stood in front of her, but she didn't look at me. She just kept staring at those drums, and I wondered if I'd made a huge mistake. I thought they would cheer her up. I thought maybe she could play for me in the evenings. I thought they'd make her happy and above all else in the world I wanted this woman happy.

"What's going on, half-pint?" I tried throwing a little humor into my voice, but even to my ears it sounded strained and scared.

She pushed the heels of her hands into her eyes and groaned. I moved in beside her and sat on the couch.

"What's up, Kelly? Tell me what's going on. You're scaring me. Why are you sitting in the dark?"

Twisting her hands in her lap, she looked down at them. "We can't do this anymore."

What in the hell was she talking about? "Do what?" Why wouldn't she look at me? Why wasn't she throwing me snark? Where were her smiling blue eyes?

"This," she said in a dead voice.

"Jesus fucking Christ! Elaborate. You're freaking me out."

"This!" she yelled back, her hands thrown out around her, like I was supposed to understand.

Her eyes were all over the room, but still not on me and my heart dropped even farther into my stomach.

"Fucking look at me!" I shouted and she jumped, her eyes meeting mine, wide and terrified.

"That's it," I whispered. I brought my big palms to her face and cradled her delicate cheeks between them. "Tell me what's going on." I was trying like hell to keep my cool. What had happened between now and the texts? Was she that upset about the drums?

Kelly had kept it together like a champ up until this moment, so when I saw the sheen of tears in her eyes, my stomach rolled.

"You can't keep taking care of me. It's not right. It's not your job."

My job? My fucking job? I took care of her because I cared for her. Because I wanted to. Because she made me happy and I wanted to make her the same. It wasn't a fucking job. It was a goddamn pleasure.

Anger boiled beneath the surface and I tried to keep it in check, I really did. I brought my forehead to hers, my hands still holding her sweet, heart-shaped face. Couldn't she see it? Didn't she understand that my job was my life? That I didn't have friends beyond professional relationships? She was it. She was everything.

"I don't do things for you because I have to, Kelly. You're not a job, or a chore, or even a burden. You're my best friend."

Air whooshed past her lips and a single tear slipped free of her eye and landed on my hand.

"I hope I'm yours, too," I whispered. A mix of anger and some emotion I couldn't put my finger on stirred inside of me as I rolled my forehead back and forth on hers slowly. "Tell me I make you as happy as you make me every day."

"I'm sorry," she choked out. "I'm so sorry." She pulled her face from my hands and threw her arms around my neck, clutching me so tightly I smiled.

"That's more like it, short stuff." I wrapped my arms around her waist and brought her body to mine.

"I'm sorry," she said again. "The drums, the apartment, you. You're just too much, Anthony. You're too good. You're too kind to me. It scares the shit out of me."

I pulled back, looking into her eyes. "Why?"

She swiped at the tears under her eyes. "It's stupid."

"If you're this upset, it's not stupid."

Her sad face peered up at me. "What happens when this is over? When the surgeries are done? What happens to us?"

I smiled down at her. She was beyond crazy. She thought once this was over so were we.

"Us? We'll always be us, Kelly. I'm not going anywhere. Are you? You're the only real friend I've had in years. You try to leave me, and I'm chasing you down."

She gave a sad laugh.

"Besides, who would feed me? Bake me cookies? Put up with my crazy mother?"

She laughed again, harder this time, more free, and I was relieved. Her face was a wet mess.

"Let me get you a tissue." I moved for the kitchen junk drawer where I'd seen a pack of travel tissues a few days before.

"Wait," she said from behind me, but I pulled the drawer open and there was a small neatly wrapped box that I knew hadn't been there before.

I looked over my shoulder at Kelly, the drawer handle still in my hand.

"That's not yours." Panic was etched across her face and I chuckled.

"It's not?"

"No."

I grinned. "Well, whose is it?"

"It's mine," she snapped out too fast.

"You wrapped yourself a present and stuck it in the kitchen drawer?" Fuck, she was cute.

"Yes?"

I pulled the package out. "You don't sound so sure. Maybe it's for me, after all?"

She tried to snatch it from my hands and I held it up, which pretty much guaranteed she'd never get it.

She glared at me and then at the present. "Fine, you can have it, but it isn't much. It's not a three-thousand-dollar drum set, that's for sure," she grumbled.

I was giddy as I took the present to the living room and sat on the sofa, the tissues long forgotten.

"I don't think anyone has ever given me a present but my mom and dad."

Her face was soft on mine. "Really?"

"Yeah," I said, holding the box in my lap.

She sucked her bottom lip into her mouth nervously before saying, "Well, go on and open it."

I tore her pretty box to shreds and looked down at the bow tie inside. The music notes on it reminded me of the ones I'd seen ten years ago along the side of her torso. I loved it.

"It's perfect," I breathed, holding it up to look closer.

"Yeah?" she squeaked from beside me.

My eyes met hers, and I saw the nerves all over her face. Wrapping my hand around her neck, I brought her face close to mine and laid a slow kiss to her cheek. "I love it," I said into her ear, before pulling back. She smelled entirely too good to be that close to. A mix of berries and vanilla. I wanted to kiss more than her cheeks. I wanted to taste her lips.

"I'm glad." Her face was happy, relieved. "I thought it was a little of me and a little of you."

Hearing her say that made my head buzz. After all, I'd had the same thoughts.

Placing the bow tie carefully back in the box, I said, "The only thing that would make me happier is if you played those drums over there."

They were like the centerpiece of the room and I'd wondered how she'd kept herself from playing them all day. And I could tell by the look on her face that she somehow had.

"I can't keep the drums, Doc. They were too expensive."

"I told you, I got a good deal. Go on, play them."

"Nope, they're going back."

"Ya know, they weren't really a gift for you." It was only part lie. I'd bought them for us both.

Her grin told me she thought I was full of shit. "Really?" She quirked a sarcastic brow.

"Really." I feigned nonchalance, picking some lint off the knee of my slacks. "I bought them for me. I've never heard you play."

"You bought a three-thousand-dollar drum kit for me so you could hear me play?"

"Yep. So get to it, lady. You don't want to disappoint me, do you?"

The playfulness that was on her face only moments before flew the coop. Her features grew too serious, too sad. "Never. I'd never want to disappoint you, Doc."

I looked away, the emotion too heavy between us. It seemed to settle on my chest, nonetheless.

"Well, then you better play for me," I said, loosening the purple bow tie around my neck and letting it hang free and popping the top two buttons on my dress shirt. I was getting comfortable. Like I said, I really wanted to hear her play.

"Okay, Doc," she said softly, leaving the couch.

She sat on the black stool behind the drum set and picked the drumsticks up that lay on top of one of the drum heads.

She twisted them around, looking like she was exercising her wrists before she finally looked at me. "The neighbors are going to lose their shit."

And then she let loose on the drums like they'd committed a crime against her. I was immediately enthralled. I couldn't take my eyes off her. Her body rocked. Her arms flew at lightning speeds, her eyes barely open like she was drugged. She played the drums like she made love all those years ago. Without inhibition, with a kind of wicked sensuality that had me so deeply entrenched in her playing that I didn't even realize when she finally stopped minutes later.

She stared at me, eyebrows raised. "Well? Was it as good for you as it was for me?"

I threw my head back and laughed before saying, "Better."

Chapter 16

Kelly

"**S**hit."

I stepped off the elevator and my box of pastries fell from my hand. I'd been jonesing for them since Anthony and I had eaten lunch at what he liked to call his Friday Café. Now, I wasn't craving much of anything except an escape route because there stood my mom and her husband, Jason, right outside my apartment door, and they looked mad as hell.

"Kelly Ann Potter, open the door to this apartment right now," my momma said through her teeth. And I was in deep shit. When my momma said my full name it was all over.

"Momma," I breathed out, taking her in. She looked good. Better than good. She looked like home, and I didn't know how she managed to do that since she hadn't had one in a long damn time. She and Jason had been retired and traveling the United States in their RV for years. But still, her long dark hair speckled with strands of gray, her long flowing skirt that covered her feet, and matching flowery top covered with long silver necklaces and even more jewelry on her wrists and fingers made me feel warm all over her. I'd missed her so much.

"Pick your jaw off the floor and open this door so I don't have to go all southern on your ass in the hallway, baby girl."

My wide eyes shot to Jason for a little support, but he only smirked and moved from in front of the door and picked up my pastries off the floor.

I looked back at my momma as I dug my keys out of my purse and opened the door, stepping inside. They followed me, my momma stomping her usually light feet all the way over to my couch and placing her bag there before returning to me quickly and wrapping her arms around me tightly. So snug I let out a grunt as my steel injected spine relaxed for the first time in months. I put my own arms around her back and pushed my nose right into the crook of her neck where I took in the familiar smell of jasmine.

"Momma," I choked out on a sob.

She rocked me back and forth in the foyer of the apartment. "It's okay, now," she cooed at me. "I'm here."

Great big hiccupping sobs burst from my mouth. Months of tears and heartache and fear drenched the collar of my momma's shirt while she held me.

"Momma's here now. Everything is going to be all right." She ran her hands through my hair.

Ainsley had ratted me out, but then again, she knew I was running out of time and I was never going to call my mother. I was too scared. I was going to kill Ainsley. I was going to kiss her. She was right. I needed my momma.

Even at thirty-two years old, nothing and no one could quite understand me like her. No one would ever quite know my fears, my sorrows, or even my love for the child I was carrying like she would. After all, she'd carried me and loved me, too.

I felt another set of strong arms come around both me and my momma. "My girls okay?" Jason laid his big head to the top of mine and I smiled through my tears. He'd been with my mom since I was seventeen and he was the best. He was good to her and that was enough for me.

We all stayed huddled together like that until my sobs had calmed. My momma was the first to pull back.

She started walking toward the sofa. "Jason, why don't you make us some tea? I think Kelly and I need to have a talk."

He smiled a small smile as he left the room for the kitchen that let me know he felt sorry for me because I think we were. at the point where my momma was about to go all southern on my ass, and I was sorry for me, too.

She sat down and patted the cushion next to her, and I took my time walking the five feet over there. I'd done wrong by not calling her. By not telling her.

I sat down, my heart heavy and my explanations nil. I'd been wrong.

She leaned back, her look casual. I knew my mom all too well and anytime she looked casual she was preparing to strike. "Why didn't you call me? Why didn't you tell me? Why did I have to hear this from Ainsley?"

Fresh tears spilled over and onto my cheeks. I used the sleeves of my hoodie to wipe them away. "I don't know, Mom." I shook my head at how stupid I'd been. Ainsley had been right. I'd needed my mom and here she was and it wasn't bad at all. In fact, it was one of the best things about now besides Anthony. And Anthony was amazing. I thought of the night last week when he'd told me I was his best friend. How much we meant to each other. Yes, what we had was definitely something special.

"It seems stupid now, but you always wanted me to travel, get a career, marry, and *then* have a baby." I scrubbed my palms over my face. "I know you didn't want me to make the same mistakes you did."

Pulling my hands away from my face, she leaned close and placed her own hands at my cheeks, cradling them gently. "Is that what you think, baby girl? That you're my mistake?"

Wetness filled her eyes and one lone tear trekked down her cheek. "You were not a mistake, Kelly Ann Potter. You were my everything." Her grip on my face tightened, not to the point of pain, but to the point of her letting me know this was important, so I was sure to pay attention. "You still are."

She used her hands to steer my forehead to her lips where she laid a long kiss before leaning back on the couch and taking me with her. I curled into my momma's side and laid my head on her chest, my forehead grazing the crook of her neck.

She dragged a hand through my hair and said, "I was so young, but it didn't matter. You were such a gift. How could you ever think I regretted a single moment of it? Those were the best and hardest days of my life, and I wouldn't have traded all the tea in China or all the stairs in Paris for a single day with you."

She stopped stroking my hair and used her hand to lift my face to hers and when I met her eyes I saw a world of love and pain and fear and pride, and I knew in that moment that's what being a mom meant.

"You were my greatest adventure, baby girl."

My face crumbled. "I'm sorry, Momma."

She kissed my cheek, her mouth close to my ear. "Was it Cash?"

I nodded. It was, indeed.

She let go of my face and pulled me into her arms again, and I let out a relieved sigh. This felt good. I needed it. I needed her.

"It's okay, honey. I'm here now. We're gonna get through this." She gave me a squeeze and said into the top of my hair, "And I'm gonna be a grandma."

I rubbed my hand over my stomach. "I hope so," I whispered

my greatest fear. And I wondered how much Ainsley had told her.

She squeezed me harder to her. "We will. Ainsley said you came here for a doctor friend of y'alls. I have faith, pumpkin. You should, too."

And just on cue, the front door opened and Anthony came barreling in, clearly straight from work as he had his backpack thrown over his shoulder and his bow tie and blazer still on. He was staring down at his phone and we were staring at him. He didn't even notice.

"Hey, short stuff," he called because clearly he didn't realize I was right here since he was responding to a text on his phone. "Did you see there's an RV double parked right out front?"

Guess it was time to meet the parents.

I sat up as I said, "Doc."

His eyes hit mine and his face fell, worry etched in the plains of it. He ditched his backpack in the foyer and darted toward me, kneeling down in front of me and taking my face in his hands the way he did so often. "Have you been crying? Why are you upset? What happened today?"

I smiled through my tears and used my eyes to motion to my mom behind me. His head turned slowly, finally registering that someone else was in the room with us.

"Doc, this is my momma, Abigail, but you can call her Abby." I grabbed Anthony's hands and pulled them from my face. Placing them in my lap, still clutched in between mine, I said, "Momma, this is Dr. Anthony Jackson."

Anthony studied my momma a beat before he stood up and held his hand out. Meanwhile, my momma sat there stunned, and my momma was never stunned.

"You're the doctor?" she said quietly as Jason entered the room with two cups of hot tea.

Anthony smiled down at her, hand still out. "I'm *a* doctor, yes."

"The doctor she came here for?"

He nodded.

Momma stood up and Anthony's hand finally dropped.

"And do you make house calls for all your patients?"

"Never," he answered easily, smiling at me.

"So, my daughter means something to you, then?" Lord have mercy, my momma was a straight shooter and I'd been embarrassed by her plenty in my life, but I had a feeling what she was about to say was going to take the cake.

Anthony didn't hesitate. "She means everything to me."

And my heart flip-flopped around in my chest at his admission. He meant everything to me, too.

"Lord have mercy," my momma exclaimed, turning to me. "Did you hear that, baby girl? This beautiful, statuesque doctor said you mean everything to him." She was fanning herself and yet here I sat hot all over, praying my momma stopped talking. God wasn't listening worth a damn, though.

"He's beautiful, Kelly, and he's a *doctor*! If I were a little younger and single"—she looked at Jason pointedly—"I'd be asking for some mouth to mouth, honey. I'd need a little resuscitating. If you know what I mean?" She jabbed me with her elbow.

I was horrified, but not surprised. I buried my face in my hands, trying to hide, but to no avail.

"You heard her, little bit. I'm a hot doctor." Anthony snickered and I wanted to crawl into the cushions of the couch and disappear.

"Helloooo, I brought dinner." I heard yelled from the foyer and looked around Anthony's legs to find his mother in the foyer. Oh, but Lord help me. This was like a bad family reunion that no one wanted.

Anthony introduced Lucy to my momma. I was still sitting here horrified and dreading what else my momma might say or do.

"I'm Anthony's mother," Lucy elaborated, and I rolled my eyes.

111

I couldn't stop myself from saying, "How nice of you to offer up that bit of information right away."

Lucy leaned around Anthony and rubbed my hair. "Oh, sweet thing, I thought that was water under the bridge."

It was, of course.

"Oh, you must be so proud of Anthony," my mother gushed to Lucy.

"And Kelly is just so wonderful. We love her dearly. You did an amazing job with her," Lucy said.

Anthony stood over me, and we just gave each other looks while our moms talked like we weren't here at all.

The doorbell rang. "Oh, for fuck's sake, who could be here now?" I was done.

My mom opened the door and grabbed a package from an older gentleman and closed the door. She studied the box for a moment and started to open it up. "Expecting a package from Miranda?"

Alarm bells went off in my brain like the ones I heard when I was in elementary school and we would huddle in the hallway and hide. Only now, I couldn't hide, unfortunately. "Oh, Momma, don't open that!"

Too late, she was peering inside with Lucy leaned over her shoulder. Nosy ass women!

"What do we have here?" Lucy said with a smile.

My momma held up a book with a hot couple on the cover, clutching each other dramatically and sensually. The tagline across the cover read "What To Read After Fifty Shades of Grey." I paled. Fuck my life. Hard.

I looked over at Anthony, horrified, and the bastard had the audacity to laugh.

"And look at this." Lucy held up a box with what looked like a small lipstick. It seemed pretty harmless except for the fact the label read, "Vibrating Lipstick—for your on the go needs."

an imperfect heart

My face flamed red-hot and I tried to snatch the box from the parents from hell. I was going to kill Miranda.

"Oh, there's a note in here, too! "For all your hot doctor needs. Love, M," my mother read.Jesus Christ, take the damn wheel right now. I was horribly embarrassed.

Burying my face in my hands, I heard Anthony laugh. "See, shortcake, everyone thinks I'm a hot doctor."

"I have dibs on the book. It looks delish," said my crazy ass mother.

"That lipstick is all mine! I don't have a man, after all. Come to the kitchen. You can help me plate dinner." Lucy put her arm through my mother's.

My mother looked back at us and turned to go with Lucy. "Aren't they adorable together?" she whispered, and I felt my eyes get big.

"They are! They argue and fight like an old married couple. You just wait and see, they are the cutest thing ever!" Lucy whispered back.

I threw myself on the couch, beyond mortified. There was a special place in hell for Miranda. And she had something good coming to her. Payback was a bitch and I'd be her dealer soon!

Anthony sat down next to me and pulled me under his big arm. I laid my head on his chest despite my embarrassment and breathed out deeply. Because I was at ease. My momma finally knew. And she was here. That was all that mattered. It didn't matter that I'd gotten the most awkward package of my life in front of both mine and Anthony's parents.

"Neither one of them can whisper worth a damn."

I laughed. "True story, Doc."

We all ate dinner around the table in the apartment, our moms cackling and carrying on like old friends over a bottle of red wine. Anthony, Jason, and I stayed quiet for the most part, enjoying their ridiculous stories about us as children and rolling our eyes at them when they'd clearly had too much to drink. No one mentioned the book or vibrator. Thank God.

At the end of our meal, I was full. Full of food, full of love, full of family. It had been a good night and when I felt Anthony's ankle settle against mine under the table, a good evening became a perfect one.

Chapter 17

Anthony

I shouldn't have started. Because now I couldn't stop. I was like some kind of crazy drug addict, only my choice of drug was Kelly Potter. And I was completely fucking strung out. But I told myself lies.

It had only been weeks since I'd shown up at her apartment and found her and my mom lounging on the sofa together watching a movie.

I'd gone home that night determined to stay away from the sixth floor.

Telling myself she was just a client.

Her daughter, my patient.

I'd hung my blazer in my closet and taken my bow tie off, running my hands through my hair roughly before finally caving and walking the stairs two floors up. I told myself I just wanted to make sure she was settled and that she didn't need anything.

Another lie.

In truth, I wanted to see her. I'd thought about her nonstop all day.

And seeing her there with my mom, it had done something to me I couldn't explain. And I was positive I couldn't explain it because I'd never felt that way before. And when my mom had leaned in and touched her face and spoken so lovingly to her, it had meant something to me. Something sweet, something different than the days I spent helping women save their babies. Something better than that. Something more and I didn't think that was possible. Because what I did for a living was pretty damn sweet.

And as the weeks passed, I found myself telling more lies. I just wanted her friendship. I didn't really have very many good friends. I was too busy with my patients. So I told myself I was going there every day after work to hang out. The early days just sitting there on the couch while she ignored me. Just friendship. That's all I wanted from her.

In truth, I just wanted to be around her. All the time.

More lies. I didn't think of our night together long ago. I didn't notice how beautiful she glowed with pregnancy. Her smile didn't make my heart beat faster. Her laughter didn't settle over my body like a thick blanket, warming me from the outside in. I didn't live for her snark, and her witty comebacks didn't make my cock hard. The brave way she loved and fought for her unborn child didn't make me proud. No, that could never happen. Because, we couldn't cross that line.

I was the doctor.

It was impossible.

I couldn't let myself feel anything for this woman. It would jeopardize her child's life.

Those were the only truths I told myself those days.

She came into the office for tests and scans and I pretended she wasn't there, and it was no easy feat with my mother skulking around, interfering, and adoring Kelly far more than I ever thought she could. And I knew what it was. She saw a bit of herself in Kelly and I couldn't even begin to think about that because it terrified me.

So, I didn't think about the coming future. I wouldn't think of the upcoming weeks when things would get harder. I refused to think of the day when I'd finally hold Kelly's most precious possession in my hands—her daughter's heart.

I wouldn't fail her. I couldn't.

Still, I selfishly marched myself up to her apartment every day after work, dying for just a drink of her company. Just a small sip. My soul felt parched without it. I was too hungry for her and far too greedy, but I just couldn't bring myself to stop.

That's why after work, I went right to her, way more excited than I should have been to sit on a couch next to a woman who wasn't pregnant with my child. I may have snuck off a bit early just so I could see her. Maybe I'd tuck my leg next to hers and feel her thigh pressed to mine. Maybe her hand would graze my own when she passed the remote and that familiar electric current of connection would zap through me. I'd cradle her face in mine, dying for the taste of her mouth. God, I wanted it. I wanted her. I lived for those small morsels of affection she fed me. I was starved for them. Ravenous for her touch.

Today, I let myself in. I unlocked the door with my key, mostly because I loved to see her face when she was all pissed off at me but totally not. She put on a good show, my girl. My girl. She never said anything about me coming right on in, but she most definitely wanted to. Her fire. Her spark. It burned me and I loved it.

Pushing the door open, I immediately noticed how quiet it was. Usually she had music or the TV or something going. Maybe she'd be banging her drums, but not this time. Dead silence greeted me and I walked in quietly, worried since I was early maybe she was napping.

But no, there she lay on the couch in a pair of black sweat pants, a tight white tank top that was pushed up over her belly and under her breasts, exposing her round stomach.

I paused, stunned. She lay there on her back, her eyes closed, earbuds pressed into her ears, her hands resting on her stomach like she was holding something precious. And she was. That baby was everything to her, and I realized in that moment that because of what she meant to her, the baby indeed meant the same to me.

And then something both beautiful and awful happened. With her eyes closed, her mouth opened and she sang the words that took me back. I was immersed so fully in the past that my breath paused.

"You are my sunshine," she sang in that sultry and sweet way that I knew she didn't mean to but couldn't help.

My stomach dropped. My eyes blurred. My head spun. And before I knew it, I was standing here, my hand pressed over my heart.

Boom, boom.

"You are my sunshine."

Boom, boom.

She just kept singing and my heart kept beating in rhythm. It was amazing. It was awful.

I felt the way I had that night, only twenty times more, and my upside down, out of focus world tipped right side up and everything became crystal fucking clear.

I couldn't do this. I couldn't be this to her and save her daughter's life. I had to choose.

Bringing my hands close to my face, I studied them, through the sting in my eyes. And they'd never looked so fragile. I'd always thought of them as unfailingly strong and capable, but no, not then. They seemed so small in comparison to the three hearts beating in that room.

I swallowed hard, sick to my stomach, terrified out of my mind.

The last few weeks played in my mind like a movie. Lunches out together. Her sweet heart-shaped face in my hands. Movie nights. Baked cookies. The drum kit. That fucking tie.

I loved her. I loved that baby. The realization hit me like a ton of bricks. It shouldn't have. I'd been lying to myself for weeks, but still the emotion bombarded me.

The moment you realize you're in love should be a moment of elation. Instead, terror filled me. Because I wasn't just in love with Kelly; I was in love with that child who carried the heart I'd have to operate on.

The night Kelly had been staring at the drums in the dark. It made sense now. She knew. She knew and I'd somehow missed it. Her terrified "We can't do this anymore" played on repeat in my mind. She'd tried to warn me. She'd tried to stop this all. I'd been so stupid and blind. So stupidly and blindly in love, I realized now. She wanted me to do the surgery. She trusted me. She'd come to me. Only me.

I clenched my big hands into fists and opened them, repeating the process as I stared down at them. Just these two hands, that's all I had. I'd have to set my *heart* aside for theirs.

Two hands, three hearts, and I had to save us all. And to do it, I'd have to make the ultimate sacrifice.

Love.

Chapter 18

Kelly

That Night Ten Years Ago

I was dreaming. Dreaming about playing the drums and Anthony was there, watching me. Looking like he wanted to eat me up. I shredded them and Anthony stared on, looking like he wanted to bend me over the kit and take me from behind. Maybe I wasn't quite asleep. Maybe I was in the sweet spot between sleep and awake where you can still hear everything around you, but it seems like it's all a part of your dreams.

A phone rang. Again and again until I popped my eyes open, the bright sunlight pouring through the windows and making me snap my eyes closed again. It was early, not terribly as the sun was pretty high in the sky.

The phone rang again and Anthony grumbled from beside

me. We'd stayed up past late and into the wee hours of morning and not just having sex. We'd talked and talked. I'd sung for him. He'd told me his dreams. I'd told him mine.

I took in his sleeping face. I'd thought him beautiful at the club last night, but it in no way compared to his beauty now. Wasn't beauty a funny thing? I learned in that moment that it really did start on the inside and radiate out because after a night with Anthony, he'd only become more gorgeous. More special. More everything. Just more.

His sleeping face looked especially boyish that morning. And sweet. We'd connected. I'd felt it deep in my skin, and I'd never felt a damn thing that deep. I was just a kid, but I knew something big when I felt it and me and Anthony, we were definitely something monumental.

The phone stopped ringing. I curled my body along the outside of his, the front of my naked thighs to the backs of his. I ran my hand through his soft blond hair. The sun was up. Was this it? Was this magical night over and so were we? I didn't want that. I'd talk to him. He had to feel the same way. I didn't know how he couldn't. We'd shared so much in just one single night. I dreamed of all we'd manage to share in days, months, years to come. It made me smile.

When he woke we would sit down and figure it out. I'd be traveling but not forever. Long-distance relationships were hard, but for Anthony I was willing to give it a try. I hoped he was willing to as well.

The phone picked up ringing again and he stretched, his long legs eating up over half of the bed and covering my own. They were firm and strong with the faintest hint of blond hairs. Even the man's legs were perfection.

He turned toward me, kissing my head. "Be back. I'll get the phone." His voice was deeper from sleep and it slid over me like thick molasses. I hoped he didn't have plans today. I wanted him again already.

I lay here blissed out, feeling drunk on sex and intimacy. I spread my body out in the middle of the bed, stretching every muscle, feeling sore in a very good way. I didn't think my body had ever been so thoroughly loved. I heard quiet murmurs of Anthony's voice coming from the kitchen, but couldn't make out what he was saying.

His footsteps thundered toward the bed and I turned, smiling. "That was quick."

Picking my clothes up off the floor, he barked out, "You need to go."

My clothes landed on the bed a foot from me. "What?"

I had to have misunderstood him. Was he throwing me out? A million questions bombarded my brain, but they all told me the same answer. I must have misunderstood him. Surely, he'd felt the same connection I had last night?

"You need to fucking go!" he shouted.

I flinched, grabbing my black dress to cover my breasts. He was scaring me.

He paced the room while I watched on, terrified. Running his hands through his hair roughly, he looked at me. I could only stare, completely stunned.

"Get your fucking clothes on and go." His face was so pained. Something was wrong.

"Doc," I said softly, reaching out a hand to him, but he flinched away like the palm of my hand might burn him.

He leaned over and into my face, his height and stature intimidating the hell out of me. "Get dressed and get the fuck out. Now," he hissed at me and it hit me square in the chest. I felt the tears burn my eyes long before they fell as I frantically squeezed myself back into my tight black dress and scoured the apartment for my panties and shoes while Anthony stormed to the bathroom and slammed the door.

I heard the click of the lock and that was that. He'd shut me out indefinitely. Our night had ended just as it had begun, with a bang.

I collected my purse and as I walked by the bathroom door, I paused, laying my hand on the outside of the door, praying this was all some sort of nightmare. Maybe I was still asleep. Maybe I'd awaken and Anthony would be petting some part of my body like he'd done all night. I'd purr and he'd smile. We'd talk, make love, repeat. It had been the most magical night of my life. This couldn't be happening. It just couldn't.

"Anthony," I said softly, my hand still pressed to the door.

A loud slam against the door that I assumed was his hand sent me reeling back.

"Just go!" he screamed and my insides hurt. His voice was anguished, crude, so fucking bleak.

Just like that. I was so expendable. What had happened? Why was he being this way? He frightened me, and I realized maybe I didn't know him at all. It had only been one night. Still, my hurt was immeasurable.

I ran from the apartment and down the steps, tears leaking from the sides of my eyes and running into my hair. It was for the best. It would have never worked out. We were on two separate paths in life. We were too different. I told myself so many lies that morning when I finally got back to my friend's house, I almost believed them. I'd be heading back to Tennessee soon, and I'd be touring with my band. I had dreams bigger than Anthony Jackson and his sparkling green eyes.

For years, I wondered what had happened that night. Who had called? Was it a girlfriend? Was he afraid of getting caught? What had made him so upset that he'd thrown me out? Screamed at me? I'd only known him a night, but it seemed so strangely uncharacteristic of him.

For years, I thought of him and sometimes it wasn't of his

screaming at me an inch from my face. No, sometimes I thought of my cheek pressed to his heart. Sometimes I thought of our young selves tangled up in the sheets, whispering to each other in the dark, and I would smile. Sometimes.

Chapter 19

Kelly

I was thirty-six weeks along and huge. I seriously felt like the marshmallow man. I was going to pop. I couldn't breathe and every time I walked or rolled over in bed, I felt like someone had kicked me right in my girl parts. That was the truth about pregnancy, and if anyone else said it was rainbows and unicorns and shit, they were fucking liars.

I told myself this misery would be worth every moment when I held my baby girl in my arms and I knew that was true, so I pushed through, but today I was feeling particularly miserable.

And there was only one person to blame. Doc. I hadn't seen him in two days. No texts. No phone calls. He'd just disappeared.

I told myself he was busy with patients, but he usually stopped by even if it was really late at least to check in. I didn't call him. I didn't want him to know how much I needed him. So, I sucked it up and entertained myself. I went about my days taking slow walks around the neighborhood, playing my drums, writing music, watching TV, and of course going to nonstop doctors' appointments. As more days went by I found myself at the craft store, an old habit of mine I'd found again.

I loved crafts like I loved music, but living in a van hadn't been conducive to making all the things with glitter. So, I splurged a little on myself and used the time away from Doc to start making a baby scrapbook for my girl.

I glittered. I cut and pasted. I used tiny letters to spell out things like first tooth, first haircut, first word. Hope. I still had it in spades. Because when that's all you had, it counted for a hell of a lot.

More days passed and finally, I couldn't take it any longer. I missed him more than I'd missed my drums. I texted him. I called. A week had passed and nothing. He didn't answer. He didn't respond.

And the feeling from ten years ago gushed over me like a bucket of cold water. Of him, throwing me out like I didn't matter. And when I thought of that, it hurt, but it in no way compared to how I felt now. Because this was a million times worse. We'd had six long weeks together, not just one measly night. Part of me didn't want to believe it. That he was tossing me away again. I couldn't even fathom it. The man who'd held my face so lovingly. The man who'd told me he'd never leave me. I couldn't believe he'd do this to me. Again.

In a last ditch effort to give him the benefit of the doubt, I called his office. I realized this seemed incredibly desperate of me, but admittedly I was at that point. I was desperate for my Doc. Our long talks. His way of easing my fears. I hadn't had it in seven long days.

Lucy answered the office phone.

"Hey, Lucy. Anthony around?"

"Hey, Kelly. He's with a patient right now. You want me to have him call you back? Anything wrong?"

I blew out a long breath into the phone. "No, it's just…It's just I haven't heard from him in days. I was worried."

"He hasn't been by to see you?"

"Not since last week."

"Oh." The shock in her voice made my stomach hurt. He hadn't even told her.

"Yeah, anyway, could you tell him I called?"

"Of course, honey. I'll let him know. Maybe he's just been really busy." I didn't like the undercurrent of pity tainting her voice.

"Yeah, maybe," I breathed.

I hung up and paced the apartment even though every step felt like someone was kicking me right down there. I was going to kill him. I was so angry. So damn hurt. No one had ever hurt me like this—ever. Not even when Cash had told me to get rid of my baby girl. In truth, I'd expected that from him. But Anthony had completely blindsided me.

I wanted to call my momma and bawl my eyes out. She'd rush over here and console me. She was only staying at an RV park across town, so she could be here in a flash. But I wasn't the call your momma and cry type of girl. I was the girl who internalized everything until I blew the fuck up, and I had to admit I'd been internalizing all damn week and I was feeling ready to lose my shit on Anthony. I was at my breaking point.

That's why I waited. Because I was overly emotional. I was giving him until the next day. Lucy would give him my message. Hopefully he'd make an effort to stop by after work and clear the air. Tell me why he deserted me after that grand speech he'd given me about us being best fucking friends. But I already knew nothing was going to make this right. He'd fucked up. Royally. He'd beyond fucked up really—he'd ruined everything.

My heart ached. My stomach churned. How could I trust him to do right by my baby if he couldn't even do right by someone he called his friend? I spent the night lying in bed and crying. I cried so much my throat felt raw, my insides, too. My head pounded and my eyes felt swollen and still I bawled my eyes out. He'd disappointed me so badly. Never in my life had one person ever let me down so epically.

I stayed up all night crying and spent much of the next day in bed, still no contact from Anthony. My sadness slipped away much like the tears I cried all night, until all that was left was anger. I was so white-hot with it, so full of rage, I wanted to hurt him like he'd hurt me and I'd never felt like that before. Maybe it was the hormones. Maybe it was the situation I was in. Completely dependent on a man who wouldn't even return my calls. Completely at his mercy. I was livid. I was hurt. I was so fucking mad.

And that night I'd had enough. He wasn't going to avoid me anymore. He was going to have to man up and tell me to my goddamn face that he didn't want me anymore. I wasn't sleeping, so it wasn't a hardship to wait until 11:00 p.m. and take the elevator down to his apartment.

I knocked on the door calmly, rationally. I wasn't going to lose my mind, I told myself. I wasn't going to be the crazy pregnant lady. I just wanted him to tell me the truth. To look me in my face when he broke my heart.

I knocked again, still eerily calm. That should have been a warning to me. I should have realized I was too calm in the moment. Looking back, I realize it was the calm before the storm. The door opened and he stood there in a white T-shirt and blue lounge pants, his feet bare, his face impassive. He looked good, healthy, normal, and all my fucking calm left the building.

"How could you?" I screamed like a crazy person. I pushed past him and in his defense he let me. He closed the door and looked at the floor and let me scream like a maniac.

"How could you do that to me?" I yelled again. I wanted his fucking eyes. I deserved them. "How could you do that to us?" I placed my hand over my stomach. Team Hope was no more. Anthony had smashed it to smithereens.

I threw my arms out at my sides. "Tell me, what kind of game were you playing? Why make me need you? Why make me adore you so much? Why? What did you get out of this? Do you know how much you've hurt me?"

His eyes stayed to the floor. It fueled my anger, his lack of eye contact. Every second his eyes weren't on mine was like throwing gasoline on an already raging inferno.

I thought I was cried out, but I was so wrong. Fresh tears spilled over and onto my cheeks, and my chest, it ached. Every bit of my hurt sat there, heavy and hot, burning me up inside.

"Look at me!" I screamed.

His head flew up, the hurt in both of our eyes clashing together like a clap of thunder.

"The apartment? The drums? What kind of game are you playing?" A sob erupted from my chest and it made me angrier. The fact he'd made me so upset. I rubbed the spot over my heart where I hurt. "You made me need you." I choked the words. My throat felt thick with emotion, my insides raw. I didn't want to feel this way. It was all his fault.

"Twice," I whispered through my tears, and he looked confused.

"Twice, you bastard. Shame on me. I let you hurt me again, but mostly shame on fucking you! Shame on you! You said we were best friends." My voice grew louder, crazed.

He reached for me, his eyes tortured, and I almost believed it. He looked so sad, almost to the point of tears, but I couldn't trust him. I wouldn't let him hurt me again.

"Don't touch me!" I screamed, moving away from him. "Don't you dare touch me, Anthony."

He stood straighter, looking like he was ready for a fight, too. "Doc," he demanded.

He moved to me and I moved toward the dining room, farther into the apartment and away from him. "What?" I breathed.

He reached for me again. "Doc. Not Anthony, it's Doc." His face reflected my pain, and I didn't want to see it. I couldn't care about how he felt right now. He'd broken my heart.

"No," I cried. Torrents of tears, now cascading down my face. "No, my Doc would never do this to me. He'd never leave me when I needed him most."

He had me backed into a corner and I squeezed in, feeling like a caged animal, ready to lash out. He reached out to me again, and I shirked away from his hand, slapping it with my own.

"Please don't touch me."

"I'm sorry," he whispered, pulling me into his arms.

"No, please, leave me alone," I cried and sobbed, pushing him away, trying to keep the last bit of sanity and dignity I could, and I couldn't do that if he had his hands on me, his arms around me. I was so devastated.

"Christ, just let me touch you. Let me hold you, please. I can't stand your tears. Please, baby, please."

My attempts at keeping him at bay were futile. He picked me up like I weighed little more than a feather and carried me to the couch. I beat on his chest with my small hands until I was too tired, too worn out, too emotionally spent to do anything anymore. I fell slack against him. He held me in his lap, rocking me, soothing me with whispered "sorrys and please forgive mes."

"Why? What happened?" I questioned softly into his chest, his heart thundering under my ear.

He kissed my forehead, the top of my head, and said into my hair, "I was scared. I'm sorry." He used his thumb to wipe the tears from my face and rocked me in his lap. "I was so scared." He repeated the words over and over, chanting them softly in my ear like a prayer.

I closed my eyes, exhausted from the emotion of it all. The

sleepless nights and my outburst caught up with me, and I wilted against his body. I let him hold me. I breathed in his scent. That smell wasn't just the hottest thing I'd ever smelled before. Now, it meant something to me. That smell was the best. It was the sweetest, too. It was the smell of my Doc, my best friend, so I let him clutch me to him one last time. I wanted all of my one last times. So I smelled him. I listened to the beating of his heart. I wrapped my short arms around his thick neck. Just one last hug. Just one more listen. Just one more of everything.

Chapter 20

Anthony

The sun was creeping up. I was thankful it was the week-end. I didn't have to get up and run off to work, and I had no surgeries scheduled. Which was good, because I would have been pretty damn worthless in the operating room anyway. I'd hardly slept all week. I was like a walking zombie. I didn't sleep last night either. Instead, I held her in my bed for the first time in ten years. I breathed in her scent and spent the night debating what I was going to do now. Because, clearly, what I'd been doing hadn't been working worth a damn for either of us.

The last week had been hell. Every night, I'd come home from work and taken the elevator up to her floor and stood outside her door, staring at it. I wanted to go in there so damn bad. Some nights I'd hear her banging on her drums and I was like a wild animal. I wanted to tear down that door and ravish her mouth—tell her I loved her.

I shouldn't have even gone up there. That wasn't the point of all this. The point was to distance myself, but I couldn't seem to do it. She called to me, this pixie of a woman with her smart mouth and her kind nature. Somehow, over the last month and some odd days she'd become so much to me. I should have known it was going to happen. After all, she'd stolen my heart in just one night years ago. It shouldn't have been a surprise, her ability to totally obliterate my soul. And she had, a little at a time, day by day, until she owned me. And I'd never wanted to be owned by somebody before until her. So, I let her take bits of me, and I gobbled up pieces of her until there wasn't a Kelly or an Anthony anymore. There was just an us. It was wrong. I saw it coming, but I was helpless to stop it.

I knew it had to have been her knocking so late last night. I'd been worried something was wrong with the baby, so I'd opened the door in a panic only to find her there so angry, so hurt. I couldn't even look at her. I was being a pussy. Every pass my eyes made over her anguished face made me sick. I'd done this. I'd caused her and the baby undue stress. I just wanted to hug her and tell her everything was going to be okay, but she wouldn't let me touch her. God, that had destroyed me. Even weeks ago, when I wasn't even sure if she liked me, she'd let me touch her. Rub her feet. Hug her. All I could think was that she hated me now. She couldn't stand me. That should have made things better, right? But it didn't. Because I still loved her. And that was where we had our problem.

I couldn't love her and save her baby's life. It was unethical. It was wrong.

I had to tell her.

I pulled her closer to my body in the bed and twined her legs with mine and laid my hand on her stomach. It was large now. She'd be here before we knew it. We had to be ready. We had the fight of our lives ahead. I wanted us to be armed with every available resource I had. I couldn't do the surgery myself, but I could make sure we had the very damn best. And I would.

She stirred beside me. She was going to be pissed this morning. I knew her through and through, so I knew she was going to wake up raging mad that she'd fallen asleep. That I'd carried her to my bed and cuddled her all night. But she'd exhausted herself. She needed to sleep and I needed to hold her. It seemed like a win-win to me. She wouldn't see it that way, of course. She was just going to have to get the fuck over it. I was done playing games. I was done wishing I didn't love her. I was done messing around. She was mine. That baby was mine now, too. It was time she knew it.

She pushed her face into the crook of my neck and I pulled her even closer, until most of her small body was draped across mine. I'd removed her sweatshirt and pants last night so she'd be comfortable. All that she was left in was a pink cami and some panties. That was going to piss her off, too. I didn't care. Besides, she looked beautiful. Pregnancy looked damn good on her.

I was readying myself for the inevitable argument. Yes, and when I got her ass calmed down I'd tell her everything. We'd figure it out together. We could do anything as long as we did it together.

Moaning a little, she stretched and I became very still, waiting for her to realize where she was, who she was with.

Her body went from languid and lazy to ramrod straight and that was my sign. She was awake and pissed.

Untangling her legs from mine, she sat up, eyes narrowed on me. I ran my hand across the stubble on my chin, trying to hide my smirk. I loved her fire. I would've stood in it all day every day if I wasn't so sure it would burn me.

She flung the covers back and looked at her legs before glaring down at me again. "Where the hell are my pants?"

I motioned to the chair in the corner. "Over there."

She shot up and over to the chair. Well, as fast as a woman that was heavily pregnant could shoot up.

She sat in the chair and started to hustle herself into her black leggings and I wanted to laugh. It was pretty damn cute.

I sat up and put my feet to the floor but stayed in the bed. I thought if I got up, she'd forget about trying to put her pants on and just take off for her apartment. "We need to talk, small fry."

She shook her head, breathing hard from pulling her pants up. "No, you don't get to do that, Anthony." She gave me an eat shit look. "You don't get to call me adorably sweet short girl nicknames anymore. Only my friends get to do shit like that." She grabbed her sweatshirt.

Her head popped through the neck of the hoodie, her angry eyes still on mine.

Finally, I stood up. She was going to leave. I couldn't let that happen. Walking toward her, she took in my bare torso and boxer briefs, and I hoped that meant she was attracted to me like I was to her.

But her eyes darted back to my chest over my heart when they stopped. She stared, and then squinted before the shock registered on her face, her eyes wide. "What the hell is that?"

Placing my hand over the tattoo that sat above my nipple and right over my heart, I just stared. This wasn't how I wanted this conversation to start. I didn't want to talk about that night.

"What the fuck is that? Is that a tattoo? Does it…" she trailed off and sat back down in the chair, placing her head in her hands.

God, I was a fuck up. She was emotionally drained and now this.

Her head came up, her eyes trailing over the tattoo again, the slight sheen of tears in them. "Does that say what I think it does?"

It did. And I wasn't sorry it was there. I was only sorry that she had to see it now. When she was already so upset.

The words *The Music Of Life* sat right over my heart. A few EKG waves and music notes scattered around the words. A little of me. A little of her. A little of him.

I nodded slowly and swallowed, scared she'd get up and run.

She wouldn't understand. That morning had been so awful, but that night had meant so much to me. That night would get me through the dark days that had lain ahead. That tattoo was a reminder of her. Of him. And of the promise I made myself the day I got it.

"How long have you had it?" She was coming toward me now and I stood so still, so quiet. I was terrified she'd run off on me and I'd never get to tell her how I loved her. How I wanted that baby almost as much as she did.

I swallowed down the fear. "Nine and a half years."

Standing close to me, she asked, "But why?" And I knew she wasn't just asking why I'd tattooed her words on me. She was asking why I'd thrown her out then. Why I'd tossed her aside now.

I couldn't make the words come. I was frozen. I couldn't tell her that her greatest fear, I'd already experienced in a sense. It would crush her soul, her spirit, her hope and we'd need an abundance of those things in the coming months. Hell, years.

She traced the music notes around the tattoo and smiled sadly, like I was already a lost cause. She knew I wasn't going to tell her. She knew I couldn't.

Cradling her face in my hands, I forced her eyes to mine. "We have to talk."

She snatched her head away. "What? You want me to find another place to live now?" She stormed through the bedroom door and into the living room. "Fine!"

"Stop, Kelly." I tried to keep my voice even.

With her hand on the front door she turned to me. "What is it? You want to break my heart a little more? Or do you want to be the one to throw me out? Is it not enough that I leave on my own?"

She was fucking killing me. Jesus, this was a fucking mess. I had a feeling no matter what I said right now, she wasn't going to listen.

Walking over to the couch, I said, "Come sit down. We need to talk about the baby."

Any anger on her face evaporated into thin air only to be replaced by fear and trepidation. Her hand immediately went to her stomach. "What about the baby?"

"Come. Sit." I patted the cushion next to me. I could do this. She was going to cry and be upset. I'd remain calm. I could do that, for both of us.

She waltzed over, her face wary, making sure to sit as far away from me as she could on the couch. I didn't care, I just moved into the center of the furniture so I could be closer. She'd need me. And I wanted to be there to lean on.

I wanted to pull off the Band-Aid quickly, so it hurt a little less. I took a deep breath and counted to three. "I can't do the surgery, honey."

Panic colored every feature of her face and I felt terrible, sick for her, but she had to know this was coming. She had to understand what I had to do. For her. For us.

Her head shook back and forth slowly. She grabbed my wrists tightly with both hands, clutching them in her fists and pulling.

"No, no, Anthony. I need you. She needs you."

I pulled her hands away from my wrists and cradled them in my own, holding them firmly, using my thumbs to caress the insides of her small palms. I wanted to soothe her. I wanted to help her get through this, but I didn't know how.

"I can't do it, baby—"

"But why?" She sobbed.

Her cries destroyed me; her pain my own.

I cradled her face in my hands. It was my way. I loved her small heart-shaped face. I wanted to plant tender kisses all over it.

"You know why, honey."

She shook her head again, tears springing to her eyes. "No, no. I don't."

I brought my face close to hers. "You do," I whispered.

"No," she said again, but I could read the emotion all over her face. I knew without a shadow of a doubt that she knew exactly what I did. That I loved her. That I loved that baby.

She knew it long before I did.

"Please don't do this. Please." She squeezed her eyes shut like she could make me disappear. Make this moment dissolve into nothing when I knew that in the years to come this moment would mean everything because it wouldn't just be the day I told her I couldn't operate on her child. It would be the day I told her I loved her, too.

"Baby," I whispered raggedly, rubbing my thumbs along the apples of her cheeks. "I can't do that surgery and you know why. You knew it before I did. I'm in love with you."

"No, it has to be you," she said. "I trust you. I only trust you. It has to be you." Her hands covered my hands, gripping hard, like she was holding onto the past. And perhaps she was. Maybe she was clinging to that day in the parking lot at the office. But so much had changed since then and we couldn't go back. We could only move forward.

"I tried. I really did, little bit. I tried to stay away from you, but I just can't." Not that it would have mattered. I was crazy thinking a few weeks would change how I felt about Kelly. She was the love of my life and part of me had known that for ten years.

"Please," she begged. I didn't know what she was begging for. Maybe she was begging me to stop talking. Maybe she was begging me to take it all back. But I wouldn't. I wouldn't take back a single minute of our time together the last six weeks. They had meant the world to me. It wasn't ideal, this situation, but it was us and we could get through anything together.

I looked deeply into her eyes so she didn't misconstrue or misunderstand me. "I can't do the surgery because I love you and because I love her." I dropped a hand and touched her stomach gently.

Tears poured down her face.

"Because it wouldn't be just her heart and your heart on that table, it would be my heart, too." I used my thumbs to angle her head toward me. "Look at me."

She opened her eyes and I hoped she saw the love, the truthfulness in mine. "It's okay, baby. I'm gonna make this right. I'm gonna take care of you. I'm gonna take care of her. I'm gonna take care of us." I pressed a chaste kiss to her tear-soaked lips. My heart bled right along with hers, but I was making the only decision I could.

"I'm good, but I'm not the best. I'll make sure she has the best. I promise. You said you trust me. So, do it. Just trust me." And I would make sure she had the best. I would call in every damn favor I could. I'd beg. I'd bargain. I'd steal. This baby girl would have the absolute best doctor I could find. I'd die trying.

Chapter 21

Kelly

"**I** want to take you on a date."

Somehow Anthony had managed to persuade me to stay over again last night. We'd spent the day cuddled up watching TV and it was exactly the kind of day I needed. I needed time to marinate on what he'd said. He loved me. He couldn't do the surgery. Part of me had already known and the other part of me was still freaking out about it. Still, I was glad I'd stayed. I'd let him wrap his long arms around my baby bump and spoon me. Doc was one hell of a big spoon, and me, well, I was an itty bitty one, but we made it work. It felt good to be held. I'd needed it. Maybe it was because my emotions were so raw from his confession yesterday. He'd told me he couldn't do the surgery. That he loved me. It was probably the most bittersweet day of my entire life. On one hand I was crushed that he couldn't do the surgery. On the other hand

I was ecstatic that he loved me like I loved him. I hadn't told him yet. I was scared to. Like somehow if I said the words everything would change. I couldn't lose our friendship now. Over the last seven days without Anthony I'd realized how vital he was to me and my happiness.

I was in the kitchen making pancakes for my big guy and he was standing on the other side of the counter, toweling off his wet hair and looking utterly delectable in a T-shirt and jeans when he sprang that doozy on me.

I looked at him like he was crazy and continued on making the pancakes like he hadn't said a damn word.

"Did you hear me?"

I looked at him again like he'd lost his mind. "Oh, I heard you."

"So?"

Flipping the pancake I answered, "So what?"

"Will you go on a date with me, Kelly Ann Potter?"

I put the rest of the pancakes on a plate and moved the skillet off the burner. "No way."

"Why not?" His look was incredulous.

"Because I'm almost nine months pregnant." What kind of harlot did he think I was? I couldn't just be going on dates. Going on dates was for women who were single and not pregnant. Women who could wear skimpy dresses and drink cocktails and laugh like they didn't have a care in the world. I had responsibilities. Like a baby and myself. That was all I could handle right now. If the past ten years were any indication, I was a far cry from adult material. I needed to mom-up, stop being so damn selfish and start thinking like a momma bear. He wanted me to add dating to the mix. I could barely handle my life right now without the added dating part. What was he thinking?

"What does that have to do with anything?" He added a ridiculous amount of syrup to his pancakes. The man's sweet tooth was out of control.

"I don't know. It's weird."

"It's only weird if you make it weird."

I gave him the look again.

He rolled his eyes. "*You're* making it weird. Pregnant women go on dates all the time."

"With their husbands," I agreed.

He leaned over the counter, his face deadly serious. "You need a ring to go on a date with me, baby?" He sounded like he was about to take me down to the courthouse ASAP.

Eyes bugged out of my head, I answered, "Oh my God, no!" I might have lied a little. I'd love for Anthony to be my husband. He was caring and sweet and the only man I'd ever loved. But he was asking me for a date, not my hand in marriage. "Besides, I can barely fit in my sweats I'm so big. I don't have anything to wear on a date."

"It doesn't matter what you wear."

"It does to me."

"Why are you so argumentative all the time?"

I quirked an eyebrow. "Then why do you want to take me on a date, if I'm so argumentative?"

"Christ almighty! You drive me insane!"

"Again, why—"

His big frame leaned over the counter and he placed his hand over my mouth. "Don't make me shut you up, little bit."

I grinned as he removed his hand. I was feeling saucy and flirtatious. Maybe it was that his hand had been pressed to my lips. Maybe it was sleeping with him wrapped around me. Maybe it was all the talk of dating. I was flattered. This big, beautiful, kind man loved me. He wanted to take me out and show me off like I was a prize even though I was anything but. "And how are you going to do that?"

His eyes heated. "I'd walk into the kitchen and I'd pin you to the refrigerator and I'd kiss you. Hard. Greedily. Really fucking kiss you like I've been waiting for what feels like forever to do. But I wanted to take you on a date first."

I licked my lips. Kisses were good. I wanted kisses. Dates, not so much. But yes to all the kisses.

"What if I want to just skip to the kissing part?"

He stared at my lips hard, considering my words. "What about if I kiss you and then you let me take you on a date?" He prowled around the counter and into the kitchen, the pancakes long forgotten.

He was like a big, stalking lion, so slow but every step so deliberate, his eyes hot on mine, and I backed toward the refrigerator, falling completely into the trap he'd voiced only minutes ago.

"What if we stay in and kiss all night?"

My back hit the fridge and his front hit mine. His hand went to the back of my neck, his face a few inches from mine.

"What if I kissed some sense into you, instead?" His deep, growly voice ghosted over my skin, making me warm from outside in. His head lowered and I held my breath. Yes, we'd shared small friendly kisses but nothing like this. Pecks, that's all. Nothing sexual, really. Not since years ago when we were young and I wasn't pregnant with someone else's baby.

His soft lips met the corner of mine, sweet, tender, like he knew I needed time. And then the other corner the same way. He was going slow and I was dying, my stomach quivering.

Once he kissed my cupid's bow.

Twice he kissed the pillowy pad of my bottom lip.

Three times he rubbed his nose along mine.

I'd kissed this man with my eyes a thousand times over the last month, but nothing compared to the real thing.

"Breathe, baby," he whispered across my lips.

I exhaled into his mouth and he moaned low into mine before giving my lips a lazy, slow lick right up the center. It surprised me. It sent my belly flip-flopping. It made me ache between my legs. It tasted like maple syrup and man. It was dirty in the perfect kind of way, that lick.

I shouldn't have been surprised. These kisses somehow perfectly personified the man who gave them. Sweet but so sensual. Thoughtful but incredibly sexy.

"Up, baby," he muttered against my mouth, our breaths intermingling, as his hand left my neck and trailed down my back to grip my ass. His other hand joined in and before I knew it I was hoisted up. I immediately wrapped my legs around his waist for leverage and because, well, I knew it would feel good. My arms tangled around his neck and his mouth finally took mine. His kisses went from slow and sweet to fast and hard, and I was right there with him, his tongue sliding along mine, his teeth nipping at my bottom lip. I groaned and the bottom of my body involuntarily pushed against his.

His body was pressed to me, and oh God! His cock was right there. Right at my center, the thick head pressed to my clit and it was so hard and big, and I could feel it all too well through the sheer fabric of my granny panties and yoga pants. And I wanted it. I wanted to push down his pants under his cock and have him slip it inside of me right here against the cold fridge in the middle of the kitchen. So, I rocked against him again and this time he didn't miss it.

"Fuck," he growled before pushing me harder into the fridge and grinding that thick cock against me, my big stomach only slightly encumbering our grinding.

It felt too good. I couldn't breathe. I hadn't done this in so long. I'd wanted him for weeks. My brain had absolutely no control over my body. I couldn't think. I couldn't speak. I couldn't breathe. All I could do was feel. I was mush.

I snapped my head back against the hard surface behind me, desperate for air. "Oh, God."

"Mmmm," he growled against my throat and he licked up the

column of it before assaulting my collarbone. He sucked there, biting the spot and then licking it better. He was driving me mad and he knew it. Every suck, every lick, every kiss spurred me on and still I continued to rock against him, my head thrown back, my eyes squeezed shut, trying to suck every bit of pleasure I could out of the moment.

"That's it, baby," he husked against my throat. "Use me."

And those words, use me, they did something awful, something amazing to me. Something unexplainable. My insides split apart at those words. I did. I wanted to use him up. I wanted to press against him until I came. I couldn't stop it. I was as helpless and wanton as the grunts and groans that seemed to echo out into the kitchen.

And he had to have known what those words did to me. It was so obvious they pushed me over the edge of oblivion into some unknown space.

With one hand still holding me up at my ass, he used the other to grab the back of my hair tight, turning my head so that my ear could meet his mouth. It started with a small suck at my lobe but turned into the dirtiest words I'd ever heard.

"Ride it, honey. Ride my cock." His words fucked my ear. "It's yours. Take it." Dirty whispers filled my fuzzy, sexed up brain. "I can feel how wet you are through your clothes." I should have been embarrassed. Instead, I pushed against him harder.

"God, you're going to come on me, aren't you, baby? And I haven't even really touched you yet. Fuck, but you're perfect."

I groaned loud.

"I remember it, you know. How tight you were. How wet you got for me. How your pussy almost felt too small for me," he panted. "Fuck, I remember it and I stroke my cock."

And the simple thought of him touching himself while thinking of me sent me racing toward my climax, spiraling down a vortex of pleasure.

"That's it," he coaxed as I curled my shaking body around him, my face planted into his shoulder, his mouth still to my ear. "Come on me. Come all over my dick." His voice was thick and rich with lust.

And then his hands were back to my ass, pushing me against his thickness. The head caught my clit, one, two, three more times and stars burst behind my eyes. My head shot back, his hand already there to protect it as my body locked tight.

Breathe, I encouraged myself and he continued to rock his body against mine and kiss the spot behind my ear, the place where my neck met my collarbone, the dip at the base of my neck. I groaned long and hard as I rode out the longest orgasm of my life before finally my body fell slack against his.

I had nothing left. Every bit of my everything had been zapped out of me. I couldn't even wrap my legs around him anymore, so Anthony carried me to the couch where he propped me in his lap and brought my head to his chest.

Anthony pushed the sweaty hair off my forehead and smiled down at me. "You're the most beautiful woman I've ever seen." And fuck if he didn't mean it. Love shone out of his eyes like the sun poured down on the Carolina beaches in the summer.

I wanted to tell him he was the most beautiful man I'd ever seen, too. I wanted to confess my love for him. I wanted to lay it all out there. That I'd never forgotten about him and our night. That it had meant something to me. That *he* meant something to me, but I was still stupidly and selfishly scared, so I burrowed further into his chest, still trying to catch my breath.

He hugged me to him and I let him. The best place in the world was inside one of Doc's hugs. For those few minutes when his arms were wrapped around me everything seemed perfect.

Ya know, until he spoke.

"I think I held up my end of the bargain, Peanut. What do you think?"

I smiled into his shirt. "What bargain?" I mumbled.

"The one where I kiss the shit out of you and you let me take you on a date."

I couldn't tell him no. I already couldn't tell him I loved him. He deserved a date. He deserved whatever he wanted. He was too good to his core, this one. I'd give him anything.

"Okay."

He laughed. "What was that?"

Rolling my eyes, I answered, "I said, okay, Doc. Calm the fuck down."

He kissed my forehead. "I love how agreeable orgasms make you. I'll have to remember that in the future."

I hid my flaming face in his chest and wrapped my arms around his middle. I couldn't even argue that point because he definitely wasn't wrong.

"Move in with me."

My body flew back and I almost fell off the couch, if not for Doc catching me just in time.

"No."

"How many orgasms is it gonna cost me?"

The loon was completely serious.

My face burned hotter. "Oh my God, stop talking about orgasms, please!"

I laid my head back to his chest and listened to his laugher there vibrating around his heart. It was the sweetest sound I'd heard in a long time, even if it was at my expense.

Chapter 22

Kelly

"Pick up, pick up, pick up." I held my cell phone to my ear, praying Ainsley answered. I needed her. After spending most of the day with Anthony, I'd come up to my apartment to get ready for our "date." Shit. I'd let him make me come against his refrigerator and then talk me into going out with him on a real date. Doc was right; clearly orgasms made me stupid agreeable. He wanted a real date. Like a fancy date with dinner and dancing or something. And I didn't think I'd ever been on a date like that. I was the girl who had quick hookups in the back of clubs I'd performed at. Or I used to be. I'd never had a serious boyfriend or a real date. I was terrified.

It seemed like I was scared of everything lately. Anthony had arranged for a doctor friend that he assured me was the best to fly in and get ready for my delivery. Between the date and the impending delivery of my baby girl, I was a mess.

The phone continued to ring and I was sick to my stomach, like I was going to puke. "Come on. Pick up, Ains."

She finally answered, sounding like she was out of breath. "Hey, Kells!"

"Oh my God, I'm so glad you answered. I'm freaking out. Freaking out, Ainsley. You have to help me. I don't know—"

She cut me off. "Calm down, crazy lady, and explain to me slowly what's happening. And of course I answered. I'll always answer when you call. You know that. I was just chasing the kids around the yard."

"God, I'm sorry to interrupt your family time. Do you want to call me back?"

She laughed. "Hell no, I want to know what the heck is going on!"

"I have a date," I whispered like anyone but she could hear me.

"What? With who?"

"Geez Louise, don't make me say it, Ains."

"Holy shit, you have a date with Anthony don't you?"

"Yes," I murmured.

"You need to give me all the details now. When did this start? Why didn't I get a call? Have y'all kissed? I'm so mad right now. I know nothing!"

I sighed. "And you called me crazy lady."

"Spill it, Potter!"

"He says he loves me. He's kissed me." I skipped the dry humping part. I could only divulge so much in one day. I'd save that tasty morsel for another day. "He wants to take me on a date. He's crazy. He wants me to move in."

She whistled long and low. "Wow."

"I know."

"You must have put in on that man."

I gasped. "Hell no, I didn't. I'm almost nine months pregnant!"

"Pregnant chicks have sex, Kelly, and they also go on dates."

Rolling my eyes, I answered, "I guess."

"I can't believe that little shit grew up to be a hot doctor who kisses my best friend."

I giggled. I already felt better just talking to her. "But what am I going to wear tonight? What do I do? I've never even been on a real date, Ains. I'm faaareaking out!"

"It's going to be fine, honey. You've been hanging with Anthony for weeks now. You're just going to be hanging with him in public, dressed up, and maybe being a little romantic."

Ainsley was my best friend. I could tell her anything, even my greatest fears. I had to tell someone. I couldn't keep it bottled up any longer. I lay back on my bed, feeling a twinge in my back that made me gasp a bit. "What if we go out on a date and he realizes this is all a big mistake?"

"What?"

"What if he realizes I'm a big mistake? That he doesn't love me. That I'm nine months pregnant with another man's baby and I don't have a job or a future. That I'm not good enough."

"Oh, Kelly." I hated the pity in her voice. "That is never going to happen. Because you aren't just some chick who's pregnant with another man's baby. You're smart and funny and beautiful, and right now you don't know what you're going to do with your future, but I have no doubt it's going to be epic because you're amazing and Anthony knows that just as well as I do. You're more than good enough."

I tried to tell myself she was right, but I didn't think I'd ever felt so insecure in my life as I did in that moment. What did he see in me? I wished I could see myself in Doc's eyes for just a moment, and then maybe I'd understand.

"Thanks, Ains."

"Anytime, baby. So what are you going to wear? Oh, wear your hair down. It's so beautiful down and around your face."

an imperfect heart

I groaned. "I have no idea what in the hell I'm wearing. I don't have anything that fits."

"What about a little black dress? Surely you have a stretchy black dress. Every girl does."

I looked down at my giant baby bump. Nope, scratch that. I was firmly out of the bump category and into the hump one. I was huge.

"I don't think there's enough stretch in the world, Ains. I'm pretty sure my little black dress would double as a tank top right now."

She laughed. "Girl, he doesn't care what you're wearing. He just wants to be with you."

The doorbell rang, and I sat up as quickly as I could. "I gotta go. The doorbell's ringing."

"Okay. Have fun tonight and don't stress. You're perfect."

"Thanks! Bye."

I looked through the peephole to find Lucy on the other side. Opening the door, I said, "Hey!" We hugged. "What are you doing here?" Not that I wasn't happy to see her, but I had a date to get ready for, and I needed a lot of time to come up with a clean pair of sweatpants that didn't look like I forced myself into them.

She held up a white shopping bag. "I brought you something to wear tonight."

"What?" How did she know about tonight and what did she bring me?

"Anthony said he was taking you out tonight and that you were worried about what to wear. He gave me his credit card and I went shopping for you."

I wanted to be annoyed that he'd once again taken care of me, but I couldn't. I was so lucky. I couldn't complain about a man who not only told me he was in love with me, but showed it, too. And I wasn't talking material things. Anthony was thoughtful, and it showed in every one of his actions.

151

"What did you get me?" I smiled and tried to peek in the bag.

"Uh uh uh, no peeking." She dashed toward my bedroom. "Come on, let's get you all dolled up. He will be here before you know it."

And for some reason, I wasn't so scared anymore. I didn't know if it was my conversation with Ainsley or Lucy to the rescue, but butterflies swarmed my belly. I was excited.

Chapter 23

Anthony

I stood outside Kelly's door and knocked. It was a date, otherwise I would have just used my key and busted on in. But I wanted to do this right. I had a feeling Kelly had never been wined and dined, and I wanted to do that. Well, minus the wine.

She was taking forever to answer, so I tugged at the bow tie she'd given me. I knew she picked on my ties, but I also knew she loved them. Why else would she have given me one? I paired the music tie with a white dress shirt and dark gray slacks. I'd thrown a little gel in my hair and put on my best cologne. I hadn't been on very many dates myself. Weren't we a pair tonight?

The door opened and there she stood in a pale pink off the shoulder flowing dress that hit her just below the knees, her gorgeous legs on display. Her hair was down and curled around her face, and I could tell she'd added a little makeup. She looked

153

beautiful. I wanted to push her back into the apartment and do an instant replay of yesterday when she'd ridden my cock against the refrigerator. Fuck, I'd been so hot, so ready for her, and she'd been so beautiful, lost in her pleasure. I wanted her. I didn't want to rush her, though. Everything would happen in time. The first being our date. She was dealing with a lot. I was trying to ease my way into her heart. The bed would have to wait, even if it killed me. And it might with her looking like that.

I pushed a hand through my hair. "Fuck, you look good." And clearly I wasn't going for dashing or debonair. I'd just used the word fuck. My face got hot. "Sorry."

Her face softened in the hallway light.

"It's just you look really beautiful." I wrung my hands.

She stepped out, closed the door, and put her arm through mine. "You nervous, too?" She steered us toward the elevator.

"Terribly."

She laughed. "Well, we can be nervous together."

She didn't have a reason to be nervous. She looked gorgeous. We shot each other quiet smiles in the elevator, and I opened the door when we reached my car.

She fidgeted in the seat next to me. "So where are we going, Doc?"

"It's a surprise."

She reached over and touched my tie, and I remembered that day in the parking lot, how she'd thumped my tie. I smiled.

"You wore the tie." It was just a statement, but it was loaded with sentiment and feeling.

I nodded. "I did."

"It looks good." Her face flushed and even though it was dark, I could see the red in her cheeks. I wanted to caress them with my fingers.

I remembered her words. A little of me and a little of you.

It wasn't a long ride to our destination and as I parked the car

an imperfect heart

Kelly studied the building in front of us. "Louisa's?"

"Yep." I walked around the car and opened the door, giving her a hand out of the low car. I could tell she was finding it more and more difficult to do the simplest of tasks. Baby girl would be here any day now. I was excited. I was frightened. I'd made all the necessary arrangements and had a doctor friend who flew in yesterday to be on standby. We couldn't take any chances. He was a damn good doctor, and I'd put every bit of my faith in him and his ability to do his job. He'd done me a huge favor being away from his family for the upcoming days until the baby arrived. I'd owe him one. But I'd owe anybody anything as long as the baby was okay.

Kelly took in the old white building that had definitely seen better days as we walked the path to the front door. My eyes adjusted to the darkness as I looked around the crowded jazz club to find an available table. Grabbing her hand, I pulled her to one of the only tables not taken.

"What is the place?" she asked, hanging her purse on the back of her chair.

I looked at the stage. "I thought you'd like to hear some music."

She grinned and looked around. I had to admit, it was pretty damn cool. I'd only ever been to Louisa's one time myself. The outside of the building sure didn't match the inside, which was the very definition of cool. Low lighting, exposed brick walls, and furniture and decor in sexy reds and blacks filled the space.

A waiter approached our table. "What can I get you?" He looked at me.

I ordered a few tapas they had on the menu for us to share and a soda water with lime.

The waiter looked at Kelly and back at me. "And what can I get your wife?"

"Oh—" Kelly started, but I cut her off. I didn't know why she felt the need to clarify or why she thought it was awkward people thought she was my wife. After all, we were together.

"She'll just have water."

"Sounds good, I'll be back with your drinks in just a moment."

The waiter left and Kelly gave me a look. "See, that was weird."

I scowled at her. "It wasn't weird. There's not a goddamn thing about you being my wife that's weird."

And there wasn't. It was my dream, to be her husband, to have that baby call me daddy. But I knew dreams could easily be crushed, so I dared not let myself voice them.

She smiled at me. "Calm down, Doc."

She loved to tell me to calm down. It almost always made her smile, and when she smiled I lost my fucking mind. That smile made me act like a lovesick idiot, so I dropped my scowl and smiled back at her.

The club darkened further and the stage lit as the performer for the night walked across the stage. I watched Kelly's face.

Her lips curved and her eyes brightened, and I wondered how I was going to take my eyes off her for one second. Her head snapped to mine.

"Mo!" she whispered with excitement as he made his way to a piano and sat down.

Her excited face turned back to the stage, and Mo started into a slow jazz piece and that had Kelly rocking in her seat slowly. That piece fed into another and another, my girl completely absorbed in the music. He pounded the keys and rocked back and forth on the bench. Some slow, some fast, but my girl's eyes never left the stage. Not even when the food and drinks arrived. I could tell she loved seeing Mo play. Her face said it all. That old man enraptured my girl. Every note he played she fell for him more and more, and every second she spent falling for him, I fell more for her. I tried to watch Mo, but instead spent much of the evening watching her. Fuck, I loved her. And I know it sounded stupid, but I wanted her to love me, too. More than anything. I wanted to hold that baby and know it was safe, and I wanted her momma to tell me she loved me. It seemed like I was asking for so little and yet so much at the same time. It felt like it was right there in front of me and miles away, the dream I dreamed.

Mo's set closed, and Kelly turned to me, giving me the biggest smile I'd ever seen. "That was amazing. That man is amazing! Did you know he could play like that?"

I grabbed her hand across the table. I wanted her next to me. "I did."

"I mean, holy shit, he's so talented. God, I loved it."

"I'm glad." And I was. I wanted her to love tonight and remember it and think of me. I wanted her to think of me always.

A warm hand on my shoulder snapped me out of my thoughts. I looked over my shoulder to see Mo standing there, black suit on, his black fedora with a red strip of silk around it perched on his head.

"Dr. Jackson." He smiled down at me. "Ms. Kelly."

Kelly flew up out of her seat and around me. "Oh my God, Mo. That was amazing. I loved it so much. Can I hug you? Is that okay?" She didn't wait for him to answer as she threw her arms around him.

He chuckled low as he hugged her back. Pulling out of her embrace he said, "You never came back and played the drums for me."

She laughed and patted her round belly. "Well, I've been kinda busy."

He gave me a look. "Well, I'm glad the good doctor could bring you to see me play."

"Oh, me, too, you're amazing!"

"Are you enjoying your drum kit?"

Now Kelly gave me a pointed look before answering, "Yeah, I'm enjoying it when the neighbors let me even if it was too much of a gift."

"Mmm," he hummed and looked at my tie. "Looking pretty smooth, brother."

Amie Knight

I grinned. "Thanks, man."

He raised an eyebrow at Kelly almost teasingly. "Looks like you gave your man the tie?"

Her man. I waited for her to deny it. To tell Mo I was just a friend. It seemed she was always trying to deny what we were growing more and more into every day. But she surprised me tonight in the most special way when her eyes got soft on me.

"I did," she said, and my chest all of a sudden felt too small for my heart. Like it might just burst wide-open.

Fuck if I didn't wanna puff my chest out and bang it like a damn caveman. That's right, I'm her man. Everybody pay fucking attention. I somehow just barely managed to rein my crazy in.

"How's Noah?" I asked Mo.

"He's good. I think he's coming into the office for a checkup, so I imagine you'll be seeing him soon. Says Lucille is gonna have a candy for him."

I laughed. "I'm sure she will." My mother spoiled rotten the kids who came in.

"Well, I don't wanna keep y'all from your date." He raised his eyebrows at me. "That is what this is, right?"

I nodded.

He laughed a little. "Well, y'all are both lookin' real good. I'd say you suit each other nicely." He kissed Kelly's hand and looked back at me. "Bring her in to see me sometime. I gotta hear this pixie play the drums."

And he was gone as quickly and as smooth as he walked up to us.

I held my arm out. "Ready?"

"Yep."

"Who's Noah?"

"Mo's grandson."

"And I imagine you saved his life, too?"

This was starting to get embarrassing, but I still answered. "Me

158

and an awesome team of doctors."

"How'd you get so damn amazing, Doc?"

I laughed.

"I'm serious. How are you so damn good, so sweet, so smart, and so damn sexy?"

My face heated at her compliments. I wasn't used to such high praise from a woman. She thought I was sexy. And, God, I thought she was, too.

I didn't know what to say, so I said nothing at all as I opened the car door for her. She paused on her way in and her baby belly pressed into my stomach as she leaned up and brushed a soft kiss across my lips. That kiss meant a fuck of a lot. She'd never initiated one between us since we'd been reunited. It wasn't the kind of kiss that was full of passion and heat. No, it was better than that because it was full of love.

"You're special, Doc. I hope you know that," she murmured before getting into the car.

I didn't know that, but she was making it clearer every day.

Chapter 24

Kelly

I spent the entire morning out with what I was now referring to as the moms. Lucille and my momma had become insepara- ble, much like me and Doc. They had such fun together, and I couldn't deny them when they asked if they could take me baby shopping. Doc encouraged me to go, saying he had to make ar- rangements for Hope and work to do. In truth, I wanted to be part of the arrangements, but there wasn't much I could do but put my trust in him. And I was trying. I really was.

Besides, I had a feeling Doc was trying to get rid of my ass for the day. I couldn't quite figure out why, but I'd find out eventually. He couldn't hide stuff from me for long.

I was exhausted, but I'd had fun even with the occasional back pains I was having. I would have said that my date last night with Doc had been the best of my life, but really it had been the only real date, so I guess it was still true. He'd known exactly what I'd enjoy, and he'd made it happen. We'd come home and gotten into bed. He'd rubbed my aching back until I fell asleep.

My Doc, he was good down to his soul. And stupid me, I was starting to believe that maybe this had all been fate. And I didn't believe in fate. But somehow this whole thing felt entirely bigger than me. What else could I call it? The way Anthony had so effort-lessly swept into our lives after all these years and fixed everything and somehow managed to love me, too. It had to be something greater than me. Something grander than him. Because together? We were pretty damn special.

The moms and I had a great day, too, but being out late and not being able to sleep much as of late was wearing me out. I'd been having these sharp pains in my back on and off for the past day or so. I was wildly restless and cranky, but still I chugged on, bound and determined to get everything we would need for the baby.

We picked out baby clothes and a small bassinet I could put next to my bed. A car seat and blankets and pacifiers. The list went on and on. My baby would be sick, so I knew there was even more I'd need to care for her. But it had been nice to celebrate her. Ever since I'd found out about her heart it seemed that every thought of her was filled with worry and fear. Today, I'd celebrated her life. Yes, today had been good. I'd needed it.

I schlepped off the elevator with a few bags of clothes feeling like I could fall over any minute, the moms behind me with boxes galore. We were going to get ready for the baby today, and I was excited. I was also worn out and my feet felt swollen and heavy. We had tons of things to assemble and loads of baby clothes to wash. I opened the door to my apartment and immediately felt some-thing was off. My drum set was gone. It was too clean, not a speck of glitter or crumbs in sight. I became suspicious. I dropped my bags on the couch and walked to the bedroom and noticed the bed was made. I never made my bed. Ever. You couldn't get back into a made bed. Everyone knew that. And I always got back into bed if I could.

I checked the closet, but it was empty, and I opened that drawer at the bottom of the dresser Anthony had so carelessly dumped all my shit in almost two months ago and it was empty, too. I growled low in my throat.

If I didn't know better, I would have assumed I'd been robbed, but I did know better and I knew Doc, too. Smug bastard. He couldn't just move my stuff! I marched out into the living room where the moms must have seen the look on my face because they looked a little scared.

They had the good sense to know you didn't fuck with a fully pregnant woman.

"Let's go," I growled. I snatched up the bags and they grabbed the boxes, and we went back down the elevator two floors while I fumed. What in the hell was wrong with him? He didn't get to make all the decisions for me. He already made all the decisions for the baby. Why couldn't that be enough for him?

I could hear the moms whispering behind me as we exited the elevator and walked into Anthony's apartment.

He was sitting on the couch, papers spread on the coffee table in front of him. "Oh, good, you're home."

I glared at him. "No, I'm not. My home is two floors up."

He pursed his lips and raised a long finger. "About that."

I dropped the bags and pushed my arm out and let my pointer finger fly. "No. No about that. You can't just move my stuff without my permission."

He shrugged nonchalantly. "And yet, I did."

"Oh my God," I groaned. The man was positively out of his ever-loving mind.

"See, just like an old married couple." Lucy snickered. "It's adorable," she whispered to my momma, but I heard everything they said because as we'd already established they were shit at whispering.

"Calm down. We decided you were moving in."

He didn't tell me to calm down. I told him to calm down.

I felt my eyebrows hit my hairline and my pointer finger turned and hit my breast bone. "I didn't decide I was moving in."

"We talked about this."

I shook my head. "No, *we* didn't."

"We did," he insisted.

"I think I would have remembered a conversation where I agreed to move in with you, Doc."

He moved over to a spot in the living room behind the couch. "I was sitting right there and you were in my lap. I said you should move in."

"Oh my God, she was in his lap," the moms said in unison and I wanted to hurt Anthony.

My eyes got wide and then narrowed at him. "Stop," I mouthed before saying out loud, "But I didn't say yes."

He raised his eyebrows accusatorially. "Oh, you said yes a lot that day, especially in the kitchen in front of the refrigerator."

The moms tittered and my glare flew to them.

They had the good sense to look embarrassed. "We'll just go make some iced tea," my momma said, pulling Lucy along as she left the room.

I pulled my gaze back to Anthony. "I didn't say yes about moving in."

He walked to me. "But you kissed me and you came for me."

I looked back at the kitchen, praying the moms weren't listening. "I didn't have a choice! My body has a mind of its own." I totally had a choice. I loved that kiss. I loved coming for him. My body heated up at the mere mention of it all.

He wrapped his arms around me and rubbed his nose along mine. "I don't know about you, short stuff, but all this kissing and coming talk is making me want to kiss the shit out of you. Maybe we should take this to the bedroom."

I wanted to drag him to the bedroom, too, but we had things to discuss and the moms in the kitchen most likely listening. "I'm not moving in with you, Doc."

He laughed. His lips were against mine. "You already did."

And as soon as I opened my mouth to object, he was on me. His tongue sliding along mine, his teeth nipping the corners of my lips, his mouth wet and hot on mine. My eyes rolled closed. God, the man could kiss and he knew it. He kissed me like he owned me. He kissed me like he could kiss me for a thousand years and he still wouldn't get enough of my mouth. Damn him. It wasn't right. He'd always get his way if he used his kisses against me. They were my kryptonite.

"Move in with me." He continued his assault of my lips when I didn't answer. "Come on, make me the happiest man in the world," he finished, his lips against mine.

Mmmm. If I moved in he could kiss me like this all the time. Maybe give me a few of those orgasms he liked to talk about so often. Every day. And he wouldn't have to leave after we watched TV at night. We could go to bed and curl up against each other. We'd done that the other night and it had been so nice. I couldn't come up with a good reason to tell him no besides my own damn pride.

"Well, I guess I'll stay since all my stuff is here."

The moms cheered from the kitchen and I rolled my eyes, but Anthony paid them no mind.

"Yeah?" He looked happy. And I decided then and there I wanted more than anything for my Doc to always be happy.

I nodded. He smiled and kissed me again. And again. And again.

Chapter 25

Kelly

It didn't matter how late we'd stayed out the night before or how tired I was. I was always up early nowadays, and the past two days I'd had some lower back pain that was wearing on me. I'd read on the good ole baby center app that it was common for sleep to evade you in the late stages of pregnancy and I was definitely in the late stages and sleep, well, it felt like I hadn't had any in ages.

Part of me was eager for this to all be over. But the smart part of me, the part of me that knew my baby girl was safer inside of me than outside of me, just wanted her to stay put a little longer. I was uncomfortable and tired, yes, but I'd be uncomfortable and tired for her as long as I needed to be.

So, I gave up on sleep around 4:00 a.m. It pained me to leave a warm Anthony in the bed, but at least one of us needed their sleep and clearly that one wasn't going to be me. I watched him sleep for a few minutes before finally leaving the bed and cleaning the dishes from last night's pasta. I immediately went to work on what felt like autopilot. I did a load of baby clothes in the sweet smelling baby detergent my momma had bought for me. I sat on the couch and folded the tiny pieces of clothes until the sun came up and the small twinge in my back began growing again.

Anthony got up around six and made us breakfast while I checked my hospital bag to make sure everything was packed. After we ate, we spent the morning putting the bassinet together and putting the freshly washed sheet on it.

As the day went on, I became increasingly agitated. My back was killing me and I was exhausted but couldn't rest. I needed to make sure everything was ready. Why I felt the need to do every-thing that day, I didn't know. I just knew it had to be done.

I was setting the dinner plates and Anthony was in the kitch-en when all disaster struck. I leaned over the table to lay a napkin next to a plate when I felt a small pop, almost like I'd sprung a leak. Warm liquid ran down one of my legs and into my sock. I looked down, shocked I'd peed on myself. Don't get me wrong, there'd been plenty of close calls over the past couple months. A baby sitting on your bladder was no joke, but I'd never actually peed on myself.

I hustled to the bathroom, hoping Anthony hadn't noticed. I pulled my pants off thinking that it sure was a lot of pee and more was still coming. And that's when I realized it. Holy shit. I hadn't peed on myself. My water had broken. Only I'd convinced myself that something like that only happened in the movies. Shit like this didn't happen to women in real life. Just the moment I realized how wrong I was, the pain in my back spread across my front and I felt like my whole midsection was being squeezed and pulled apart simultaneously.

"Fuck," I grunted and held on to the bathroom counter while I crouched a little. That seemed to help. After a minute or so the pain passed, and I managed to get my pants and underwear off. I was going to keep my cool. I was not going to freak out. We were having a baby today and people had been having babies since the beginning of time. I could do it, too.

I found some panties and pants in the bedroom and slipped them on. "Doc," I called.

"You ready to eat?" He came into the room.

I still sat on the bed, trying to get dry socks on my feet. It was no easy feat, let me tell you.

He took the socks from my hands and kneeled down in front of me. I would've objected, but I was in labor. He rolled them onto my feet.

"I'm in labor." I never was one to beat around the bush.

His eyes flew to mine. "What?"

"My water just broke all over the dining room." And another contraction rolled through me. "Shit," I groaned.

"How far apart are the contractions?"

I leaned forward and rested my elbows on his shoulders. It felt better curled up like that. "How the hell am I supposed to know? I didn't even realize I was having contractions until my water broke. Maybe five minutes?"

"Fuck," he said sharply into my ear, holding me through the pain.

"I know. I think I've been contracting for the past day or so. I didn't realize it felt like back pain. I've never done this before."

He rubbed my back. "I know, baby. We need to get your bag and get you to the hospital."

He was right. All of the numerous doctors I'd met with had all agreed that a natural birth was best for the baby. A trip through the birth canal made sure the baby lost all the extra fluid on her body and in her lungs. It was best for her. She'd come that way. And then I'd get to hold her for just a few moments before they took her straightaway to surgery. Most babies born with this particular heart defect didn't experience problems until fifteen minutes to twenty-four hours after birth. So, I'd have just a small amount of time with her. And I was more than happy with that. I'd take the minutes with her right after birth.

The contraction passed, and I got off the bed further embarrassed. The spot I'd sat in was soaked and so were my pants again. Who the hell knew having a baby was so damn messy?

"I'm sorry, Doc." I was near tears.

He pulled me into a tight embrace. "There's nothing to be sorry about. We're having a baby today."

We.

That word washed over me in the best possible way. We. Me and Doc. Team Hope. God, he made me so happy. He was too damn good to me.

Tears sprang to my eyes. "I know, but now there's a wet spot on your bed."

"Our bed."

I wasn't touching that subject with a ten-foot pole right now. We had enough on our hands.

"It's ruined. And in the dining room."

His hands settled on my cheeks in that way I'd grown to love and had become so familiar with. He smiled down at me. "Everything is fixable. It's okay." He placed a soft, close-mouthed kiss to my lips and let me go.

I walked to the closet to get my bag while Anthony packed his own. Another rip-roaring contraction shot through me and I wobbled on my feet. I'd never experienced a pain so raw, so completely real in my life. It almost brought me to my knees. I blew long breaths, trying to get through it, and that's when I felt it. A sort of drop, like a bowling ball was sitting right between my legs. My pants and socks were even wetter now, and I started to panic about Anthony's car, but I didn't know if that was going to matter because it felt like the baby's head was right there, getting ready to come out any minute. I braced my hand on the wall and shouted, "Doc!"

He entered the closet just as I hit my knees. I couldn't stand anymore. I was in too much pain. Something was wrong. Why did it hurt so much? I hadn't quite prepared myself for so much pain.

"What happened?" he said, squatting down next to me.

"I don't know," I panted. "But I don't think we are going to make it to the hospital."

"What?" His eyes darted around the closet in a panic. I knew he was thinking the same thing I was. We couldn't have our sick baby in a closet. Even if it was a large and beautifully smelling one.

A sudden unexplainable urge to push came over me and I leaned forward onto my hands and rocked my body back and forth on my knees. I should have been embarrassed, horrified at the situation, but the pain overshadowed everything. All I could think was I needed to push and I'd feel better.

"I have to push," I grunted. Sweat poured from my hair and onto my forehead.

"No, baby, you can't push. We have to get to the hospital."

Oh, no, he couldn't panic now. A baby was coming any minute. I knew it. "No, Anthony. The baby is coming. Do you understand me? I have to fucking push!"

My harsh words snapped him out of whatever panicked state he was in, and he dashed to the cell phone.

"I need an ambulance. My girlfriend is in labor. Now. The child has a heart defect. Hypoplastic Right Heart Syndrome. We need an ambulance immediately." He rattled off our address, but I barely noticed. The pain was making me feel dizzy and sick to my stomach.

And then he was back in the closet with me, his own sheet of sweat on his forehead. He kneeled behind me and ripped my pants and panties down my legs. I lifted my feet so he could get them the rest of the way off.

"Lean forward and spread your legs a little."

I leaned forward, laying my forehead on my arms as a fresh

new pain swept through me. I groaned and blew air through it, praying this would end soon. Terrified it would end in the wrong way. I should have been horrified at Anthony behind me, kneeling between my legs, but I just couldn't feel anything but panic and pain.

"What do you see?"

"Nothing yet."

"Okay, that's good, right? Maybe the ambulance will get here in time. Everything is gonna be fine," I said more to myself than Anthony.

"I don't know, baby. Your contractions are really close together." He crawled around to my head to look me in the face. "I haven't delivered a baby in a long time, not since my residency."

Tears leaked out the sides of my eyes. What if they didn't make it in time? What would we do? Terror tore at my insides. I couldn't have my baby here. Anthony was right. We needed the hospital. We needed medical professionals and not just my Doc.

"I'm scared, Doc."

He sat down at my head and pulled me up under my arms until I was kneeled over his lap and face-to-face with him, straddling his thighs.

"I know, baby, but everything is going to be okay. I promise." But I saw the hint of fear in his eyes. Just the smidge of distress he tried to hide from me. But I knew his face almost just as well as my own.

Another contraction took hold, and I widened my legs over his lap and panted into his chest, curling my body around the front of his. "Fuck, I have to push. I have to," I panted.

"Then do it. Push," he said calmly.

I wanted to wait until the ambulance came. I wanted to give my baby girl the best fighting chance and the more medical personnel here, the better. I shook my head, my hair now soaked with sweat. "I can't. I'm too scared."

He grabbed my chin, bringing my eyes to his. "Someone once told me that if you aren't scared, you aren't dreaming big enough."

Tears poured down my cheeks as my lips trembled wildly. My sweet man. He didn't know. Those were the words of a young, naive girl. A silly fool. It was beautiful that he remembered and awful, too, because this wasn't a dream.

"This isn't a dream, Doc," I cried. "This is a nightmare." My baby was sick and there wasn't a damn thing I could do about it. And she was about to be born in a closet. She could die here. All of this and maybe we'd never even stood a chance. Maybe fate hadn't been on our side after all.

His grip was firm on my chin, his eyes fierce, his face that of a fighter, a warrior. "No, Kelly. Not your dream. My dream. You and that baby. You're *my* dream."

I wondered how big of a dream it was. "How scared are you?" I whispered.

"Terrified," he answered sharply.

More tears squeezed from my eyes. "That's an awfully big dream, Doc."

His face was savage. I'd never forget how it looked in that moment, so forceful and wildly beautiful. So scared and so fearsome. "Then you better not let me down."

Never, I conceded. I'd never let him down. I placed my forehead to his. "I love you."

His eyes closed slowly, like he was savoring the words, tucking them somewhere safe deep in his heart, before he opened them. "I love you, too. Team Hope," he whispered.

"Team Hope," I said back.

"Now push."

And I did. And I kept pushing, until I felt a burning that made small tears leak out the sides of my eyes, but I didn't stop until I felt Doc's big hands under me, his voice telling me to wait.

"Okay, one more." He kissed my forehead. Burning, fire, and

a long scream accompanied by a big push and all of a sudden I felt strangely empty.

"There she is!" Doc cried out. He pulled her up and between us and stuck his finger into her mouth, making sure nothing was there. I looked down shocked at how small she was between us, especially in Doc's big hands.

Why wasn't she crying? Why wasn't she moving?

"What's wrong with her, Doc? Why isn't she crying?" Panic climbed up my throat.

She was strangely quiet as Doc grabbed a shoe lace from one of the shoes in the closet. I watched him tie it around the umbilical cord, feeling like every second was an hour, scared out of my mind. I was tired, but so frightened. Why wasn't she crying? He pulled a dress shirt off a hanger in the closet and wrapped it around her, rubbing her back vigorously while he held her against his chest until I heard the sweetest sound I'd ever heard in my life. My baby girl's loud cry.

She was pink and mad as hell as far as I could tell, and he put her in my arms and pulled me close so he was holding both of us.

"She looks like you. She's beautiful." He had tears in his eyes. "She looks good. She's a nice color." His pointer and middle finger covered her heart for a few seconds. "She's a fighter. Like her momma."

His face held an enormous amount of pride I couldn't even begin to comprehend.

I held her to me. She did look like me. Her hair was dark and she was so tiny. She screamed and cried, and I hiccupped a laugh. "She's perfect," I breathed.

The whirr of an ambulance sounded in the distance, and I was relieved. And sad. I wanted to stay in the closet forever, me and my baby and Doc. They'd take her from me soon.

Doc kissed me all over my face a thousand times with the baby held between us like the precious gift she was. I didn't know how we'd ever let her go although in mere minutes we'd have to.

Doc told me time and time again in low whispered words how amazing I was, how proud he was of me. How awed he was by me, until finally the paramedics banged on the door and he went to let them in.

Anthony cut her umbilical cord, and they took her from us and loaded us all into an ambulance while Doc shouted orders at them I didn't understand. But I didn't need to. I trusted him implicitly. She was as much his as she was mine, and I knew he'd never let her down.

Chapter 26

Anthony

Waiting is awful on a regular day. Waiting for news on a baby that means more than the world to you is a special kind of hell.

All of the favors I'd called in were coming to fruition and yet I still felt so incredibly helpless. The ambulance ride had been too quick. They'd taken her from us too fast, whisking her to surgery, which had always been the plan, but it felt so wrong. She should be with us, not with strangers. Not with people she didn't know. People who didn't love her like we did.

"What's her name?" They'd asked when we finally got Kelly settled into a hospital room and looked over.

We'd looked at each other and laughed until tears sprang to our eyes. We'd never even thought about names. Our thoughts had been too full of other problems, other worries. So we'd cried tears of laughter at our thoughtlessness. Those tears wouldn't stop and then they'd changed to a different kind of tears. The terrified kind. We cried together and held each other, both so damn frightened we didn't know what else to do.

"Hope," Kelly had said when we'd finally quieted. "Abigail Hope, but we'll call her Hope." Her tear-filled eyes looked at me for confirmation, and I nodded. How could I argue with what seemed so very perfect?

Now we waited. And I wasn't used to it. Kelly lay quietly in the bed next to the chair I sat in. They called the room with updates almost every fifteen minutes.

"She's in the OR."

"We've intubated her."

"The first incision has occurred."

And we waited, each time the phone rang, making us practically jump out of our skin. Every phone call seemed too damn important and pivotal and it was. I knew how fast it could all go wrong. How quickly we could lose her. I wasn't used to it. I knew Kelly wasn't either, but I really wasn't.

It was different being on this side of things. I was so helpless, so very out of control. I wanted to march down there and demand to be let in. Demand to see that they were doing the very best for Hope, but I'd already been warned away. There couldn't be any emotional ties in that operating room and what I felt for Hope was beyond emotional ties. She was mine. It was in my bones, my love for her. I loved her like she was my own, and if I had anything to do with it, she would be.

So, I stalked around Kelly's hospital room feeling like a goddamn failure because I couldn't oversee the surgery. Because I couldn't make this better for Kelly. I paced. I went from anger to tears. I ran my hands through my hair and barked orders at the nurses like a complete asshole. I decided I was really bad at being on this end of things. And it was only going to get harder.

This was Hope's first surgery and it wasn't even one that was going to help her. It was only a small fix to give her heart time to grow bigger so we could do this again and then again until her heart was fixed. We had a long road ahead of us and it was a scary one. There was no guarantee she would pull through. I saw it all the time. Babies were so fragile, so susceptible to infection. A million things could go wrong and I went down a bad path that day, one I shouldn't have traveled, obsessing over every one of them.

That's how I missed it. I was being too selfish. Too caught up in my own grief that I didn't notice how oddly solemn Kelly was. How strangely quiet and distant she'd become over the hours.

Then she voiced it. I was pacing the room, pulling at the roots of my hair when I heard her. I almost missed it she'd said it so quietly.

"It was something I did."

I paused, finally really seeing her for the first time since we'd arrived at the hospital and they'd taken Hope from us.

She looked tired but still so beautiful, and already her stomach was smaller where she'd carried Hope. It made me sad. Hope had been so very safe in there.

Kelly had been the kind of brave today I'd only seen in movies or read about in books. I shouldn't have been surprised. I already knew she was the type of woman who would walk through fire for her child. She'd shown me that by showing up at my office months ago.

I walked to the foot of her bed and stared down at her. "What did you say?"

She wasn't looking at me either and I realized all day she'd been lost in her head, too. She still was. Immediately, I felt sick. I hadn't been there for her.

"It was me. It's my fault," she said to the wall behind me. I didn't like the look in her eyes. It was too vacant, too gone. She wouldn't look me in the eye.

Walking around to the side of the bed, I asked, "What's your fault?"

I ran my hand over her forehead and her eyes finally met mine. "It had to have been something I did, right? Or something I didn't do?" She stuttered the sentence and it came out stilted and cluttered, the words seeming to trip over one another.

My eyes burned at the emotion behind those words. I knew what she was asking me, but I hoped against hope I was wrong.

"That's why she's sick." Tears poured down her face. "It was me. I didn't eat enough vegetables or maybe I had a drink before I knew I was pregnant. I did this to her, right?" She sobbed at me, her voice becoming louder and heavier with remorse every sentence.

I climbed into bed next to her, shoes and all, and lay on top of the covers. I was way too big to fit, but we would just have to make do. We needed each other right now. We needed to be as close to each other as possible because clearly apart we were a damn mess.

That was us. Together we were unstoppable. Apart, we were hopeless.

Pulling her head onto my chest, I said, "No, baby. We don't know why these things happen, but this is not your fault. It's no one's fault. It just happens sometimes and it fucking sucks, but you are not allowed to blame yourself. Do you understand me?"

I breathed in the scent of her hair while she wrapped her arms tight around my middle. She didn't answer me, but she sobbed into my T-shirt and her cries broke me because if that baby didn't make it, she wouldn't make it. Maybe I wouldn't either. It would break us all.

I knew firsthand how losing someone you love could rip a family apart. How grief could inevitably crush a family's soul beyond repair if you let it.

I vowed from that moment on, I wouldn't get lost in my head anymore. I'd be there for her. I'd be strong despite how weak I felt.

I held her to me and petted her in the way I knew she loved

while more phone calls came in with news of Hope's surgery. My mother and Kelly's arrived and we all waited together, cuddled up on that bed; every one of us wrapped around each other, holding one another together, making sure all of our pieces stayed intact.

It was one of the hardest days of my life. The waiting. It does a weird thing to a person. We prayed and begged to a God we hadn't talked to in a very long time. We made promises. We bargained. We pleaded.

In the end, God came through that day.

Hope and faith won, and our pleas were answered.

Hours later I wheeled Kelly down to the Pediatric Intensive Care Unit, where there lay our Hope almost completely unrecognizable. Kelly cried again as she held Hope's tiny hand.

And me. I just stared at Hope. I couldn't quite believe it, how I'd seen hundreds of babies like that. The tubes that seemingly came from everywhere, the gauze covering the long incision on their chest. The intubation tube that almost seemed as big as she was. My heart hadn't ached for those babies like they did for my Hope. My eyes hadn't burned with emotion for them.

Tears poured from Kelly's eyes endlessly as she looked her baby over. I wanted to soothe her. To make it better, but there wasn't a better in this situation. It just was. And we just had to make do. The nurse on duty worried for Kelly and eventually covered Hope with a small blanket up to her chin, rubbing Kelly on the back, telling her it was sometimes too hard to see and that she should take a break.

I hated this feeling, the sadness. The worry, I loathed it. Being on this side of things was excruciating. And the weeks to come would try us beyond anything we could even imagine. They would test our faith. They would push our limits. They would make us question everything every second of the day. But we'd lean on each other. We'd cry together with worry. We'd smile at every small accomplishment. And we'd get through it all.

Together.

Chapter 27

Kelly

Hours turned into days, and days turned into weeks. I floated along through them all on autopilot. Doing what I felt I had to just to get by. Most days counting every hour a blessing. Most nights hardly sleeping from the worry. Hope's first surgery was just a quick fix. Just enough to make the half of her heart that wasn't working get by for the time being. We spent a week in the Pediatric Intensive Care Unit before we were transferred to a step down unit. There, I spent weeks learning how to care for my sick baby. Checking her oxygen. Her temperature. Learning to feed her through a tube since she wasn't able to actually eat yet. Anthony spent the nights and evenings with us when he could. He took time off to be with us as much as his schedule allowed, but I knew how important his kids were to him, so I sent him back to work when I felt capable. He spent his days saving everyone else's babies and spent his nights trying to save ours. When finally a month later they allowed us to go home, I should have felt ecstatic. Instead, I was scared as hell.

Here, the doctor and nurses were only steps away. At home, Hope would solely depend on me during the day while Anthony was at work. At least I would have him and his medical expertise at night, I told myself.

At home I thought maybe we would rest better and sometimes we did on those days when the moms would come by and help so we could actually take a nap in peace. A nap where I wasn't worried something would happen to Hope while I was away from her. It was true, there was so no rest for the weary. I lay in bed at night exhausted but too scared to sleep. Instead, I'd get up and check on Hope. Was she still breathing? Was her temperature too high? We were exhausted and barely surviving and it seemed like there was no end in sight. It felt like our lives were just going to be a series of doctors' appointments and tube feedings, and oxygen checks and recording it all in a book with times. Even diaper changes were on record. Our lives were in a binder. Every damn bit of them. But still, I'd do it, every day for the rest of my life if it meant more days with Hope.

But every day, it got easier to be this way—to live this life. It became routine, the new normal, and Anthony and I settled into a daily schedule. We lived more like roommates than lovers. Probably because we hadn't really been lovers in ten years. And, God, I may have had a sick baby that I would gladly devote every moment of my time to, but I wanted to feel normal. Like a woman. I wanted to remember how my Doc loved me, lusted for me.

I'd look at the refrigerator in the kitchen and think of the day he'd pushed me up against it and made come against him. I wanted that. I wanted him.

I wanted it all. I wanted motherhood. And I wanted Doc, too. And not just the daddy version of him. Don't get me wrong. I loved seeing him with Hope. He was perfect with her. Whenever I was panicked over something, he took over, knowing exactly what to do. And at night when he held her against his big bare chest, God, I'd ache for him in ways he didn't even realize. Because my man was sexy. And with my small baby girl propped against his large chest I'd feel my ovaries ache. He was attentive and caring and loving, but for some reason he never tried to take our relationship any further than nights curled around each other in bed. Comforting, sweet, much needed nights, but I still wanted more. Maybe I was selfish, but why couldn't I have it all? I'd wait for him to slide his hand up my thigh or maybe under my shirt, but it never happened.

Six weeks went by. I thought maybe he was waiting for the all clear from the doctor but after eight weeks of waiting for him to finally put the moves on me, I was done. I needed to do something about this shit. I was over it.

So that night when I knew Doc was coming home from work, I changed into my favorite pair of black workout booty shorts. I also made sure to put on a form-fitting tank. I was pretty sure I was wearing the equivalent of mom lingerie. I looked like I was headed to yoga. Hopefully I was headed to bed. I brushed my hair, which I admit some days I just didn't really get around to. I even put on some lip gloss and checked myself over in the mirror.

I thought I looked pretty damn good for a chick who was eight weeks postpartum. My body was mostly back, minus the stretch marks and a few inches on the love handles. God, I hoped they got some love tonight.

Doc came in from work like he did every evening and headed straight for the dining room where we had a makeshift hospital room set up for Hope. Her hospital scale, hospital grade crib, took up the small space now, the dining room table long since in storage.

He walked right past me and my sexy shorts. I couldn't believe it. I looked damn good.

He picked Hope up and grinned down at her. "Hey, Hope, it's

me. Your Doc, I'm home. How's my girl this evening?"

She was just starting to give little smiles that I couldn't quite decide whether it was gas or the actual real deal. Her mouth curved into one of those smiles and I realized she must be really smiling nowadays.

"Did you see this, little bit? She smiled!" he exclaimed over his shoulder.

I came up behind him and put my arm around him. "I did. She's growing so fast."

He changed her diaper and cooed at her and gave her a feeding, recording everything in the book.

He was completely enamored with Hope, so helplessly in love with her, I couldn't even be mad that he'd failed to notice my sexy mom clothes. I heated him up a plate of leftover food in the microwave and told myself I'd try another time. Maybe a day when he was off work.

He sat on the couch with Hope and baby talked to her while she stared up at him like he hung the moon and I guess to her he probably did. They did this every night and every damn time I'd feel the familiar sting of tears in my eyes. She didn't understand all he'd done for her. For us. How Doc might not have done the surgery that saved her life, but he'd made sure her momma was safe. Made it possible for her to have the best doctors at no expense. He was the reason she was here and as healthy as she could be.

One day, she'd realize and it probably wouldn't make a lick of difference because I knew, she'd already think the world of him. He'd stepped into the role of Dad like he was born for it.

He never said the words, daddy or dad, and I didn't either. I was too scared of the pressure it might put on him. After all, those were big words, meaningful ones. I wanted him to be absolutely sure he was in this for the long haul before saddling him with the responsibilities that came with the word father. That didn't stop me from thinking them, though. It didn't stop me from daydreaming. It didn't stop my thoughts from wandering to the future where I saw Doc teaching Hope to ride her bike for the first time or them on the way to her first daddy daughter dance, her in a frilly pink dress, him in a pale pink bow tie to match. Oh, I was full of fantasies.

The evenings were all the same. He'd come home and gently lift her from her crib and say, "Hey, Hope, it's me. Your Doc, I'm home." I wondered if ten years from now he'd still come home and say those same words, only she'd be healthy and climb up in his lap and wrap her arms around his neck.

And Lord have mercy. If I thought my sweet man couldn't get sweeter I was wrong, because there was nothing in the world more pure and good than Doc and Hope together. They were it for me, those two.

"Your food will get cold," I called from the kitchen and his answer was the same as it was every night.

"It's okay. I'll just hold her a bit longer. I don't mind if it's cold."

And I did what I did every night and put tin foil over it and stuck it back in the warm oven. I had to admit, if you'd asked me ten years ago about being a stay-at-home mom, I would've laughed in your face. I'd wanted the fast life then, but I was realizing the slow life was sometimes richer. I wouldn't have traded a day of stardom for a minute of being able to stay home with Hope and care for her.

The doorbell rang and my eyes shot to his. "Your mom coming by?"

He smirked as he carried Hope to the door.

Lucy came in like she always did, like a damn hurricane, chatting, boisterous, and loud, before she took Hope from Anthony.

"Give me that sweet baby." She cradled Hope to her chest and kissed the top of her head. I never felt so lucky as I did when I saw Hope with Doc and his mother. Our family had grown leaps and bounds over the last several weeks.

I leaned over the baby and kissed Lucy on the cheek. "To what do we owe this visit?"

Anthony interrupted. "I asked her to come by and keep the baby so we could go out for a bit."

That was a great idea. I would've loved to go out with Doc and have an evening to ourselves, but hell no, I wasn't leaving my sick baby, even for a couple hours.

Shaking my head, I said, "That's not a good idea. Something could happen while we're gone." I was completely fine with us having a date night in. Leaving the baby and going out on the town was absolutely out of the question.

Pulling my body into the front of his and wrapping his arms around me, he whispered, "I thought we'd take a few hours up two floors in your old apartment."

I raised my eyebrows. Maybe he *had* noticed my booty shorts. I wanted the sexy time, but I still wasn't convinced leaving Hope was a good idea. "I don't know, Doc. Anything could go wrong."

He kissed my lips softy. "And we'd only be two minutes away and Mom would call immediately if anything did." He kissed me again. "Come on, baby. You deserve a night off."

I smiled up at him. "Well, I did brush my hair today."

He ran a hand through my strands. "You always look beautiful."

"Okay, okay. You wore me down with your flattery." My eyes shot to Lucy. "But you call right away if anything is even a little off."

"Of course," she said, not looking at me at all but smiling down at Hope.

"Come on, gorgeous. Let's get you upstairs," Doc said, motioning me to the door, meanwhile all I could think was 'come on, let's get you naked.'

I called over my shoulder, "Seriously, call me if anything happens."

"Yes, yes." Lucy waved me away. "I get it, now go and have fun."

We rode the elevator the two floors up while I rocked on the balls of my feet and eyed Doc's red bow tie. I was going to rip it off with my teeth.

Anthony unlocked the door to the apartment and I'd never been more thankful his friend was going to be gone for a couple more months still. Maybe we could sneak away every now and then when the moms were around.

I walked into the room and smiled. My Doc. He was trying to romance me. Rose petals covered the floor in a path that led to a bottle of champagne chilling and more roses that led to the bedroom.

He didn't know I didn't need romancing. I wanted to jump him right now. Roses and champagne wouldn't make a damn bit of difference.

He poured the champagne while I hugged him, my chest to his back, my hands roaming the large expanse of his chest. I would've kissed his neck, but I couldn't reach it. The man was a giant. God, he felt good.

He turned and planted a long kiss on the top of my head before handing me a glass of bubbly. I smiled up at him as I sipped. I'd just have a little. I wouldn't overindulge. I always had to be ready for anything when it came to Hope, like surprise trips to the emergency room.

Grabbing my hand, he pulled me from the dining room and through the bedroom straight to the big bathtub I'd enjoyed when I first moved in. It was full of steaming water, bubbles, and more rose petals.

This man. He'd planned this for me. He must have come here straight from work.

"Kiss me, Doc," I whispered.

His lips pressed softly to mine. A quick, sweet kiss when I wanted raw, primal, barbaric.

"Take a bath, baby. Relax for a while." He took my champagne glass from me and set it on the edge of the tub and started to walk out of the room.

Where the hell was he going?

"Wait," I probably yelled a little crazily because I was feeling insane or sexually deprived, whatever you wanted to call it. "You aren't getting in with me?"

I mean, it would be a tight fit with Doc's size, but I was more than willing to take one for the team and squeeze my ass in that tub with him.

He smiled. "Baby, tonight is all about you. I wanted to give you a baby free night, where you could take a few hours for yourself."

But I didn't want a hot bath and champagne! I wanted the D! It had never occurred to me until that moment. I wasn't an insecure type of girl. But maybe he didn't want me anymore. Maybe he didn't find me attractive. He had delivered a baby for me and seen everything. And when I said everything I meant *everything*.

I looked at the bath water, the bubbles and petals floating on the top, and realized he wasn't romancing me. He was just giving me a night off. I was an idiot. I wasn't getting laid. I was getting a nap.

My face fell with the realization that maybe Doc hadn't put the moves on me because he just wasn't interested anymore.

"What's wrong?" He came to stand in front of me while I wracked my brain trying to figure out exactly what about me he didn't like anymore.

"Is it the weight?"

The small line between his eyebrows creased. "What?"

"I know I've gained a little weight and the stretch marks aren't that hot—"

He cut me off, crowding me into the wall behind me. "What the hell are you talking about?"

"I…I," I stuttered, feeling like maybe I'd said something wrong because Doc was looking especially primal at the moment.

My back hit the wall and Doc's front hit the front of mine. He looked down at me like he wanted to eat me alive. "You think I don't want you?"

Reaching behind my neck, he wrapped his large hand around it firmly. "You don't think I think about being inside of you, putting my mouth on you, tasting every inch of you every fucking moment of every day?"

Holy shit. I was so unprepared for this. And he was serious as a heart attack. I squeaked out a, "Maybe?"

He laughed sarcastically. "Fucking maybe, she says."

He used my neck to guide me toward the bathroom door and into the bedroom. "Get on the fucking bed, Kelly, and I'll show you just how much I *don't* want you."

Oh, he was pissed at me, I thought. He was scarily sexy in that moment. I didn't know whether to get naked or run for my life. "But..."

"Get on the fucking bed, shortcake." He gave me a filthy dirty smile that instantly made my panties soaking wet. "Doctor's orders."

Chapter 28

Kelly

I was getting the D! Finally! Only, if he did want me, how come he hadn't put the moves on me before now? I was a question girl and Anthony had the answers, so I couldn't stop myself as I stepped out of my booty shorts and down to my black sexy panties I'd worn especially just for the occasion.

"If you want me, then why haven't you taken me?"

"Less talking, more getting naked," he growled at me while pulling my top over my head.

"But why?" I shouted.

"Jesus, you've always asked too many damn questions."

I grinned. "You like it."

"I love it." He came around behind me and unfastened my bra before moving my body to the bed with his. He placed his hand in the center of my back and pushed me down on the bed until I was bent over, face in the comforter, ass in the air.

His knees hit the floor and I felt his smooth hands at the sides of my underwear, sliding them down and past my legs and off. "How could you think for one second that I don't want you?"

I felt his hot breath near my ass cheek before the sharp bite of teeth. Fuck. No one had ever bitten my ass before. And, God, I liked it. I wiggled under his ministrations, wanting more.

"I feel like there wasn't a time in my life that I didn't want you. I was giving you time. I didn't know if you were ready, but I've been ready. I was ready ten years ago and I know I fucked it all up but, I'm ready now. And I don't know if I've made this clear to you, but you're the love of my life, so my guess is I'll never not want you, baby. You understand?"

I groaned into the comforter.

He bit my other ass cheek and chuckled before rubbing his hands over both globes. "Seems like you're getting it now. Now, up on your knees." He pushed my legs up and under me until my ass really was up in the air now. Pulling my legs apart, he growled low. "Fuck, you're so wet for me already."

He brushed one finger over my clit lightly and grunted. I thought he'd touch me more there, maybe slide a finger inside, but of course he loved to surprise me. The man was full of fucking surprises, so I shouldn't have been so shocked when his hands gripped my hips harshly, separating my folds, and pulled me back onto his face where he lashed his tongue against my clit. But I damn sure was.

"Oh, fuck. Oh, God," I moaned while he sucked my clit into his mouth and swirled his tongue around it before slipping it up to my entrance.

"I've been thinking about tasting you since that day in the kitchen against the fridge. I wanted to drop to my knees right there and fuck you with my tongue," he said against my slit. He bit my thigh and I cried out. "But you were too eager. You couldn't wait, so

I let you ride my cock instead. Did that feel good, baby?"

Oh, God, I'd almost forgotten how filthy the man could talk. Doc could go from sweet to dirty in point five seconds in the sack. I was so glad he'd reminded me. His words alone could make a girl come.

"You almost made me come in my pants like a goddamn teenager."

I could feel him stand up behind me as he gripped my ass in his hands. "I'd really like to take you just like this from behind with your ass in my hands, but I think I'd like it even more to see your face when you come."

And then I was flipped over and onto my back, knees spread with my blond Greek god standing between them. I watched as he pulled at the red tie that for some reason I thought I'd remove with my teeth. I should have known he'd be running the show. He was slow removing his shirt and then belt. His eyes danced down at me like he knew I loved watching him get undressed and he held my gaze as he pushed his pants and underwear down past his heavy erection. Standing up, he reached between his legs and wrapped his hand around the length of his cock, giving it a few tugs that had my face burning hot and my body on fire. Fuck, but he was gorgeous. Even better than I remembered from our younger days. His body was more defined, bigger, and broader, a little hairier. His cock just as exquisite as I remembered it. The years had been fucking amazing to Doc.

He moved closer to the bed between my legs and stared down at my body, his gaze burning across my breasts down to my stomach where my hands seemed to move of their own accord. The stretch marks, the small bit of extra baby weight that I just couldn't shake; I didn't want him to see it.

He grabbed them in his own. "No, baby. You don't cover yourself from me ever. I love every bit of you. Especially this part," he said, moving my hands aside and touching my belly. "This is where the proof that you carried the other love of my life is. Don't you dare hide it from me."

And that was all it took for tears to fill my eyes.

He leaned down and kissed the small slope of my stomach. "Every bit of you is beautiful," he whispered against the skin there. "But this part, it's especially gorgeous."

He kissed the spot below my belly button, above it and to the sides before moving up my body and to my chest with the kind of excruciating slowness that could drive any woman wild, especially one who hadn't had sex in almost a year.

"Please," I begged as he licked up the center of my chest like we had all the time in the world.

"You never have to beg, baby. You just tell me what you want and it's all yours," he growled out as he drew one of my nipples into his mouth and sucked hard while pinching the other between his fingers, teasing me mercilessly.

"Oh, God, please. Please."

He squeezed my breasts together and alternated nipples, biting, sucking, licking, driving me completely wild. He smiled up at me from my chest. "I've been dreaming about these for ten long fucking years. Don't rush me."

But it didn't take long for him to become impatient, too. "God, I need to be inside you." He ground his pelvis against mine. His cock ran up and down the wet length of me as I wiggled beneath him, anxious for him to fill me up.

Kneeling up and away from me, he grabbed his pants from the floor, removing his wallet and then a silver packet.

He rolled the condom on slowly and breathed heavily. I got the impression he was trying to rein himself in as he settled over me. Positioning himself at my entrance, he kissed me slowly, sweetly before pushing in delicately like I was something fragile.

A deep, growly groan slipped past his lips and into the air around us when he was fully seated. He laid his forehead against my chest, breathing deeply before lifting his head and gazing into my eyes.

His elbows planted on either side of my head, he cradled my jaw in that way he always did, his thumbs meeting right in the middle of my chin. "Okay?"

A small blip in my heart, like it skipped a beat because of this man's pure goodness. I smiled up at him. "I'm okay." I was better than okay. I was in love with the best man I'd ever known. And he loved me, too. He was the type of man who could love a child who wasn't genetically his own. He was the type of man who came home after twelve hours of work and never complained about caring for said child. He was the type of man who asked the woman he loved if she was okay while he was making love to her because he never wanted to hurt her. Yeah, I was better than okay. I was wonderful.

His eyes gazing down at me said it all, but it didn't matter, his lips did, too. "I love you, little bit."

Tears slipped from the corners of my eyes and onto the bedding beneath me. "I know," I whispered, leaning up to capture his lips with my own. "I love you, too," I said across them.

And he held my face and kissed me again while he moved inside of me, slowly, leisurely, painstakingly unhurried. I gasped into his mouth and he moaned into mine. I met his every thrust with one of my own. We were heated flesh to heated flesh, sweat slicked skin to sweat slicked skin, thundering heart to thundering heart.

And when I was close, his lips pressed to my ear, his hands still holding my face. "You're close, aren't you? I can feel how tight you are around me. Are you going to come on my cock? You are, aren't you?"

And just like that his dirty words sent me over the edge and flying apart.

"That's it. Give it to me. Give me everything. I want it all." His hands tightened on my face as he picked up speed, thrusting into me harshly. "Fuck, I'm coming," he grunted above me, his eyes still eating me up.

Three more long hard thrusts inside of me and he stilled above me, dropping his forehead to mine, panting like he'd run a marathon.

He ran his lips along mine before smiling against them. "Should I call Mom and tell her we're going to be late?"

And then I smiled against his lips. "Absolutely."

Chapter 29

Cash: We're going to be in the Raleigh area in a few days.
Cash: I need to see you.

Those were the first texts.

Fuck. It hadn't paid off to keep up with some members of my band. They were my friends for over ten years, so I'd kept in touch with most of them. Not Cash, though. Looked like they'd ratted me out anyway. I never expected Cash would try to contact me ever again. We'd never been romantic. We'd simply fucked from time to time when it had suited us. And he'd been as clear as day how he felt about me having a baby. I ignored his messages.

A day later more texts.

Cash: We need to talk.

I ignored the texts as long as I could. He was coming to town and I was terrified he was going to somehow find out where I lived and show up at the apartment and set Anthony off. My Doc, he was the sweetest, but I also knew he'd go absolutely savage on that man if he ever met him. Things were just getting normal again and not so damn crazy. We were settling into life. It wasn't an easy life. Some days were really hard having a sick baby, but I wouldn't have changed a hair on Hope's head. She was perfectly imperfect. I was finally settling into motherhood, even finding that I really liked it. I couldn't have him rocking our fragile boat.

Cash was no good for anybody if he was still in the state I left him months ago, drinking, drugging, fucking. He definitely wasn't father material. Some might have told you a year ago that I wasn't mother material, but I'd changed. For her. Cash would never change. I knew it in my heart. He loved the lifestyle too much. Partying, working odd jobs, performing when he could and just scrounging by; he lived for it.

So, I gave him the address to our Friday Café. It was the closest place I could think of and the quietest. I told him I'd meet him there at noon and I made arrangements for Mom to come over and watch Hope. I'd meet him there while Anthony was at work. I'd find out what the hell he wanted and I'd get rid of him. That would be the end of this.

My momma arrived right before noon and could immediately tell I was on edge.

"What's going on, baby girl? Where you going today?"

"Just having lunch with an old friend."

Her eyes narrowed a little, but she only said, "Okay, well, have fun," as she picked up Hope and gave her a kiss on the forehead.

I, too, kissed my angel's forehead and headed out the door. I hadn't dressed up for him. I personally didn't give a shit how he thought I looked. I'd thrown on some jeans and a T-shirt that I was ninety-nine percent sure Hope had spat up on before I'd even made it out of the house.

Spring was fully in swing, the weather beautiful. Blooming

trees and bushes lined the sidewalk along the street, but for the first time since I'd moved here I didn't notice. I was too focused on making this go away. Making Cash go away. He had the potential to ruin everything. I couldn't let him destroy all I'd managed to build in the past couple of months.

The café was slow today and Cash was easy to find amongst the empty tables in the back. I walked toward him feeling sick. I started to question everything as I saw him sitting there. He was slouched down in the booth like he hadn't a care in the world, his long dark hair in his face, his five o'clock shadow out of control. His black T-shirt was wrinkled over his lanky frame. I rolled my eyes at the leather jacket he was sporting. It was seventy degrees out.

I used to think this man was mysterious and sexy. Now, I knew different. He was an asshole, a douchebag, and a total disappointment, and I immediately wanted to yell and scream and lay into him. I wanted to take out all of my frustrations from the last few months on him. All of the pain. All of the stress. I should have brought Anthony. He was the voice of reason in our relationship and I had a feeling I was going to be anything but that.

I slid into the booth, trying to keep my cool. I could smell the stale cigarettes coming off him in waves even from across the table.

He didn't say anything, only observed me from behind his sunglasses.

The bastard couldn't even show me the courtesy of removing his shades. I was fuming.

"Well, I'm here, Cash."

Before he could respond, Isabelle appeared to take our orders. "Kelly! What are you doing here?" She leaned in for a hug. Fuck. I'd been hoping she wasn't working today. Now, I was hoping she didn't tell Doc about this. He'd lose his shit.

I couldn't muster a smile. I was upset, and pissed, and scared, and mostly I just wanted to get back to my sweet, sick baby.

"Just meeting a friend for coffee."

She studied me hard, like she knew something was off before smiling at Cash. I didn't introduce them. It was rude, but she didn't need to know Cash.

"How's Hope doing?"

Now I smiled. I couldn't help it. When I thought of her adorable little face, I always smiled. "She's good. Thanks for asking."

She put a hand on my shoulder. This woman knew what I was going through. She'd lived it and her son was healthy. "Good, when she's feeling up to it, bring her in to us. Okay?"

I laid my hand on hers and squeezed. "Of course."

"Good." She looked between the two of us. "Are you guys ready to order?"

Cash looked at the menu through his stupid sunglasses like he was ordering lunch. I wasn't going to be here that long.

"We're just gonna have some coffee," I made sure to say before Cash could order.

Isabelle placed her notepad back in her apron. "I'll be back with your coffees."

As soon as she was out of earshot I asked, "What do you want, Cash?"

He smiled at me. "You look good, Kelly."

I didn't smile back. "Great. Now what do you want?"

He finally had the decency to remove his absurd sunglasses. His eyes were bloodshot and I wondered if he'd been up all night or was simply stoned out of his mind. All those eyes did were reaffirm something I already knew. This man couldn't be associated with Hope until he got his shit together.

"Fuck, chill out. I was in the area and I wanted to see you. I've missed you."

"You missed me?"

He reached across the table and tried to take my hand that was lying on my side of the table. I snatched it back and slid it into my lap underneath the table.

I couldn't believe this shit. "You missed me?"

"Of course I missed you, Kells. I went from seeing you every day for over ten years to never seeing you."

I was completely dumbfounded. Was he serious? Every moment in his presence that he acted like he hadn't impregnated me. That he acted like we didn't have a daughter together made me want to lean over the table and throat punch him. Every moment across from him, I felt my temper climbing. "Are you fucking serious right now?"

He let out a shocked laugh. "What do you mean?"

I leaned forward over the table about to let him fucking have it when Isabelle brought our coffees. She gave me a concerned look as she asked if we needed anything else. I waved her off and she left the table with another concerned glance over her shoulder.

Cash took a sip of his hot coffee like he didn't have a care in the fucking world and I guess he didn't and it made me even more mad. I cared. I cared too much. I stayed up all night worried my baby might stop breathing. Worrying I wasn't feeding her enough. Worried her heart might not make it another day. He hadn't even asked about her.

The sound of his coffee cup settling back against the table snapped me out of my thoughts.

"You seem pissed. I just wanted to stop and see you since we were in town."

He didn't have a damn clue how pissed I was. "Aren't you even going to ask about her?"

He ran a hand through his hair and looked down at the table.

What the fuck? "You weren't, were you?" I slammed my hand down on the table. How could she be my everything and his nothing? I just couldn't understand it. "You weren't even going to ask about her! What the fuck is wrong with you?" My lips curled, disgust for him settling over me, making me feel dirty.

How could he not want to know her and love her? I couldn't

even imagine not wanting to see her face every day. "Do you even want to know her name?"

The bastard wouldn't even look at me.

"Why the fuck did you come here, Cash?"

If he hadn't come about her then I didn't understand why he was even here.

"Yeah, Cash, why the fuck *are* you here?" I heard Anthony's voice from beside the table. I looked up and there he was in all of his knight in shining armor glory. Except he wasn't shining. He was mad as hell. He gave me a look that said we'd talk about this later and I knew we would.

He muscled his way into my side of the booth and slid his arm around my shoulder possessively before looking across the table at Cash.

"Introduce us, Kelly." It wasn't a request. It was an order. Oh, Doc was pissed.

I fidgeted with my coffee cup on the table and swallowed hard before saying, "Doc, this is Cash, this is—"

"Doctor Anthony Jackson," Doc interrupted me. "Kelly's boy-friend," he finished.

I swallowed again. Oh, yeah. He was mad.

Cash's lips curled and he threw his shades back on over his eyes, studying Anthony behind them. I knew what he saw. A well dressed, beautiful man who had his shit together.

"So back to Kelly's question. What are you doing here, Cash?"

Cash's jaw ticked and his head turned to me. I could tell he was checking me out behind his glasses. He shrugged. "Just wanted to see an old friend."

Anthony's nostrils flared and his hand gripped my thigh. "That's where we have a problem, buddy. It doesn't look like Kelly is feeling too friendly toward you."

He wasn't wrong.

He was also incredibly jealous.

"I don't think you need to contact Kelly unless it's about the child you fathered. A child who requires around the hour care. A child who's very sick. A child who'll be very sick for some time to come. So unless you're here to help care for Hope, to be an active member in her life, then what are you here for?"

He paused and studied Cash's face, his own face hard and unreadable.

"Ah, I see now. You're here for my girl." Anthony chuckled darkly and I bit my lip. I'd never seen him so pissed. My Doc was as cool and as calm as a cucumber and if you didn't know how chill he was on an everyday basis you'd probably never guess he was so pissed now. There wasn't a doubt in my mind I was in deep shit.

He removed his arm from around me and leaned across the table, his height and his girth to his advantage. He was intimidating as hell.

Cash seemed to shrink back in the booth, away from Anthony.

"You're not a smart man, Cash, so I'm going to lay it all out for you, make this real fucking plain. You didn't take care of what was yours. And now it's mine. Hope and Kelly belong to me now and unless you plan to step up and be more than a sperm donor then I'm going to need you to stay the fuck away from me and mine."

He moved out of the booth and held out a hand for me. "It's time to go."

And when pissed off Anthony said it was time to go, it damn sure was. I gave Anthony my hand and scooted out of the seat and didn't spare Cash even a glance.

We walked out hand in hand, although Anthony was more dragging me behind him. His steps were entirely too big for me to match and he seemed to be walking at warp speed.

"Geez, slow down, Doc."

He stopped on the sidewalk, the sun bright in his light hair, but his face; man, only one word could describe it. Irate. Irate as hell. His jaw ticked as he glared down at me.

His hand flew to the door of the restaurant. "What the hell was that, Kelly?"

He hardly ever used my given name. I was always some adorably cutesy short girl name. The Kelly of it all hurt, but I knew I undoubtedly deserved it. I'd kept the texts and the meeting from him. I would've been hurt, too.

"I'm sorry." It was all I could think to say. What else was there? I reached my hand up to rub his face, but he shrugged me off.

"What if Isabelle hadn't called me? Would you have told me? Would you have kept lying to me? How long has he been contacting you?" He ran his hands furiously through his hair. "What else are you keeping from me?" he shouted.

I flinched at his last question like he'd slapped me. Doc never yelled or lost his temper at me, but we'd never ever really had a real fight. Was that what this was? We were fighting because I'd made a terrible mistake.

I grabbed the sleeve of his pale green shirt. It matched his eyes so perfectly. Only this morning, I'd leaned up and kissed his lips and whispered how it was my favorite shirt and that I couldn't wait to take it off him when he got home. I'd royally fucked up. Judging by his pissed off expression a lot had changed since that kiss this morning.

"I'm sorry. I was just trying to make him go away. I didn't want to upset you. Everything's been so good lately."

The torment on his face said it all. I'd hurt him.

"I didn't think we were the kind of people who kept things from each other. I thought we were a team."

He knocked me over with those words. They struck me right in the stomach.

This time when I touched his jaw, he leaned into it. "We are," I said softly.

He pulled away from my hand and took a step back before looking back at the restaurant and then at me. "It sure doesn't feel that way."

Tears sprung to my eyes. I'd upset him and never, not in a million years, did I ever think I'd hurt this man who'd done everything for me. Who'd helped me when no one else could. Who'd loved me at a time when I thought I wasn't deserving of love.

"I love you, Doc. You know that, right?"

His eyes seared me through. "I do."

"I'm sorry. Please forgive me. I just wanted him to go away. I just want to be with you and Hope."

His eyes left mine and strayed off into the distance and I knew he wasn't seeing anything but my betrayal, me sitting across from Cash in *our* restaurant.

"I should get back to work. I'm really stretched today and I shouldn't have left to begin with." His voice was sharp, all of the emotion seemingly sucked out of his words.

And if I felt bad before, I felt even worse taking him away from his kids. I knew what they meant to him.

"Okay." I swallowed the lump in my throat down and blinked back tears. I'd fucked up.

Before I knew what was happening his big arm wrapped around me and I was jerked into his chest, our fronts pressed together and his lips on mine roughly. His mouth claiming mine harshly. His tongue slipping along mine possessively before biting my bottom lip with a pinch that made my eyes snap open.

"You're mine." He growled against my lips and my lids slipped closed again as I leaned up on my toes to press my lips against his again.

I was his. In a lot of ways, I'd been his since I was twenty-two years old.

He didn't give me his mouth again even though I was practically begging for it.

"You understand me? You're mine." His hand grasped my waist firmly. "Only mine."

My hands went up and around his jaw, just like he so often cradled mine and calmed me. I wanted to soothe his fears. I wanted to still his anger.

With his face held in my palms my eyes landed on his and I hoped they said everything I wanted him to hear. That I'd always be his, even when he made me mad or when I made him angry or when things weren't perfect and when they were. "I'll always be yours, Doc."

His jaw ticked once, twice, three times, his breath heavy, his nostrils flaring, his hands heavy at my waist, before he smashed his lips to mine harshly once more, then letting me go and turning on his heel. The harsh sounds of his dress shoes echoing on the concrete as he walked away.

I decided right then and there I never wanted to see him walk away from me again even if he did look damn good doing it.

Chapter 30

Anthony

I'd had the day from fucking hell. My day started with two nurses calling in sick, so I'd been constantly behind all day. I didn't like keeping my kids waiting, but every appointment had been at least thirty minutes behind with no end in sight of me catching up. To add to the total shit show that was my day, Isabelle had called from the restaurant to say Kelly was there with some questionable guy who seemed to be really upsetting her.

I'd immediately known it was Cash. I don't know how, but I just knew Kelly wouldn't keep something from me unless it was big and bad and Cash was both of those. Seeing them sitting there together had made me see red. Seeing my girl upset had nearly made me toss the table that separated them. I'd done everything to keep myself in check and I thought I'd done a damn good job considering.

It had hurt. That Kelly had kept something from me. Something as important as a meeting with her child's father. I thought we were in this thing together. We were a team after all and had been for what felt like forever.

And then I'd kissed her like a crazy person, but I couldn't help myself. I wanted her to know she was mine and I was hers and no Cash or any other man was going to take her from me. I didn't have the words. All I could do was grab her, and kiss her, and hold her to me, praying she understood, hoping she knew I'd never be able to let her go.

I walked back to the office feeling like I was fire. Like I could burn down the world with my love for that woman and her child. I'd fight for them. If Cash wanted to be a part of Hope's life, I'd deal with it, but he'd never have Kelly. Over my dead body.

Lucille hit me up as soon as I walked into the back door. "Ian Hughes is being transferred to the hospital by ambulance."

"Fuck." My day was going from bad to worse. "Cancel my appointments for the rest of the day." I only had a few left and I needed to get to the hospital to check on my little buddy.

I practically jogged the block over to the main hospital and into the ER. I passed the nursing station calling out, "Ian Hughes? He was transferred by ambulance."

The nurse's face fell and I knew. I'd seen that kind of face too many times. The sad face. The fucking terrible news face. My stomach turned at that face.

"I'm sorry, Doctor Jackson. He didn't make it. He was DOA."

I stood here, stunned. I'd expected something different. Not that. Maybe that he was in ICU or terribly sick but no, I'd just seen him a few weeks ago and he was doing great after his final surgery.

I hated losing someone. It never got any fucking easier. Every child lost hurt me to the quick. It somehow always seemed to blindside me, shocking me and devastating me all in one foul blow. I wanted to scream.

Instead, I searched the halls for Deanna Hughes. We were

practically friends. It was what happened when you did three consecutive surgeries that spanned years on people's children. We'd all been through so very much together.

I found her in the room with her son's body, sobbing. I hugged her for what felt like hours but was probably only minutes. He'd complained of chest pain and she'd immediately called the ambulance. She'd done everything she could for Ian, just like I had. Sometimes, we had no control over these things. That's what I told myself on the walk back to the office.

I was feeling grim, helpless, completely out of control. I thought my day couldn't get any worse, but I'd been fucking wrong.

I spent the evening pouring over paperwork and trying to catch up. Maybe I was avoiding going home and the inevitable argument I knew was waiting there. I was still so pissed at Kelly and since then my mood had only soured with my day.

It was 8:00 p.m. when I got the call that would change everything. It was the perfect ending to a terrible day, which was to say it wasn't perfect at all.

I picked up thinking she'd called to see if I'd left work.

I didn't even get the chance to say hello.

"Doc, Doc. She has a fever. It's 103. She's so lethargic. Something's wrong."

My world spun. I stood up from my desk feeling disoriented and off-kilter but still I managed, "Put her in the car. Get to the Emergency Room now. Hurry!"

I hung up feeling a sense of dread hit me like a semi. It slammed into me like a freight train and nearly knocked me over as I made my way down the dark office hallway toward the door to lock up. My hands shook around the key and it took me twice as long to secure the office.

I jogged back to the hospital feeling like I was in some sort of dream. No, a nightmare. I'd jogged this route already once today. I couldn't get it out of my mind how it had ended. I couldn't lose

Hope. I'd already lost too much. I would've told her to call an ambulance, but we lived so close. It'd be faster to just load her in the car seat and get her here.

I stood at the emergency room entrance pacing frantically, pulling at the strands of my hair and sweating even though the day was unseasonably cool for spring. I didn't know what else to do. I'd never felt so out of sorts, so impatient, so frantic.

Kelly's car pulled up and I ran to the back door, opening it and retrieving the bucket seat with Hope inside. "How long has she had a fever?" I barked the question. I was crazed. This was my baby girl. I ran my finger over the apple of Hope's cheek and she felt so hot.

Kelly walked quickly alongside me as I carried Hope in. "I don't know. She felt warm earlier, but I thought I was just cold. I took her temp and then called you."

I walked past the front desk and pushed my way through the double doors. I ignored the nurses behind the desk farther down the hall and pulled back curtains like a mad man, searching for an empty room. Only finding rooms full of startled people instead.

"Dr. Jackson!"

Someone yelled my name, but I barely heard. I had one single objective. I needed to get my baby help.

"Dr. Jackson! You can't just come back here. We're full."

I spun to the nurse. I knew her name. I did, but I couldn't think of it. My mind felt fuzzy. "Our baby." I held out the carrier with Hope sleeping in it. "Help me." It was all I could get out. All of my medical training had fled the fucking building. I couldn't think of one goddamn thing to do to help her. I was a mess.

The nurse gave me a sad look as she took Hope from me and called a doctor over.

"I'm gonna need you to wait here while we take a look at her. Okay, Dr. Jackson?" the nurse giving me pity eyes said.

I knew why they were throwing me out. I was losing my shit. I pulled on the strands of my hair again as the doctor and nurse looked for a room for Hope.

Kelly followed them with a small worried glance over her shoulder at me. "I need him with me," she begged the nurse.

The nurse patted her back. "Give him a minute to collect himself."

I leaned against a wall in the hallway nearby, trying to catch my breath. Trying to breathe myself to calm. Only the longer I was there the more panicked I became. I tried counting. I tried deep breaths. I tried everything. I needed to be there for Hope today. I needed to be there for Kelly. But my thoughts took hold, racing through my mind like someone was changing the channels on a TV too quickly.

Hope could die, just like he did. Hope could die just like Ian. And then Kelly would break. I'd fall. We both would never be the same. I knew what losing a child did to a family. It had the ability to ruin everything, to tear it all apart.

Pressing the heels of my hands into my eyes harshly, I rocked back and forth against the wall, feeling like this giant hospital was too goddamn small. The beige walls that had felt like home for so many years now felt like they were closing in, like they were getting closer and closer to me. The smell that once was the comfort of a familiar place made the acid in my stomach churn. The soft chatter of nurses and doctors, the beeps of machines nearby that once proved nothing more than the background noise of my workmates now were a cacophony of sounds that made my head pound and my eardrums burn. I held my head in my hands and prayed for some measure of peace, but it never came, no matter how long I stood there breathing deep.

Before I knew it, I was at a dead sprint. Running out of the sliding glass emergency room doors and across the parking lot, down a block and to my car, ripping the confining bow tie off my neck and wiping the sweat from my brow. With shaking hands and blurry eyes, I barely managed to unlock the car.

I felt the first tear slip free as I pulled out of the parking lot and onto the main road. I cranked the radio up loud to drown out the pain thundering in my head and pounding in my heart, but it didn't work. I pulled onto the interstate and drove south. At the time I didn't have a clue where I was going. I barely payed attention to the roads, but I knew where I'd end up. I needed to talk to him.

Chapter 31

Kelly

It was 3:00 a.m. in the morning. Where the hell was Doc? Hope was settled and the doctors had finally managed to bring down her fever. I sagged against the wall in the Pediatric Intensive Care Unit. I felt like I'd been put through the wringer. And I had in a lot of ways. God, what a fucking terrible day. It had gone from bad to worse. It seemed like Cash had been some kind of bad omen for what was to come because I'd gotten home and noticed that Hope seemed especially tired and cranky. But babies, they couldn't tell you when something was wrong or if they felt bad, so I'd been extra watchful all day after I'd sent my momma home.

It was late in the evening when I'd taken her temperature. A temperature like that with a baby with a delicate heart such as Hope's was dangerous. I'd immediately packed her in the car seat and called Anthony. I'd known we had to get here, even before he'd told me.

I'd remained calm despite my panic. I'd surprised myself, honestly. I'd thought in the face of Hope's illness and being alone, I'd lose it, but a calm had swept over me. I'd known what I had to do and I'd done it. This momma intuition was an odd thing.

Only Anthony had been the opposite. He'd looked pale and crazed when I'd pulled up to the emergency entrance. He'd wrenched the door open and grabbed Hope before I could even get around the car. I'd left him in the hall to calm down. Only when I'd finally gotten baby girl settled he'd been gone.

Now I was out of my mind worried for two people I loved with all my heart. Doc had been gone for hours and so I'd sat at Hope's side by myself freaking out that she was going to get worse, worried as hell for Anthony. I'd tried calling his phone and texting him more times than I could count. It may have been three in the morning, but I didn't know what else to do besides call Lucy and pray he was with her.

"Hello?" Her croaky voice came over the line.

"Hey, Lucy."

"What's wrong? Is Hope okay?" She sounded more than wide awake now.

"We're at the hospital. She has a fever. They think maybe an infection. Listen, is Anthony with you?" I wondered if my voice sounded as desperate to her ears as it did to mine.

It must have. "I'll be there in twenty."

I paced the room and checked on Hope and those twenty minutes seemed like the longest of my life. And when Lucy showed up in a T-shirt and yoga pants with flip-flops on her feet I thought she had never looked so good, not even when she was in her fancy ass shoes and fancy ass suit.

Her gentle eyes took me in and immediately wrapped me in a hug and held me tight. How did moms do that? How did they just know what you needed when you needed it, even if they weren't technically your mom?

Tears streamed down my face. All of my worry from the entire day spilled over onto my face and landed on the shoulder of her T-shirt. "Where is he?" I sobbed.

She pulled out of our hug but grabbed my hands. "Let's sit and you tell me what happened."

And I told her everything. The awful meeting with Cash. The fight afterward. The harsh, claiming kiss. And then I told her how he'd stormed the ER desperately trying to get Hope help.

Her face fell before she smiled sadly at me. "My boy had a very bad day. The worst actually. After he got back from meeting with you, we found out one of his favorite kids was being transferred by ambulance with chest pain."

My stomach dropped. "Oh no."

She nodded slowly. "He didn't make it, Kelly. He passed away before Anthony got here."

More tears fell from my eyes as I processed the news. Oh God, my Doc really had an awful, terrible day. No wonder he'd lost his mind about Hope. He was barely hanging on. Hope being sick was the straw that broke the camel's back.

"Any idea where he's gone?" I choked out. I needed to make sure he was okay. I couldn't leave here, but I'd send Lucy to find him. She needed to bring him to me so I could make him feel better.

Lucy moved her chair closer to mine, until our knees were touching. She squeezed my hand tightly before saying with a sad smile, "I bet Anthony hasn't told you about Charles yet, has he? He treats him like some kind of special secret and I suppose he is. He was very special to us, our surprise baby boy."

Charles? I was so confused. "Charles?" Why were we talking about someone I didn't know instead of trying to find Doc?

Her free hand moved to my face, her thumb brushing over my cheek. "Oh, from the moment I met you, I adored you, sweet girl. And I know it may sound crazy, but I saw so much of myself in you.

Scared. Terrified. Elated. I experienced it all, too."

I hung on her every word, trying my hardest to understand what she was telling me. What she was trying to make me understand.

"Anthony was already twenty when I found out I was pregnant with Charles. Could you imagine? I was over forty years old and having a baby? It seemed ludicrous at the time."

And somewhere in the back of my mind, I remembered that night. Me telling Anthony I was an only child. Him telling me he had a brother. I searched her face, wanting to ask a million questions but knowing I needed to give her the time to tell her story.

"I didn't want to start over with a new baby. Anthony's father and I, we were already struggling to hold onto our marriage, but Anthony, he was ecstatic. He was twenty years old and having a baby brother. The kid was over the moon."

Anthony had a baby brother, but where was he now? I had a feeling my night was about to get worse. Lucy's eyes were shiny with sadness when she spoke of Charles.

"That's why Anthony picked the heart, you know? Just when I'd finally come to accept that I was going to have another baby boy, they saw it on a scan late in my pregnancy. A heart defect, the same one our Hope has." She looked over at sleeping Hope in the crib with all the wires attached to her again and wetness spilled from her eyes. "Oh yes, Kelly, you reminded me so much of myself, long ago."

"My baby boy, Charles, he didn't make it to the third surgery." Her words were like razor blades across my heart, slicing me up. She'd lived my every fear, my worst nightmare. This beautiful, kind woman had lost her baby. My heart was broken for her.

I pulled her into me for a hug. "I'm so sorry, Lucy. I'm so, so sorry."

She rubbed my back while we cried together, arms holding each other tightly. "It's okay. I've made peace with it." Pulling out of my embrace, her eyes met mine, perseverance burning in them. "Back then, I was so terrified, but Anthony was so sure medicine would save Charles. Ever the optimist, he was." She turned to look at Hope. "I thought it was so incredibly perfect that you named her Hope. When I sat in waiting rooms terrified out of my mind that my baby wouldn't make it out of the operating room and I would feel so helpless, Anthony would say, 'Never lose hope, Mom. There's always hope.'"

She smiled at my sweet, sick baby sleeping in the crib near us. "How right he was. So, we held on through two surgeries and then my Charles got really sick. Medicine has come a long way in ten years, Kelly. He didn't make it to his final surgery, died in the middle of the night in his crib. Anthony was so smitten with him. It broke his heart. He was on the cusp of great things. He was twenty-two at the time, just finished college and getting ready to head to medical school. We called him in the morning, woke him up and told him. He was devastated."

Realization dawned on me even as I heard her words. That morning, ten years ago. He'd been so carefree, so happy. He'd kissed my head before answering the phone. And he'd come back ravaged, his face anguished, and I left. I'd left because I'd been a stupid, stupid, young, naive girl. I should have stayed. I should have stayed and hugged him and loved him. My soul ached for young Anthony Jackson who'd just lost his baby brother, but there wasn't a damn thing I could do about it now. I was too late. I'd failed him. I'd failed us. I felt sick. And now I had no idea where Doc was or how I could help him.

"I'm so worried about him," I cried fresh tears. I was worried about everyone. Hope, Anthony, Lucy, Me.

She touched my cheek again. "Oh, honey, he'll come back. He just needs some time." Her gaze wandered the room until they landed on my angel snoozing in the corner. "You know, for a long time I was sad. So sad, I thought I'd never not feel sad.

Until Anthony finished school and hired me at his office. Where I get to watch him every day save all the children. Where I got to watch him help save Hope. It's where we've healed, that office. Yes, Anthony saves children every day, but every day those children save us, too."

Chapter 32

Anthony

Three hours and a half later and I was parked outside of a cemetery in Columbia, South Carolina. I rubbed the grit from my eyes and pushed the car door open. It was pitch-black outside, but I didn't need light to know where I was going. I'd been here enough times to know where my baby brother was buried. I traversed the path through what felt like too many graves to count before coming up on the familiar headstone.

Charles James Jackson. There he was. I leaned down on my knees at the head of the grave, the dew on the grass seeping into my pants, but I didn't care. I reached into my back pocket and fished out my wallet. In the little pocket beneath my ID was where I kept him.

His little face, just two years old, his soft hair blond, his eyes green like mine. It was the last picture I had of him. Now it was all

I had left of him.

Sitting his picture on the headstone, I said, "Hey, buddy."

I hadn't been to see him in a long while, probably over a year, and shame flared through me, but I kept him there in my pocket always, all of my love for him in one single photograph.

His deep dimples smiled at me from the photo and a single tear slipped down my cheek. "I'm sorry it's been so long." I laid my palm on the headstone next to his picture.

I'd loved Charles long before he was born. I'd always wanted a sibling. I was twenty at the time, but better late than never, right? I'd only had him for a mere two years, but in just that short time, he'd managed to impact my life more than any other person.

I'd always known I'd be a doctor, but I chose the heart because of him. I was going to go to school and learn everything I could. Become the best to make sure he and my mom had the best.

It had all been in vain, though. He wouldn't make it to his third birthday and it had come as the greatest shock. I'd been with Kelly the night before and had the most amazing time of my life. The call had broken me. I'd wanted to cry and scream and tear my apartment apart, but I couldn't with her there. I couldn't grieve. So, I'd tossed her out, convinced I was doing it for her own good. Seeing me like that would scare her. She wouldn't understand my grief, after all, we hardly knew each other. She didn't know and love Charles like I did. How could she possibly understand?

The months that followed now seemed like a dream. I'd drifted through them dazed, and grieving so terribly. I felt like I'd failed him. So, I worked harder, became better. I'd never fail anyone again, I told myself. But medicine, God, faith, they didn't work that way. Some things were out of my control and I lost kids all the time, my only consolation that I saved more than I would lose.

"You remember that girl, right, buddy? The one I told you I got the tattoo for? The one I was with when Mom called? She's back. And I love her." I thought of the night I'd gotten the tattoo only six months after Charles' death. How I'd driven to the tattoo parlor knowing exactly what I wanted. Him. Her. Me. I missed us all. I'd been so long, but I'd promised myself that night that I'd try. I'd always try for Charles. For all the children like him.

I used my shirt sleeve to wipe the wetness from my face because I couldn't see him. I couldn't see him through the tears. His smiling face and messy hair.

"We have a baby. Her name is Hope. She's beautiful and perfect like her mother, but she's sick, bud. She's sick like you were and I'm so scared. So fucking scared because I love her, too, and I think I'd die if something happened to her." My voice caught on a sob at the end. But saying it, saying how scared I was, was almost a relief. I hadn't been able to tell anyone. To voice it. I'd been protecting Kelly and my mother. I couldn't tell them how I woke in the night with racing thoughts of Hope's impending death. How in my dreams I sometimes lost her.

I thought of my mother and how sad and worried she was all the time after Charles was born. I'd been a naive kid. Twenty wasn't really adult yet and I'd been the optimistic one telling her we'd get through it. How the doctors would help him. But I understood now. I understood her worry, her despair. I was living it, because when it was your child it was different, and Hope wasn't mine biologically, but she was mine in every other sense of the word. I couldn't have loved her more even if she were of my blood. She was mine. It was a different kind of worry. The love you feel, it's unexplainable. I hadn't been able to understand my mother's undying love and devotion to Charles until I'd held Hope between Kelly and me in that dark closet the day she'd been born. When she'd cried, my heart had soared.

If I lost her, I would lose part of myself.

I finally sat on my behind, the grass soaking me through, but I didn't care. I needed to think. I just needed to be for a few minutes without the chaos of beeping machines and sick babies. I needed to breathe. I needed to know how to make this better. I sat there for a long time thinking.

"I don't know what to do." I stared at his dancing green eyes, expecting answers I knew he couldn't give me. I just wanted a sign, something. I needed to know Hope was going to be okay. "I can't visit her here. I just can't," I cried into the night. I refused to walk through a slew of graves to get to her. I couldn't do it.

I thought of how stupidly optimistic I'd been and I'd still lost Charles. In fact, I lost people every damn week.

"Mom must have thought I was so ridiculous, always thinking the doctors were going to save you. Save our family. You were gone and Dad left. I still haven't talked to him in years."

I let out a chilling laugh. Fuck, I'd been so young, innocent, so unassuming of the real ways of the world. You couldn't guarantee anything, especially life or health. They could be snatched away from you any moment. The next day, the next minute, the next second were never a sure thing.

"I miss you, bud. I think of you every day." I smiled sadly down at the only piece of him I had left. "I used to tell Mom you were our miracle. We weren't expecting you but that didn't mean you weren't the best surprise ever."

I thought of how much we immediately loved him even knowing we might not get to keep him forever. Medicine had progressed so much in the last ten years, especially hearts. Back then, the type of surgeries I did now were just in the early stages and a lot of babies just didn't make it.

My mom had been terrified every time he'd gone into the operating room. I remembered sitting there with her, my arm around her slender shoulders. "Mom always knew. It was like she knew you were too good for this world, but not me. I was always blindly hopeful. Every time you were in surgery, I'd tell Mom, 'Never lose hope. There's always hope.'"

Hope. My breath stopped. I felt like my heart might have

paused, too. Never lose hope. I hadn't thought about saying that to Mom in years, but I had. I'd said it time and time again. And now I had Hope. I looked at that precious picture of my brother that held all of my love and memories and thought that maybe he had sent me her. Hope.

I'd hated how the night with Kelly had ended, with me yelling at her, screaming to leave. But if it hadn't, I wouldn't have Hope. And God, I loved her as much as I loved her momma.

"Never lose hope." I smiled down at the headstone. "I have to go, buddy. I have to go find Hope. I love you."

I grabbed his picture off the headstone and placed it back in my wallet carefully behind my driver's license. I'd show Kelly him. I would because I loved her and I wanted her to know how this two-year-old boy I adored had unknowingly mapped out the last ten years of my life and given me Hope.

I laid my hand to the gravestone one more time, the granite cold against my fingers. I ran to my car and jumped in the driver's seat, scanning the car for my phone. "Fuck," I banged my hands on the steering wheel. The damn phone was back at the office. I felt sick. I had to get to her. I'd been gone for hours. And I had no way of knowing how Hope was. I was sure Kelly was worried out of her mind. God, I was a fuck up. I had no idea why she put up with me. It could only be love.

I started the car and hit the interstate. I had to get home. Home to Kelly and Hope.

Chapter 33

Kelly

W e had finally been transferred to a room and while Hope rested on, Lucy beside her sleeping in a recliner, I sat in my own recliner, unable to catch a wink.

It was almost dawn and still no Anthony. Lucy was worried, too. She tried to act like she wasn't, but her sleep was fitful and I noticed because I hadn't slept at all. Where was he? I thought for sure he would have contacted me by now, at least to check on Hope. It was so uncharacteristic of him. And I'd called him for what seemed like a million times during the night only to get his voicemail.

Hope was doing better. She was on IV antibiotics and they were controlling her fever with meds. She already seemed more like herself, a little more alert. I'd even managed to get a smile or two.

My eyes drifted closed finally as I leaned my head back. I'd had a hell of a day and a night and I was worn out despite my worries over Doc. I couldn't fight sleep anymore. I'd wait for the sun to come up and call my momma and let her know we were in the hospital with Hope. She'd want to come up and check on her today. I'd try calling Doc again, maybe have Lucy go check the office and the apartment. Those were my thoughts as I drifted off into a light sleep.

It was the sound of quiet humming that woke me as the very beginnings of dawn came through the window. I creeped my eyes open slowly. I thought I was dreaming, him standing there in front of the big window behind Hope's hospital crib. That green shirt I'd kissed him goodbye in yesterday morning was untucked and unbuttoned, revealing the white cotton T-shirt beneath it. His hair was a damn mess and I knew why; my Doc loved to tug on those golden locks when he was upset. He was holding our baby to his chest, the beginnings of daylight peering through the window and just barely shining on them. He looked like an angel, a big, strong angel holding my baby. I felt like all I'd done was cry for the last twelve hours and still more tears poured from my eyes. Relief swept through me. I didn't care where he'd been or why he'd gone, only that he was here now.

"Doc," I said before I could stop myself. I wanted to make sure this wasn't some dream. I wanted to make sure he was here with us.

His head turned my way, his eyes meeting mine. "Shh," he said quietly. "You'll wake her." He placed Hope in her crib carefully before smiling at his sleeping mom in the chair next to the crib.

He walked over to me and kneeled at the foot of the recliner. "Hey there, shorty."

I ran a hand through his disarray of hair. "Hey, Doc." And the tears kept coming. I tried to smile through them.

He laid his head in my lap. "I'm sorry," he said softly. "I'm so sorry." He pushed his hands past my seated legs until they gripped me low on my waist, between my lower back and the recliner, pulling me closer.

Pushing my hands through his hair, I said, "It's okay."

His head shook back and forth against my legs. "It's not."

"I have things I should tell you. My brother. He—"

But I cut him off. I didn't want him to have to tell me. I didn't want him to have to relive that right this moment. He could tell me everything when he was ready. "I know. Your mom told me."

His face rose from my lap and he smiled up at me. "Of course she did."

I giggled softly.

"I heard that," came Lucy's croaky morning voice from across the room.

Anthony laughed low and deep before standing up, stretching, and walking toward his mother, who met him in the middle of the room.

He wrapped her in a deep, heartfelt hug that had me hoping and praying Hope loved me like Anthony Jackson loved his mom. Their relationship was the stuff that dreams were made of.

"Thanks for taking care of my girls," he said into the top of her head.

She leaned back, smiling up at him. "Hey, they're my girls too. Stop being so greedy," she joked.

They hugged again and she stepped out of his embrace before leaning forward and straightening the collar on his shirt. "Did you go see my baby?"

"I did." His answer was so unashamed, so sweet, Lucy's eyes shone.

She bit her trembling lip and I wanted to hug her. "And did he help you?"

Doc nodded. "He did, Mom." His own eyes full of heartache and love all rolled together.

She pulled on Anthony's collar again. "Well, of course he did. I have the two best boys ever." She looked over at me and then at Hope. "The two best girls now, also. I'm a lucky old lady."

She kissed Doc's cheek. "I love you, honey." And then she turned toward me and was on me, hugging me tightly. "I love you, too. I should go. I'll be by later to check on Hope."

And she was gone, like she hadn't just broken and then healed my heart in the last five minutes.

"Your mom's pretty damn amazing, Doc," I said through my tears.

"I know. You're pretty amazing, too."

I stood from the chair and made my way to stand in front of Hope's crib. My face flushed at his compliment. If I was only half the mother Lucille Jackson was then I was doing pretty damn good.

Doc came up behind me, laying his hands on my shoulders. "I'm sorry. I wasn't there for you guys last night when I should have been."

"It's okay." I'd already told him it was okay. And it was. I understood.

He let out a long breath. "It's not okay, Kelly. I don't want you to think I'm like Cash because I'm not. I promise I won't ever let you down like that ever again. I love you and I love Hope and I'm in it for the long haul. I want to call her daughter and I want her to call me daddy. I want you to call me husband. Do you understand?"

I turned to face him. "I do, honey." I rubbed the scruff on his chin and he pulled me into his chest where I could smell and feel him, the only man who could comfort me like he somehow did.

"I'm still so scared, Doc. We still have two more surgeries. I don't know if I can dream for that long. I don't want to be terrified anymore," I said into his chest, my eyes leaking all over his shirt.

His palms met my cheeks and I closed my eyes. This. This was what I'd missed last night. His big hands on my face. His thumbs on my chin. His face a breath from mine. His caress sweeping me away for just a mere second, but it was enough. It would always be enough.

"No, baby. We're not dreaming big anymore. We're living big.

We did it. We're doing it every day. And we'll do it tomorrow and the day after that. We're not dreaming, we're making memories because at some point your dreams can't even touch the miracle that is your reality. And look at our miracle." He turned us to face Hope. "Wake up, Kelly. You're here. You did it."

He was right. Looking down at my daughter, I realized all we'd accomplished. She'd made it through one life-threatening surgery. And we'd get through two more together. I wasn't wishing or dreaming anymore. I was here and fear was keeping me from missing it all, but I hadn't done it alone.

I grabbed Doc's hand in mine. "No, *we* did it."

His grinning lips met mine. "We did," he whispered against them.

Chapter 34

Seven Months Later

Anthony

The heart is amazing. Other doctors might tell you different. A psychologist will tell you the mind is an unyielding, intricate place. And he wouldn't be wrong, but the mind didn't have anything on the heart. An obstetrician will tell you there's nothing in the world better than babies, but I'd just tell her there wouldn't be babies without hearts. A pulmonologist will go on and on about the respiratory system, but I'd just tell him to stop blowing hot air. Damn, I was funny nowadays. And while all of those doctors have very valid points. Nothing. Nothing, is as exquisite as the heart.

The thump thump sound everyone adores about the heart is the sound made by the four valves of the heart closing. Pretty cool background music, huh? And because the heart has its own electrical impulse, it can continue to beat even when separated from the body as long as it has adequate oxygen. It's true, I've seen it with my own eyes. I've held it in my own hands.

The heart is beautiful and strong.

The heart is the most powerful organ. What besides the heart could break, heal, and become stronger again from it all? The heart knows things that mind can't quite explain.

Yes, the heart is brilliant.

Nearly half of the deaths due to congenital heart defects occur during infancy; younger than one year of age.

As I watched Kelly hold on to Hope's tiny hand, I realized how damn lucky we were. It was two days after her second surgery. She was already looking better, stronger. This was the surgery that fixed her poorly formed heart. We were two down, and one to go. Our girl was a rock star and Kelly was hogging every bit of her attention.

I sat across the room eyeing my ladies, the loves of my life; the women I'd die for.

"Marry me," I said from my spot propped by the window. I'd just thrown it out there, not thinking. Not planning it at all, but it was so us. We didn't really plan things.

The hospital room was small so I knew she heard me. She was rocking Hope in a chair in the corner. She always ignored me when she thought I was being too rash or excitable, which I was admittedly known to do.

"I said, marry me."

She pursed her lips as her eyes met mine. "Oh, I heard you, Doc."

"Well?" I smirked. I loved our dance. Our battle of words. Our bickering. They made me smile. They made me laugh. They made me hard.

One half of her mouth tipped up. She was trying to hide that grin from me. "I don't know. It depends. Was that a question or an order?"

I chuckled. "Which one is gonna get me the answer I want, tater tot?"

Giggling, she shook her head. "Tater tot—that's a new one. You have an endless supply of short girl names, you know that?"

She was putting me off. I walked to her side of the room. "You have an endless supply of evasion strategies. What's it gonna be?"

She grinned down at Hope, who was looking up at her smiling. "What do you think, boo boo? We gonna marry your Doc or what?"

Hope turned her gummy smile on me like she knew exactly what we were talking about.

I leaned close to Kelly's ear and whispered, "Come on, Kelly, how many orgasms is this gonna cost me?" I made sure to sound exasperated even as I smiled.

She turned wide eyes to me and placed her hands over Hope's ears. "Oh my God, Doc. Watch your mouth around the baby."

"She didn't hear me. Besides, she doesn't even know what orgasms are."

Her eyes got bigger if possible. "Let's not give her a lesson this early, then."

"Well?" I waggled my eyebrows suggestively.

"I don't know if you have that kind of stamina, Doc."

I laughed loudly. "I'm willingly to give it a try if you are."

Her face softened, her heart in her eyes. "Yes."

"Yes to orgasms or yes to you'll marry me?" I asked even though I knew. I could read it in every ounce of love on her face.

"Yes to everything."

Epilogue

Anthony

Four Years Later

Everyone was there. Well, everyone who mattered to Kelly and me. The waiting room was littered with our people. Miranda and Ainsley had driven up early that morning at 4:00 a.m. so they could arrive for Hope's final surgery. They sat there, chatting quietly to each other, clutching balloons and flowers in their hands. Their husbands, Adrian and Holden, had stayed home with their herd of children. Our mothers sat nearby, their own flowers and stuffed animals tucked around them while they talked not so quietly.

And my girl, she was seated beside me. Her leg bounced next to mine and I lay my hand on it. She was nervous. So was I. But we were in the home stretch. With two surgeries under our belts already this should have been old hat. In truth, it never got any easier. Every time our baby underwent surgery we sat on pins and needles, waiting for news. Open heart surgery was always risky business.

But this was it, Hope was four now. This was the last of the three surgeries that would finally fix her heart. And ours. Long, sleepless nights of feedings and watching our baby girl in pain would come to a close soon enough. She'd probably never run track, but she'd run. Her prognosis was good. It was all we could ask for.

"It's okay, baby. She has the best doctors in the world in there working on her." I said the same thing every time our baby went under, but even the best failed. I was terrified, too, but I'd hide it for her.

She gave me a close-lipped smile. "I know. But I can't help but worry, and I'm not feeling so great." She lay her hand to her round stomach. She was almost thirty-seven weeks along. It was another girl. A healthy girl. We were ecstatic, if a little scared, but it was time.

Hope was still a lot of work but soon that wouldn't be the case. The past three years seemed to have flown by in a flurry of doctors' appointments and hospital stays and surgeries. Kelly was a rock star stay-at-home mom and me and Lucille we still spent our days saving the babies. In between surgeries and work when Hope was feeling well enough, we did manage to squeeze in a small wedding ceremony at the court house. We put Hope in a white dress and Kelly tucked tiny little flowers into her hair. They'd stood in our small three-bedroom house near the hospital in white dresses and I'd never felt so damn lucky in my life. She'd told her momma she thought she looked like a princess. I'd thought both of them did.

"You want some water? A snack?" I got up and started walking to the vending machines across the room.

"Anthony," she hissed out and I turned around. I should have known something was wrong the minute she'd said my name. She never called me by Anthony unless she was pissed or upset. I was her Doc.

"What's up, shortstop?" I walked back over to her. I got down on my haunches and put my hands on her knees. A sweat had broken out along her forehead and her face was flushed. I started to worry. "What's wrong?"

She leaned close to my ear and whispered, "I think I'm in labor."

I rocked back and almost fell onto my ass. "What?"

"I think I'm having a baby," she whisper yelled at me.

"Why are we whispering?" I said softy.

She gave me big eyes. "Because I can't have a baby today. I have to be here when Hope gets out. This can't happen."

I grinned at her and grabbed her face in my hands. It calmed her and I knew she needed to chill out. "You know as well as I do that you don't get to pick the times these things happen." I looked around the room. "Hey, at least this time we are actually at a hospital."

Oh, that look. My girl could give me go to hell eyes like no other.

"Now is not the time to be cute," she deadpanned, before leaning over clutching her stomach.

"How long have they been coming and how often?"

"Every four minutes now, lasting about a minute," she groaned.

Fuck, my girl really *was* in labor. And we all knew how fast Hope had come. They said the second one was even quicker.

I felt a hand on my shoulder. "Everything okay?" Mom asked.

I looked over my shoulder and smiled up at her. "I think we might have a little bit of a situation."

Kelly sat up. "Nope, no situation." She tried to smile, but it came off more a grimace.

"She's in labor."

Kelly shook her head. "Nope, I can't be in labor. I have to be here for Hope."

Lucille looked at us both like we were crazy before coasting out of the waiting room and saying, "I'll go get a nurse."

"Doc, we can't have a baby today."

Wrapping my arms around her, I hugged her to me. "We can. We can do anything, baby. You know that better than anybody."

"What's the problem?" Miranda piped in behind me.

I let Kelly go and stood up. "She's in labor."

"Shit!" Ainsley said. "You people have the worst timing for these things."

My girl laughed and I was relieved. And it was true. We didn't do anything the conventional way. Our lives were always crazy, but we loved it.

"Move aside." Abby pushed through and knelt down in front of Kelly like I had. "It's okay, baby. Lucy went to get a nurse, and you and Anthony will go have the baby, and me and Lucy can stay here. We'll be here when Hope gets out."

She shook her head. "No, Momma, it has to be me." Her eyes went to mine. "Or Anthony. One of us has to be there when she comes out."

"Then I'll stay. I'll be here when she wakes up, baby, I promise." I offered up.

Kelly swallowed and looked at her mom and Ainsley and Miranda. "Then I guess it's just us ladies in the delivery room." She looked scared, but firm in her resolve that I stay with Hope. She was the best mom I'd ever known.

Miranda lay her hand on Kelly's shoulder. "We got this, girl. My vagina has been a freaking revolving door for years. I'm a professional."

"Miranda!" Abby scolded and we all laughed.

Lucille entered the room followed by a nurse with a wheelchair.

"Let's get you in this chair, Mrs. Jackson, and you over to the birthing wing." The nurse smiled.

We knew everyone around here. I felt like our entire family was here at this hospital more than we were at home.

We got a contracting Kelly into the chair and they started to wheel her out and into the hallway.

"Doc!" she called out.

I met her in the hallway and kneeled down in front of her. "What's up, little bit?"

She took my face in her hands. "I love you."

"I love you too, baby," I said, kissing her lips one last time. "Now bring it in."

She rolled her eyes. "Not this. Not now."

"Come onnnn. Indulge me and bring it the hell in." I brought both of my bunched fist up and waited on her to bring hers up to mine. I tapped our fists together lightly. I laid my forehead to hers. "Team Jackson," I muttered against her lips.

"Team Jackson," she breathed back.

A different version of Team Hope but much the same. Our team had evolved and grown over the years and now we were about to add a new member. I was sad to miss it, but I knew where I was needed and I'd never leave Hope without her daddy when she needed him.

She already had one dud of a father. At least Cash had eventually done right by her by signing away his parental rights and letting me adopt her. He didn't have a desire to see her and hadn't tried the first year of her life. Drugs did that to a person—made them miss out on the best things that life had to offer. His loss was my gain, though, because when Hope was eighteen months old she became officially mine. It was just a technicality, though. She'd always been mine, even before she was born.

They wheeled Kelly down the hall and I went back to the small family room and waited. I thought of my sweet brown-haired, blue-eyed Hope with her small, imperfect heart. I loved that heart. It had given me everything. Without her broken heart, I wouldn't be husband—a father. I owed everything to her and that heart.

It wasn't long before I was called into a small conference and a doctor friend told me that my daughter was fine and the surgery was successful. Only a few minutes after that, I sat at her side in the recovery room until she woke up. It was four hours later when Hope and I finally got to meet our newest team member. A nurse wheeled my exhausted looking wife with our baby in her lap into the NICU room Hope would be staying in the next few days. Hope had already deemed our new bundle Faith months ago. "They just go together," she'd said. Who were we to argue, besides she wasn't wrong and she pretty much ran the show around here anyway.

"She looks just like you," Kelly said, tears rolling down her face as I held Faith for the first time and she did. She had green eyes and blond baby fuzz covering her head. Her nose my nose. Her mouth mine too. She looked like Charles. I smiled down at her while Kelly held Hope's hand as she slept.

We'd had a hell of a day. A hell of a couple of years, really, but I was learning that everything would be okay as long as we had a little Hope and Faith.

Things weren't perfect by any means. We knew the greatest gifts life had to offer often weren't the big and easy things. The amazing things were sometimes as hard as steel. But if you looked closely, you could see through all the bad straight to the good where imperfect things become impossibly perfect. Where grief is a road that sometimes leads you astray, but the memories and lost love bring you back home. Where a huge loss doesn't always mean the end but maybe a new beginning. And where broken hearts go to get second chances and become healthy and whole again.

The End

Authors Note

So many tears. I can't believe this series is finally over. I have to say I am very happy with Kelly and Anthony's story being the final in this series. All of the heart references just seemed to round off these books perfectly. I tried to do as much research as possible for this story. I'd like to give a huge thank you to my friend Dené, whose baby actually was born with the same syndrome as sweet Hope. Dené opened her heart to me, telling me her personal accounts of what happened to her sweet baby and her struggles emotionally as a momma with a very sick baby. I tried to stay as medically accurate as I could without taking away from the story, but of course it's fiction, so I had to take some liberties to keep readers entertained.

It's funny, because honestly when I wrote the first book in this series, See Through Heart, I wasn't really expecting there to be a series. See Through Heart was a deeply emotional book that was written straight from my heart and about my own personal experiences with substance abuse and grieving. But my readers begged for Miranda's and Kelly's stories and I am so glad they did. Because I grew to love this clan so very much. In truth, I didn't know Anthony and Kelly's story, and what happened that night ten years ago in the first book in this series was as much a mystery to me as it was to you guys. Because of that, this one took me a bit longer to write, but I am so, so happy I did give them a story. I love them and Hope.

So, this is a big thank you for taking a chance on my very first series. I hope that with every book you took away a little of the points I was trying to drive home in each. Every heart book I wrote had an underlying message of loss and grieving and how it affects our lives and shapes and molds us, sometimes strengthening our relationships, sometimes destroying them, but tragedy is always something that we overcome with a little time and tenderness.

What I'm saying is that whether your heart is See Through, Steel, or Imperfect you are still so completely deserving of love and all the healing properties it holds. So, soak it up. Bathe in it. Love is always the answer.

If you loved this book or not I'd love a review. Good or bad, reviews are so important to us indie authors! Thank you so much for taking the time to read.

Acknowledgements

Tony: You're amazing. You're also the best damn PA money can't buy. Thank you for all you do. I love you bigger than the sky.

My kiddos: I lucked out. I seriously don't know how I ended up with the most amazing children in the world, but I did. Nothing makes me prouder than you guys being proud of me. I love you.

To my beloved Beta Readers: Jamie, Renee, Danielle, and Kim: Thank you for taking the time to do this for me. You guys give it to me straight and you make my books better, which is invaluable to me.

Kelly: To the crazy lady who still made time to beta for me even though she'd just had surgery. And that sentence makes it abundantly clear why you are so dear to me. Virtual hugs. Because I suck at the real ones.

Megan: Thank you for all your hard work on this book, friend. I can't wait to return the favor one day.

Miranda: Thank you for dropping everything to help me get this book done in time. This year is your year. I can feel it in my bones.

Aly and Ashley: I'm gonna treat y'all like one person, because ya'll kinda are. I love you guys. You make me laugh and you listen to me cry. And you don't even judge me when I drink too much. How did y'all get so perfect? Thank you for being wonderful friends to me.

Hang Le: This series has my favorite covers in the world and that is because of you. Thank you for all your hard work.

Amor Caro: Thank you for your help and support every book, friend. You rock!

Amber Goodwyn: I couldn't release a book without your help. Thank you from the bottom of my heart.

Tania Baikie: The images you took the time to make me are beautiful. Thank you so much!

DND Authors: I don't even know how I ended up in that crazy group, but I've never felt so lucky. You guys make me laugh and give me a safe space when I need one. I'm so glad I have y'all.

Sarah and Jenn at Social Butterfly PR: Thank you for taking on a new author still trying to find her place in this indie writing world. You guys have made my releases epic and I can't say how much I appreciate it.

Stacey Blake of Champagne Book Design: Thank you for making my books as pretty on the inside as they are on the outside. You are amazing!

Bloggers and Readers: I want to list so many of you individually, but I know I could be here all day doing that. I read every review. I see every share. And it means the absolute world to me. Thank you, thank you, thank you.

About The Author

Amie Knight has been a reader for as long as she could remember and a romance lover since she could get her hands on her momma's books. A dedicated wife and mother with a love of music and makeup, she won't ever be seen leaving the house without her eyebrows and eyelashes done just right. When she isn't reading and writing, you can catch her jamming out in the car with her two kids to '90s R&B, country, and showtunes. Amie draws inspiration from her childhood in Columbia, South Carolina, and can't imagine living anywhere other than the South.

FACEBOOK: www.facebook.com/authoramieknight

TWITTER: www.twitter.com/AuthorAmieKnigh

GOODREADS: www.goodreads.com/AmieKnight

INSTAGRAM: www.instagram.com/amie_knight

WEBSITE: www.authoramieknight.com

GROUP: www.facebook.com/groups/amiessouthernsocial

NEWSLETTER: eepurl.com/cPHIuT

OTHER TITLES
See Through Heart
A Steel Heart
The Line

85125676R00140

Made in the USA
San Bernardino, CA
16 August 2018